Alana

Alana

a novel

Nancy Ferguson

FITHIAN PRESS, SANTA BARBARA, CALIFORNIA
2001

Printed in the United States of America

Published by Fithian Press
A division of Daniel and Daniel, Publishers, Inc.
Post Office Box 1525
Santa Barbara, CA 93102
www.danielpublishing.com

LIBRARY OF CONGRESS CATALOGING-IN-PUBLICATION DATA
Ferguson, Nancy.
Alana : a novel / by Nancy Ferguson
p. cm.
ISBN 1-56474-361-6 (pbk : alk. paper)
1. Motion picture actors and actresses—Fiction. 2. Hollywood (Los Angeles, Calif.)—Fiction. 3. Retirees—Fiction. 4. Texas—Fiction. I. Title
PS3556.E7165 A79 2001
813'.6—dc21 00-010187

To my cousin Allan,
who, for some strange reason,
never lost faith in me.

O beauty, are you not enough?
Why am I crying after love?

—Sara Teasdale

Alana

I

The legendary actress, Alana Paige, has offered me an opportunity that comes once in a career. Why me? I don't know; we've never met and I know little about her, aside from marvelous movies I've seen on TV and that her name is frequently spoken with awe. There was some kind of scandal or tragedy in her life and she disappeared from Hollywood at the height of her glory, a long time ago.

At any rate, possibly because she liked my book about Lombard and Gable, she evidently feels I am the author she wishes to have record her life story—whether as a nostalgic search into her personal history or simply because so many others are doing the same thing I have no idea.

I had no time to get to Hollywood for intensive research before I came: she contacted my publisher to find me, called, and asked that I come here with as little delay as practical; perhaps not the best timing for me, but too good a chance to miss.

Thus I find myself ensconced in a comfortable room in the Hilton, on the site of the old Scarbauer Hotel in Midland, Texas, a town split into districts, as are most—one new, gleaming with contemporary buildings and glossy shops, the other clearly surrendered to hard times.

The sleek office buildings that housed five hundred oil companies until the crash of '87 are only partially occupied; some of the exquisite homes built by oil earnings are deserted, the former owners gone to greener pastures after salvaging what they could from the debacle. However, all of that is changing as recovery and growth have begun in this new decade.

As I drive my rented Toyota through the older section of town, I'm intrigued; this is where the beginning action of the book I will write took place.

The streets here are quite deserted, with occasional stray pieces of newsprint blowing by theatrically in the traditional winds of the area. The theater on what was the main street in earlier times has broken glass in the windows that once displayed the advertising boards for every movie imported for what was then the few thousand residents of this West Texas community.

The area resembles nothing so much as an abandoned movie set.

And there is Alana Paige. Her glorious hair is cropped and silver gray; a few fine wrinkles map the delicate skin of her still lovely face. She looks perhaps forty-five, though she must be nearing sixty now. She walks slowly, limping slightly, from arthritis, I would guess. She is upright, however, her carriage remaining as regal as in her young days. Her eyes are bright and alert, even merry, though occasionally a sadness seems to emanate from the depths of them when she gazes over my shoulder into the past.

She offers me wine, which I refuse, then tea, and serves it in porcelain from France. The living room in this small, slightly shabby house is furnished sparsely, but with fine pieces and some remarkable art on the walls. The rug on the scrubbed wooden floor is Aubusson.

She doesn't object to my tape recorder but seems slightly nervous, though open as well as friendly. We sip our tea. She begins to talk.

~

My real name is Billie Jo Payner. You know how it was in Hollywood: names were rarely one's own, and for some strange reason the studio thought Alana was properly glamorous for me, perhaps because of Lana Turner, also blond and so highly praised in *The Bad and The Beautiful.*

Or perhaps simply because I looked like an Alana to whoever was in charge of such things. Why they picked Paige is another mystery.

So I was stuck with it; they changed it before I had my first starring role, when I might have had some say in the matter. I didn't mind, though it certainly wouldn't have been my choice. I remember thinking that, with a new name, the folk back home would never know it was me, even assuming they saw my films, since my whole look was so different. I was a natural blond, of course—well, eventually my hair had a little help—but since I appeared about twenty with the make-up and the new way I had of walking and the way I tossed my head—but you know all that. I'm supposed to be telling my story, not describing what you've seen photographed so many times. Well then....

I was born in Texas. Quite a few stars came from here, as far back as Bebe Daniels: Susan Hayward, Ann Sheridan, Mary Martin; all beautiful and famous.

We had one theater in my hometown then, and if there was enough money, Mama took my sister and me to an early Friday movie every week when the feature changed. She would lean over to us and whisper, "See her? You'll both be just as pretty when you grow up. You can be like her if you want to." I was too little to understand, but I had favorites even then: Mickey Rooney, who made me laugh as Andy Hardy, then made me cry in *Boy's Town*; Laurence Olivier, who thrilled me in *Rebecca*, though I didn't know why and didn't understand the story; Veronica Lake, whose hair I envied; and Spencer Tracy, who was the father I wanted to have, whatever the role he played.

The town was Midland, properly named since it was halfway between Dallas and El Paso on what just might be the flattest stretch of land in the whole country. It was a booming town then. Oil was spouting from the ground like buttercups and everyone was rich. Almost everyone, that is. Somehow we never quite made it. We had enough to eat and I had new clothes sometimes, but we didn't have the kind of money many other families in town had.

I remember being invited to a sixth birthday party. It was held in the Scarbauer Hotel, the big—well, so it seemed to me—and only hotel in town. The birthday girl, Mary Lee, was Mayor Farly's daughter. The main gift she received, among many, was a white bunny-fur coat. Oh, how I longed for that coat. I stroked its soft fur and lay my cheek on it and whispered, "Someday I'll have a coat like this."

That was in 1943. We certainly should have been well off then, because with the bombardier school on the outskirts of town and the bigger than ever boom in oil—there was a war on, you remember—money was flowing like tap water. But my family usually seemed to be just a little short of cash.

I never quite understood what my father did for a living, though I knew there was something different about him. Other kids would ask, "What does your daddy do?" and I'd answer, "He works for Uncle Sam," not really knowing who Uncle Sam was; then I'd turn up my nose and walk away before they could ask any more questions.

When I was growing up in Midland, during a war I knew nothing about, my life was considered "normal." My parents were still together, my older sister, Fay Ann, was a nuisance only some of the time, and for the most part we all were healthy, aside from the usual colds and childhood ailments.

I remember a lot of incidents from those years, some good, some not so good.

The earliest was standing in my crib in the room I shared with my sister, light just beginning to erase the corner shadows that scared me so much. I was calling for Mama. My feet got tangled in the sheet; I fell and cut my lip against the side of the crib. I screamed at the top of my lungs, as you can imagine. Fay Ann never woke up.

I remember my surprise better than the pain of the cut lip, when Mama came running, still in her sheer nightgown; I'd never known hair grew anywhere except on people's heads.

There was blood everywhere, and Mama panicked. Then my father came in and calmed her down while I sobbed, "Nasty bed," and hit it with my fist. Mama went for some ice to try to keep the swelling down. It didn't work very well since I wouldn't hold it against my mouth. So I had a Ubangi lip for a day or two, and my playmates laughed and pointed. My four-year-old brain registered the laughter; that must have been when I decided that no one would ever laugh at me when I grew up.

The little scar my fans always found so appealing was from that accident.

Have you ever seen a centipede? They are ugly worm-like creatures with the hundred legs their name describes. Mama hated bugs. One day I was out making mud pies in the back yard, and playing with my pet horned toad that everyone said would make warts on my hands (you know how silly that is; the directors always made sure my hands were in as many takes as possible; they thought them beautiful), when

I heard a scream from the house. I ran in, expecting to find it on fire. Mama was cowering in the corner of the kitchen. On the floor was the largest centipede I'd ever seen. Fay Ann came dashing in with Daddy's rifle, which was almost as long as she was tall. She took careful aim at the floor and *boom*. Mama screamed louder and I clapped my hands over my ears. A huge, ragged hole appeared in the linoleum with splinters from the wood beneath flying in all directions. There was nothing left of the centipede.

My sister was good with that .22. She had a friend from school whose father owned a ranch, as well as half the oil land in the Permian Basin. She often went with Emma Sue to visit the ranch and swim in the water tank and ride one of the horses. This time there was to be a roundup and cattle drive, just like the one in my first picture, *Texas Belle*.

I was so jealous I hated her. She packed up a bedroll with an extra bit of clothing and off she went, while I stayed behind, watching her out the window of the living room, thinking, "Someday she'll have to watch me go somewhere she wants to go and I'll just laugh."

She came back all sunburned and full of importance, telling about the chuck wagon and the wonderful food the cook was able to prepare in that seemingly impossible situation, and the cowboys with their spurs and ten-gallon hats, riding those sturdy horses to keep the beautiful red Herefords from straying. She slept under the stars, giggling the night away with Emma Sue, then rose with the others at dawn.

When she went for her horse she heard the dread rattle that proclaimed a snake nearby. Instead of screaming for help, like any sensible person would do—after all, there were cowboys everywhere—she ran for Dad's .22, which she had brought along against Mama's orders, and shot that critter dead.

You can imagine the fuss everyone made over her. She was a heroine, and never let us forget it, from that time on.

But as often as she was a pain, she was a blessing. When I got caught in the bedroom we shared, with my panties around my ankles playing doctor with the Byer twins from next door, it was Fay Ann who talked my mother out of beating me with a switch. She said, "Mama, you know how Jim and Jesse are; it wasn't Billie Jo's fault. Besides," she added from her twelve-year-old wisdom, "they're too little to know what they're doing anyhow."

That made me take notice; I really didn't know we were doing anything forbidden, and if we were I sure wanted to find out what it was. I asked Fay Ann later. She said, "You're too young; when you get old enough Mama will tell you." So I was even more curious, but I couldn't get any more from her, and Mama was out back, killing a chicken for dinner. I hated watching her chop off its head, the headless body running around in circles, bloody drops flying from its severed neck until it finally gave up and dropped dead.

By the time she came into the house I must have been busy with my dolls; I forgot all about asking her to solve the mystery of why I wasn't supposed to play doctor. I remember wondering if it was only boys I wasn't supposed to play it with or if it was a game I couldn't play at all. I had sort of enjoyed showing the boys my bottom. We hadn't gotten far enough for them to show me theirs.

It snowed one winter. Snow in West Texas is as strange as snow in Los Angeles, maybe more so. We all ran out to watch the flakes drift towards the ground. I couldn't believe Mama when she told me that where she came from there would be mountains of snow all winter and that no two snowflakes were ever alike. I was enchanted with the snowflakes' beauty, wanting to preserve at least one to savor its crystalline perfection. But each time I caught a flake it melted before I could study it.

Mama said, "Let it fall on your coat sleeve; then it will last long enough for you to look at it."

She was right; I saw the geometric form, each angle and branch, with tiny sparks of light glinting like the diamond on Mary Lee's mother's finger. Then it was gone, as if it had never been. I was much too young to see how similar it was to human life.

The snow lasted all night; in the morning we built a lopsided snowman, threw snowballs at each other, all four of us, Mama, Papa, Fay Ann and I, and got thoroughly soaked; our clothes weren't made for this kind of weather.

By late afternoon the snowman was a pyramid instead of a body, and though overnight it froze in that shape, it was gone the next day. I didn't cry; it never seemed to solve anything.

Strangely, it was Daddy, not Mama, who made me go to Sunday school. I hated it. I hated it as much as I hated regular school and for the same reason. When a teacher called on me to answer a question I just seemed to shrivel into a mute, quivering lump. It didn't matter whether or not I knew the answer; I was simply too shy to talk.

That must surprise you if you've seen my movies and read any of the trash that has been written about me. At that age I was dreadfully shy and hated to be in the spotlight. That condition, or neurosis or whatever the psychiatrists would call it, didn't last long, once I got a taste of applause. There was a vast difference between answering when I was called on as myself, and playing someone else on screen or stage.

The only person outside my family with whom I was completely at ease was my father's friend, Lester. He looked just like Van Johnson in *Two Girls and a Sailor.* I wanted to grow up to be June Allyson and marry Van—or Lester—and live happily ever after.

I adored him. He would let me sit on his lap, which Daddy no longer allowed because, he said, "you're too bony."

I didn't know why, one day, we all piled in the car heading for the airfield outside of town. When we arrived there were three people with several suitcases on the ground beside them, standing by the building that was designated "Airport."

One of the three was Lester. He shook hands with Daddy, gave Mama a big hug and kissed Fay Ann. Then he turned to me.

"Are you going away?" I asked.

"Didn't your daddy tell you? I have to move up north. I have a new job. I thought you knew."

He was squatting next to me, holding my hand. I couldn't speak; I felt the tears scorch my eyes and brushed them away; they wouldn't keep him here.

He pulled me close to him and said loudly, "You'll come visit me in Chicago. We'll have a great time, you'll see."

I nodded, looking into his blue eyes; I saw only sympathy, not reassurance. He released me, picked up his bag, and walked towards the airplane, which was parked sedately, waiting for its passengers. Mama took my hand; the three people climbed the boarding ladder and a lady in a blue uniform closed the door. As the engines sputtered to life the propellers turned, then whined into a silver blur; the plane taxied to the end of the runway, a clearing down the length of the barren field. The motor roared as the pilot dipped the ailerons and waggled the rudder, then moved, first ponderously, then with increasing grace, finally lifting off, soaring higher and higher into the cerulean sky until it became a mere flash of light in the distance. Lester was gone.

Later that year Grandma and Grandpa Payner came to visit. They had saved their gas coupons for months to make the trip and drove from Charleston in a 1937 Chrysler that had spare tires mounted behind the front fenders.

While Grandma and Grandpa were visiting, Daddy never went out at night. It was a wonderful time. Mama was happy, my grandparents were doting, and Fay Ann was busy with her first boyfriend so I didn't have her telling me what to do all the time. And with her away from the house I got all the attention.

They brought presents for everyone: a brown sweater for Daddy, a silver bracelet for Mama and dresses for Fay Ann and me. Mine was pink with a white Peter Pan collar and white cuffs on the puffed sleeves. Fay Ann's was navy blue, her favorite color, with a narrow belt and patch pockets on the skirt. To my astonishment, both dresses fit. It didn't occur to me that Grandma had asked Mama about the sizes.

They also brought a very special gift for the whole family: a camera. I didn't think to ask who would buy the film after my grandparents left; as usual, we were low on cash. I knew that; I heard my parents arguing about it.

The camera was put to work the minute it was out of the box. I was sent to the drug store with the first roll of exposed film, and we all waited anxiously for it to be returned. Except for school pictures we hadn't seen any photographs of ourselves since Fay Ann held me on her lap when I was two months old.

"Look at that child," said Grandma, pointing a finger gnarled with arthritis at me. "She's right beautiful with all those curls and that dimple in her chin."

Mama beamed and Fay Ann glanced at the picture as she was flying out the door. She scowled at me and made a face.

"I hope Jimmy sees you like that," I screamed at her.

"Hush, now. Don't be mean to your sister," said Mama, who hadn't seen the grimace. "She's just as pretty as you; you're like two sides of a coin, one dark, one blond."

That didn't make me too happy since I wanted to be the prettiest. Daddy was laughing from his seat in the recliner.

"Let me see my girls," he said, reaching for the print. He was *with us* in a way I didn't remember ever feeling before. "They are both beautiful; you're right," he said, as if it had never occurred to him before.

"They'll break some hearts when they grow up."

"Looks to me like Fay Ann is already growing up," said Grandpa. "Just thirteen and with a boyfriend already. I'm surprised you let her go out, especially with all those servicemen in town."

"Jimmy lives down the street and they're just going to a movie. I don't worry like I would if we were in a big city."

"Why would you worry in a big city?" I asked my mother.

Mama got a puzzled look on her face. "It doesn't really make much sense, when you think about it. Bad things happen in small towns too. But. . . ."

"What kind of bad things?"

"That's enough, Billie Jo," said Daddy and I knew I'd get no more information on that subject.

When Grandma and Grandpa left, everything was just like it had been before: Daddy began leaving the house in the evening again, and Mama got sad. Fay Ann went to the movies with Jimmy, and I played house and paper dolls and hopscotch with Mary Lee after school, which I hated as much as ever even though I was getting good grades.

Mama took me to see Bing Crosby in *Going My Way;* I liked the way he looked with his collar on backwards. *The Song of Bernadette* made me squirm and I never liked Jennifer Jones after that. I wasn't allowed to see *Laura*, with Gene Tierny; and *Gaslight*, with Ingrid Bergman, who Mama said was the world's greatest actress, scared me half to death.

Then Judy Garland came in *Meet Me in St. Loius*—it stayed two weeks but I only got to see it once—and I spent the rest of the week singing, "Clang, clang, clang went the trolley." Finally Daddy said, "If you don't stop singing that damn song I'm going to lock you out of the house." That was the only time I ever heard him swear at me.

I was terribly insulted. Mustering all the dignity a seven—almost eight—year old could gather, I said, "You'll be sorry when I'm a big star. I won't sing for you," turned on my heel and stalked from the room.

II

Midland was bulging with soldiers in those days. They wore khaki uniforms with silver wings on their chests. On Saturdays, when Mary Lee and I would walk to town, to the park, or wander down the street to the drug store, we would see dozens of them. We would climb on the tall stools with wire backs shaped like big hearts and order sodas (or if I didn't have enough money sometimes Mary Lee would order a sundae and ask for an extra spoon so we could share.)

The drug store buzzed with strange accents, soldiers released from camp for the weekend, but with no place to go. We would watch them from our stools, trying to figure out where they had come from and where they were going. It was fun because we didn't understand that they had come from everywhere and they were going, oh, so many, to their deaths.

One day, as we started back towards the dirt road that led to our houses, we saw a heap of flailing bodies; they were yelling words we mostly couldn't make out, except I do recall it was the first time I had heard the word "fucking." I didn't think it was important until I repeated it to Daddy and he said, "If I ever hear you use that word again, I'll whip you." When he whipped me it was as bad as when Mama used the switch, so I paid close attention.

But that was afterwards. When Mary Lee and I saw the fight, for that was obviously what it was, we backed into the doorway of the dry goods store. Mr. Green was trying to call someone on the telephone, screaming for help as loud as the soldiers who were fighting. It was only a couple of minutes later that a jeep came tearing around the corner, screeching to a halt. Three of the largest men I'd ever seen jumped out, running. They all had bands around their arms that said MP. I recognized those bands from the movie *Bataan* which Mama hadn't wanted me to see, but I stole a quarter from her purse and sneaked in when she went to her part-time job at Woolworth's.

That's how I knew those men were some kind of police. They broke up that fight in a hurry and hauled everyone away. When I got home Mama and Daddy were already talking about the fight; I heard the words, "nigger bastard," from my Dad, then Mama shussing him, "Quiet, here's Billie Jo."

"What happened, Mama? How did you know there was a fight?"

"Your father was driving by and saw it start. Where were you?"

"Mary Lee and I were just walking home from the drug store. What were they fighting about?"

"Some of the soldiers didn't want the *Negro*," she glanced at Dad, "to be in the drug store with them."

"But he's a soldier too, isn't he?"

"Yes, Honey, but people don't always stop to think about it like that. It's sad, but that's the way some people are."

All this time Dad just stood there with a sour look on his face, saying nothing. Now he gave a snort of disgust and said, "I'm going out. I won't be back for dinner."

"But, Harry...." Mama stopped. Dad had picked up his hat from the little round table in the front hall and was walking out the door.

"Don't be sad, Mama. I'll stay with you."

She hugged me tight and kissed my forehead. "Were you scared, Billie Jo?"

"Not until the policemen came."

"The MPs?"

"Yes. They were so big."

"I guess they have to be to keep the soldiers in line."

"Well, I wasn't scared 'til then. When we saw them, Mary Lee and I ran home."

Mama wasn't really a southern lady; she was born in Connecticut. When she was twelve the barn caught on fire and her father was trapped inside. Grandma tried to get him out and was hit with a piece of timber that fell from the loft. They both died.

Mama was sent to live with Aunt—my great aunt—Nell, in South Carolina. She arrived with northern notions and never did pick up the form of bigotry of those bred in the south. She always said *Negro* instead of *nigger* and was as polite to a black as to white folk.

She was pretty and lively and did well in school but her new friends in Charleston thought she was a little strange and "northern" in her ways. She used to tell me that while some southerners retained a great deal of the antebellum—I didn't know what that meant then—attitude of owning their blacks and therefore treating them kindly and with care, people in the north frequently were more prejudiced than southerners. They were unkind and often worse. Sometimes I think that times haven't changed much since then.

Mama went to college and would have graduated if she hadn't met my father when she was a sophomore. He was handsome and romantic, with dark flashing eyes in a coppery face; there must have been an Indian somewhere in his background. He had black hair, was tall and broad and his chin was cleft. That's where I got my brown eyes and the dimple in my chin but I got my blond hair from Mama.

Daddy moved to Charleston from Virginia; he had a falling out with his parents that didn't heal until Fay Ann was born.

He was twenty years old and it was 1929. You know what times were like then: the great market crash in October, much worse than the October '87 crash we had a few years ago; the suicides and bread lines; and Hitler gearing up for his venture into genocide. It was also the year of the first Academy Awards. I know that; when I was nominated in 1961 for my role in *Royal Interlude*, I planned to mention it if I won. I've never forgiven Liz Taylor for winning that *Butterfield 8* Oscar.

Daddy was so lucky. He got a job with the Federal Farm Board and was eating when others were starving. He and Mama met at a church picnic in September the next year. It didn't take long for them to fall in love and Mama was pregnant by New Year's Eve. So, of course they got married.

Daddy asked for a transfer; in those days if the baby was born before nine months after the wedding it was a scandal. Now it doesn't seem to matter when the baby is born or, for that matter, even if the woman is married at all.

But times were different then and they were happy and in love and didn't really care much where they lived as long as they were together and had a home where they could bring their child.

For some reason the government cooperated and the Payners moved to Atlanta. Fay Ann was born there. When she was two the family was transferred to Midland. It was all right: they were still eating.

Mama was so much in love that she glossed over the defects in Daddy's character. Don't we all do the same thing? She only saw the broad shoulders and striking face and seemed to ignore the number of times he didn't show up for dinner or went out in the evening and didn't return until dawn.

The night of the fight in town I was dreaming about the MPs. They were beating the soldiers with clubs and there was blood and broken bones and men with smashed faces. I heard them screaming and I woke, my heart pounding with terror. It was worse then. I could hear Mama crying and calling out for, "Harry, Harry."

I woke Fay Ann who grumbled until I shook her and yelled, "It's Mama. She's crying and I don't know what to do. I'm scared."

My sister was up like a shot; I followed her to Mama's room but stopped in the doorway, afraid of what I'd see if I went in.

"What's wrong, Mama," asked Fay Ann. "What's the matter?"

Mama tossed on the bed, clutching a handful of blanket to her chest and moaning, "Oh, Harry, no, I'm losing it."

"Losing what?" I asked in a voice almost as strangled as hers, looking wildly around the room. "What's she losing, Fay Ann?"

"Shut up and go call Dr. Crane. Tell him we need him fast."

I raced for the telephone, praying that the operator would be there in the middle of the night; I'd never used a telephone at night before. When she answered I almost collapsed with relief and my knees were shaking. "Please, operator, get Dr. Crane. My Mother's sick."

"All right, Honey, tell me the doctor's number."

"I don't know his number," I screamed. "It's Dr. Crane and he lives on J Street. Hurry, it's a 'mergency."

"Calm down now, Honey, and I'll find him. But you have to tell me your name and where you live."

That seemed the first sensible thing she had said—why didn't she know his number? She was the operator—so I told her where we lived, slammed the ear piece into the hook and raced back to Fay Ann who was crying herself and trying to comfort Mama at the same time.

It seemed like an hour before there was a knock on the door; it had grown unnaturally quiet in the room and I thought Mama was dying but was too afraid to ask.

"Well, don't just stand there, stupid, answer the door."

Dr. Crane, a short, burly man with old fashioned side whiskers, was usually affable and had lollipops for me each time I had an ailment. Not this night. He growled at me when I let him in, and barked, "Where's your mother?"

I led him upstairs to her room; he sent Fay Ann and me out and closed the door in our faces.

We looked at each other and I suppose I was as white as my sister. I grabbed her hand and squeezed it so tight she winced. I was still afraid to ask any questions so we both just sat there and waited.

When the doctor came back out of the room we popped up like the jumping jack which had been my favorite toy when I was three.

"All right, girls. Your mother will be fine, but I'm going to drive her to the hospital now. Where's your father?"

A chorus, "I don't know."

He nodded as if that were what he expected and asked, "Will you be all right alone for the rest of the night? I can't take you to the hospital with us."

"We'll be fine, Dr. Crane," said Fay Ann, "I'm thirteen now; I can take care of Billie Jo. What's wrong with Mama?"

"I'll tell you some other time. You just take care of each other and I'll see to your Mother; I told you, she'll be all right."

He went back into the bedroom; we watched from a distance, forbidden the presence of the person who kept our world spinning in the right direction. The doctor helped Mama into a warm but tattered bathrobe and half carried her down the stairs and out the front door to his car where he carefully deposited her, then went to the driver's side, slid onto the seat and drove away. She didn't wave.

We were restlessly waiting until it was late enough to call the hospital, the sky just turning a glaucous blue, when Father got home around six o'clock. At first he was angry, asking several times, "Well, what was wrong with her." Then he broke down. It was the only time I ever saw him cry. He turned away, towards the bedroom, trying to hide the emotion that had taken him—and us—so unaware. But he stopped in the doorway with a gasp. "Oh, my God."

When we looked past him towards the rumpled bed we saw the dried blood where Mama had lain.

It took several weeks for Mama to recover from the miscarriage. She was never as strong after that. Sometimes I wonder how different my life would have been if I'd had a younger sibling.

My father made promises Fay Ann and I would occasionally overhear, like, "I won't ever do it again, Jeanne." If I'd been old enough to think of it I would have suspected other women. Whatever it was, for some reason, even though I didn't understand what he was promising not to do again, I didn't believe him.

It wasn't until I was nine that I found out about the gambling. The problem wasn't that Father's earnings were too little. Compared to the average American who had lived through the disasters of the depression years he earned a fortune. But he gambled it all away.

It was Fay Ann who told me. I was complaining about wearing one of her old, badly made-over dresses to a party.

"At least you have something different to wear," she hissed viciously. "I'm stuck with the same thing I wore to the prom last year. Daddy's been shooting craps again."

That was more than a revelation. It hadn't occurred to me that anyone could play a game and lose their money and make a family poor. I finally understood why Mama looked so sad. And why, sometimes when I'd wake in the middle of the night I'd hear my parents yelling at each other in those strained, "Quiet, the kids will hear you," voices.

But that was later. Other things happened in the years before that.

Mary Lee moved away. My best friend, the one with whom I had played since long before I could remember, with whom I walked to school and town, who shared with me, not only ice cream when I was needy but also confidences and gossip, joys and sorrows, plans and hopes and dreams.

She was moving to California.

"Promise you'll write. Promise."

"I'll write, Billie Jo, 'course I will. And you can come visit me. There's a beach. We can go."

"'You'll come visit me.'" Yes, I had heard that before.

She left on a Thursday. I was in school so I didn't get to wave goodbye. I remember the date. It was April 12th. Franklin Delano Roosevelt died that day. So everyone grieved.

III

The day in May that signified the end of the war in Europe is a day I'll never forget. We went to town, the Payners and everyone else for miles around. The youngsters in uniform were lifted to sturdy shoulders and carried down Main Street; everyone kissed everyone, sometimes strangers; it didn't matter.

Yes, there was still Japan to finish, but even I, not quite eight, was aware that this great day was the end of something awful, so I celebrated with the rest. Daddy lifted me to his shoulders, a rare privilege, so that I sat level with the soldiers as we paraded in a trail back and forth across the streets and sang and shouted like demented fools on a Mardi Gras of joy.

We lost Fay Ann and Mama gave up and retreated to the drug store to wait for us. On our third trip by I could see her through the window, perched on a stool just as Mary Lee and I had done so often. I hadn't been for a soda since my friend had left.

Daddy was sweating and panting. "Down you go, Billie Jo. You might be skinny but you're too heavy for any more of this."

I never wanted to get down. The excitement, the noise, the happy faces, Daddy's hands holding me so I wouldn't fall, it all was a sort of magic. I never wanted it to end.

When he lowered me to the sidewalk he looked at me in surprise. "Where are your braids? What did you do to your hair?"

"I curled it, like Jane Powell. Mama let me." I had been curling it for two weeks and he'd never noticed. "Do you like it?"

"It makes you look older. You really are. . . ." he broke off.

"I'm what, Daddy, I'm what?" I longed for him to tell me I was beautiful, to lift me again and hug me, to keep his promises to Mama so she wouldn't look sad anymore.

"Nothing," he said. "Let's try to find Fay Ann and go home. I've had enough celebration."

I have my father to thank for being able to remember so much of what was going on in the world in those early days. When I was about four he decided that I must learn to read without waiting for school to teach me. He would sit me on his lap and take the newspaper, and we would "study" together, always the headlines, until I began to understand what the words meant. It became a sort of game to see if I could figure out what was happening in France or Japan before my father did. I became somewhat of an addict—a headline addict, you might say. It makes me laugh to think how seldom, even now, I delve below the most basic information. I'm not sure that's all bad.

We had one of those old fashioned radios, the kind that peak like a Gothic arch, with rough textured material behind a fancy wood design on the front. Fay Ann was a Sinatra fan and searched for him on the radio all the time when my parents weren't listening to the news. It got to a point where I couldn't stand Sinatra. I'd beg her to find Betty Grable or Deanna Durban but she kept telling me that they were in the movies and not on the radio. I didn't understand. Then she explained that we'd need records to hear those singers but we didn't have a record player and it wasn't likely that we'd have enough money to buy one.

After that I would sneak into the music store in town and hang around just to listen to whatever happened to be playing: Ella Fitzgerald with Louis Armstrong, the piano of Art Tatum, Nat King Cole singing anything. Also there was Toscanini, Rubenstein, Arthur Feidler and the Boston Pops Orchestra; I got my first exposure to classical music in those days. What luck!

But my greatest pleasure was the Lux Radio Theater. All the actors had such beautiful voices. It seemed to me that the most elevating thing I ever could do would be to act on the radio. And everything sounded so real. It wasn't until years later that I discovered cellophane and pieces of wood and the other few tricks that created all those sounds. It still amazes me that they could have used so little to make so much reality.

When mushroom clouds put an end to World War II in August, our celebration was quieter than the one for the end of hostilities in Europe. In our household, at least, it was like a breath long held and gently released. The war had brought prosperity to our town; Midland was rich, one of the richest towns in the United States and would continue to be for several years—until long after I had left—rising to an astounding high before the 1987 oil market crash.

None of this changed our circumstances in the slightest, for Daddy continued to break his promises to Mama and to break her heart in the process.

Gone with the Wind came back. Mama said, "This is history, Billie Jo. We'll all go tonight."

On a week night?

"It's long. I hope you don't fall asleep."

Mr. Lowell, the theater manager, started the projector at six o'clock sharp. At ten fifteen, when the lights came up, I was still glued to the screen, wide awake, tears rolling down my face for the ill-fated Melanie, aching for Scarlett, madly in love with Rhett, and so transported that it took Mama several minutes to convince me that what I'd seen was a movie.

"Billie Jo," she shook me, "come on. It's late."

"Come *on*, Billie Jo," cried Fay Ann, pulling my sweater around me. "Let's go home."

I tried to shake myself free of the spell. Now, when I look back, I think it was at that moment I knew I wanted to become an actress. For the first time I began to listen when Mama told me I was pretty enough to go to Hollywood. I started watching more carefully at the Saturday matinees, where I now went by myself or with friends. I looked at the makeup and the way the stars carried themselves. I began to see the difference between being beautiful and having a sexy—a term I wasn't capable of using then—body, and actually seeming to *become* the person portrayed in the story flashing on what we still called the silver screen.

It was a haunting time; the drug store bored me, my toys seemed stupid, my family made me angry, and I didn't want to help with chores. Daddy got mad.

"What's wrong with you?" he yelled. "You aren't helping your mother. You had better shape up, young lady, or there will be no more Saturday movies for you."

This, of course, was a more dire threat than he could possibly know and therefore effective. I shook myself free and promised that I'd be good. Missing the Saturday movie would be like starving and I would end up like the people in Europe we'd seen pictures of after VE day.

My world expanded slowly. I had one letter from Mary Lee, telling me that she lived near a beach, in Santa Monica, not far from Hollywood, and that she had seen Judy Holliday and Cary Grant one day when her mother took her to visit Columbia Studio. Maybe we could go there when I came to see her.

In October organized baseball grew up when the Brooklyn Dodgers hired Jackie Robinson to play shortstop; November, in Nuremburg, the first trial of Nazi war criminals began.

The holidays passed; it was 1946. People talked about strikes and the United Nations, refugees and riots in India. The cost of eating grew suddenly more expensive, since sugar was the only food remaining under price control.

I went to the movies and did my homework, played, and generally drifted as nine-year-olds do.

We were in the middle of a hot spell that had the whole town groaning. Just getting to school was an ordeal and by the time homeroom was over everyone had wet patches under their arms and across their backs. It was so hot we didn't even have a turkey for Thanksgiving dinner. Mama made salads and we ate outside. It wasn't until December that the temperature broke and everyone could breathe again.

Over the months we had heard about more riots and more strikes, the Iron Curtain, spies and A-bomb tests. In Nuremburg they hung nine Nazi war criminals. W.C. Fields died on Christmas Day; and in Vietnam the French were about to begin a disastrous war that no one dreamed would someday engulf America.

In April Texas and Oklahoma had a terrible tornado, but luckily it never reached West Texas; the world's worst air crash killed forty people—I can still see that headline: "forty"; ironic these days, isn't it?

There was to be a play the last week before summer vacation. It had been written by Mr. Janus, the high school English teacher; he had asked our grammar school to allow some of the younger children to take part. Though I was terrified, a part of me ached to be chosen. When the teacher called my name my heart turned over.

I would play one of the four seasons: Summer. Mama brought home some light green material to make a costume; I was skeptical: she didn't sew very well.

We rehearsed after school and on Saturdays. Mama brought me and stayed to watch; those rehearsals kept me rapt: the contained excitement, the confusion, the stumbling through lines and search for the proper chalk mark onstage.

Mr. Janus, as director, frequently lost patience with the actors and shouted as Fay Ann said he never did when he was teaching English. I loved it all.

Watching the stage crew paint sets was a revelation, for when I walked to the back of the auditorium, they had created an outdoor scene that looked almost real. And when I tried my costume on for the first time and saw myself in the hall mirror I thought I looked like Ginger Rogers in *Lady in the Dark*—as well as I could remember, for I'd seen that picture when I was seven.

The headdress had real sequins on it and the bodice of the dress too. And there were more sequins on the skirt, which was very short, since "Summer" had to be scantily clothed. Mama had put snaps down the back. Zippers weren't yet readily available and buttonholes too difficult. Oh, how I loved that first costume; it transported me to mysterious Hollywood where all the magic took place.

My part had two lines: I said, "Your Majesty, I bring sunshine and flowers," and later, "I bow to my cousin, Autumn."

The night of the show we all were excited. Even Daddy was coming and Fay Ann had talked her current boyfriend, Steve, into sitting with her instead of with his friends, a great concession.

My two lines were certainly not a problem to remember. The butterflies in my stomach were pleasantly disturbing and I watched our sixteen-year-old "lead" and her anxiety with bewilderment. She was wringing her hands like someone facing a firing squad.

I was "on" early. I walked to the designated spot with confidence, turned and faced an audience for the first time. What a shock: past the first couple of rows I could hardly see them. Even though I knew where my parents were seated, they were invisible in the gloom of the darkened auditorium. But they were there, I knew, and my first line was delivered complete with grandiose gesture. As I threw my arms wide I felt the snaps pop open down my back; that certainly had not happened in dress rehearsal.

Panic! My face grew hot and my knees began to shake. "Spring", standing next to me, looked up in alarm; she probably thought I'd suddenly been paralyzed with fear. Of course she was right, but for the wrong reason. I was supposed to bow to the Queen, turn and retreat upstage. If I bowed, my costume would come off. If I just stood there I'd be in the way of the six-year-olds who were supposed to dance across the stage.

I dipped my knee towards the floor in the first attempt at the curtsy I would later practice for my meeting with the Queen of England after *Royal Interlude*, and with arms still wide-spread, backed off into the wings, the entire cast looking on in amazement.

Mr. Janus was furious. "What do you think you're doing?" I was too frightened to speak so I pointed over my shoulder, then turned my back to him.

"I'll be damned," he said. "How did that happen?" His anger had evaporated instantly.

My voice returned. "My mother doesn't sew very well," I answered in a whisper.

He was now making funny noises behind me, which I suspected were stifled laughter but he only said, "Let me fasten you together. Then we have to get you back onstage somehow so you can say your line. You did very well to get off that way—great presence." It was the first time I'd heard the expression. I liked it.

I never told Mama why the way the play was staged got changed.

That summer I fell in love.

You know my birthday; at least you think you do. Actually it was always stated incorrectly since the studio wanted it July 4 instead of

June 30, so they simply moved it a few days. Studios still had the clout to do that kind of thing when I got to Hollywood in 1953, though as everyone knows, their power was on the wane by then.

At any rate, that year we had enough money to have a birthday party. What a thrill! First planning the date and figuring out whom to invite, then writing the invitations, buying favors and paper plates and the anxiety waiting for RSVP. I felt very important writing those initials when Mama explained that they stood for French words and that all polite people would *"respondez"* if we requested it.

Everyone did, too, and they all accepted, which was a surprise; ever since Mary Lee left I had felt I didn't have many friends anymore.

The big day arrived; my present from Mama and Daddy was a new dress that I thought was about the most beautiful dress anyone ever had worn. I remember it: white, with a ruffle at the bottom and a sweetheart neckline. As to shoes—even if we'd had the money there was still rationing; I had to borrow party shoes from Fay Ann. They were old and too big but they were white so I didn't mind.

One of the boys I'd invited had not been in Midland long. He was from Ohio so he sounded funny to us. But he didn't look funny. He was tall for his age and slender. Red hair fell on his forehead and his blue eyes had an alert expression as if he were always just a little ahead of our slow Southern ways.

I hadn't paid much attention to him before school let out but he was friendly and Mama suggested it would be nice to invite him since he was new.

When he arrived, hair unnaturally slicked and in a *necktie*, I was struck dumb. My heart went bumping along and my hands grew wet. What was happening to me? It's funny now, of course, but then it was staggering.

I barely remember the party; we played games and had ice cream and everyone was traditional and brought gifts, a novel experience for me. But my heart was wound around Jack Wilson and every time he looked at me I quaked in my borrowed shoes like an aspen in the wind. It's a good thing we were too young to play Spin the Bottle; I never would have been able to survive kissing him.

The rest of the summer became a series of false trips to the drug store, walking the long way through town in the hope of a glimpse of Jack Wilson. If I got lucky I would see him before he saw me so I'd have time to prepare myself for the encounter. I'd straighten my shoulders and lift my head high, glancing in the store windows to be sure my hair was combed. If Mama had allowed lipstick I would have worn it but she insisted I was much too young. Always too young; I'd like a little of that youth now. We never appreciate it when we're there.

Each encounter was a little different from the one preceding it. Jack always said hello. And that was all. He wasn't smitten as I was. I realized he had no particular desire to be close to me—*me*—so I thought that if I were different he might become interested. First I tried Judy Garland, fresh, peppy, bouncy. When that didn't work I tried Lana Turner, stealing into Fay Ann's drawer for her mascara and leg makeup but not brave enough to try stuffing one of her bras. Finally I graduated to my version of Mae West, always back in reruns at our one theater. Hand on hip I would begin my swagger if I spied Jack coming towards me, swaying my hips and pitching my voice deep into my throat. Nothing worked. Then, one fatal day I got mad. We bumped into one another on Maple Street, in front of the stationary store. I didn't even say hello, I just tore into that poor boy, screaming, "I don't know why you don't pay more attention to me; I've tried every actress I know of and all you do is just say hi and keep going. Why don't you like me? What's wrong?"

I can still see the look of astonishment on his face as he answered with the scathing, indisputable fact, "But you're a *girl*."

The year had vanished and suddenly I was starting fifth grade; I liked it, which surprised us all. Jack Wilson and his family moved on and I didn't even miss him.

As I grew older Fay Ann and I grew closer. Not so close that we didn't fight, of course, but there was a new community of "family" which felt good. She helped me with my homework and advised me on the latest fashion in hair styles and generally didn't seem to be as constantly annoyed with me as she had been. Except when one of her increasing number of boyfriends came over and I stuck around too long, teasing him and trying to climb on his lap.

In spite of all the strikes, The Ford Company had started producing new cars. That was no help to the Payner family; we continued to drive the same 1938 Chevy, now faded from navy to a purplish blue. It didn't matter. There were still a lot of old cars on the streets, mostly owned by servicemen or passed down to sons and daughters as wealthy parents bought the rapidly appearing new models.

Over a period of several months I saw Fay Ann with the same man more than once in the front seat of a new Ford Sportsman. He was a boy I'd never seen before. I started teasing her about him. "Who's that guy you've been going out with? Is he your latest boyfriend? He looks old enough to be your uncle. Besides, he's ugly."

"Ugly? He looks great in his uniform. You really don't know anything, Billie Jo. Now leave me alone. I want to go to sleep." She flipped over her pillow and burrowed her head into it. I decided to pay more attention. I hadn't noticed the uniform because he was sitting in the car.

"What's his name, Fay Ann?" She lifted her head and stared at me, then turned away and pulled the pillow over her face. She was acting strange. When I thought about it, it also was strange that she was going to sleep so early. Maybe she had those mysterious "cramps" that neither she nor Mama would explain. I couldn't figure out the puzzle so I curled up and went to sleep myself.

A few nights later I tried again. "Who is he, Fay Ann? He hasn't ever been over to meet Mama. He must be rich to drive that car. Do you like him?"

Fay Ann groaned, "Leave me alone Billie Jo, just leave me alone."

"Well, if that's the way you're going to be!" I turned to the wall and pulled up the covers. In the morning I had forgotten all about it.

Fay Ann was crying and Mama was wringing her hands when I stumbled into the living room earlier than expected from playing after-school baseball, my nose bloodied from stupidly sliding to first base on my face.

Surprise made me stop short; I asked what happened.

"Go to your room," said Mama, apparently without noticing the blood dripping onto my jacket.

"Mama, my nose is bleeding."

"Get some ice and a washcloth and go to your room."

"You don't care what happens to me. You don't love me at all," I moaned dramatically and headed for the Frigidaire. Ice wrapped in a dishtowel, I sneaked through the back door, letting it close gently behind me, then carefully worked my way around the corner of the house to the side where I knew I could hear if the window were cracked just a tiny bit.

"Maybe you're wrong, Honey. Maybe you're just late."

Fay Ann was shaking her head. "I don't think so, Mama."

"But you *can't*, Fay Ann, you're only a baby yourself.

Muffled sobs hid most of Fay Ann's answer but the last two words were, "...have to."

"Have to what?" I wondered.

"You don't even know him. He might be—well, anything, how can you tell?"

"How can you ask such a stupid question, with the way Papa treats you?" shrieked Fay Ann, almost knocking me off my precarious perch on the rough edge of siding to which I was clinging.

Mama's answer was too quiet for me to hear but she was crying too. My nose was still bleeding; I had forgotten it. There was blood on my hands and the dishtowel was pink. I raised it to my nose, lost my single-handed grip and tumbled into the bushes.

It must have been noisy for the next thing I knew Mama was shaking me and yelling, "Eavesdroppers hear no good about themselves. I said go to your room and I meant it." She had never sounded so angry before, so I went, no better informed than I had been and much more curious.

The next day Fay Ann told me she was bringing a boyfriend home to dinner. "Be nice to him, Billie Jo, and don't climb on his lap, either. Please."

She seemed so serious and so sad that I resolved to behave.

The night he came Mama put on the white tablecloth that we saved for holidays and set the table early, fussing that the glasses didn't match and that the only set of dishes we had were the ones she had collected from the theater by going regularly every Friday night. It was obvious that this dinner would be very special.

When Fay Ann's guest arrived he turned out to be the man I had asked her about a few days earlier. He wasn't at all bad looking, just a little chubby even in his uniform, with sandy hair and light blue eyes. His name was Alton Fawcett. I could feel my eyes get round when Fay Ann introduced us. The Fawcetts were among the richest families in town. He smiled at me and then shook Mama's hand awkwardly, and

Daddy's, saying, "I've been looking forward to meeting you, Mr. and Mrs. Payner."

That sure sounded funny but no one laughed at him. Mama seemed nervous and Daddy cross. I wondered if Daddy knew what it was Fay Ann had to do.

Dinner was very quiet. Everyone seemed embarrassed until finally Mama asked some questions, got Alton talking about his plans for opening a new Ford dealership on Main Street as soon as he got out of the service. (I thought that meant he was someone's servant and had to clarify it after he left.)

That's about when I tuned out and just watched Fay Ann grow more and more still and silent until she seemed to sort of disappear, even though she sat in her usual seat in her best blue dress with the white collar, the one she had said would have to get her through all the rest of the parties till the end of school.

After dinner Mama sent Fay Ann and Alton to the living room to talk to Daddy and me to my room to do homework.

"And if I catch you eavesdropping tonight, you'll not go to a movie for a month," she hissed as I left the kitchen.

I was almost asleep when my sister finally came in. She threw herself down on the bed and started to cry. "What's the matter, Fay Ann?"

"Oh, Billie Jo, I don't want to get married," she said, her voice warped with misery.

"Married!" I sat straight up. Married? Fay Ann was only sixteen years old. She wouldn't even graduate from high school 'til next year. "You can't get married."

"I have to. There's no choice. I'm pregnant."

"Pregnant? You mean like having a baby? How could you?"

"I could. I could and I am. And I'm lucky Alton will marry me; I don't think he really wants to."

I didn't know what to say. What would it be like to have my sister married? And with a baby of her own? I couldn't imagine it. No movie had told me what having a baby would be like, not even *Gone with the Wind*, except that it hurt a lot and sometimes you almost died. Would Fay Ann die? And who would take care of the baby if she did? That scared me. Mama didn't seem strong enough and I didn't know how and we certainly couldn't depend on Daddy.

"Are you going to die?" I asked in a whisper.

"I wish I could," Fay Ann groaned, then she laughed while she was crying and asked, "What made you think of such an awful thing?"

"Well, Melanie almost did, so I thought you might."

"Oh, Billie Jo, things aren't always like the movies. Those are just make believe, not real life. Real life is bad enough."

She didn't know, of course, just how bad real life could be, for with all the problems of finances and gambling and a broken hearted mother, until now we had been sheltered from all the worst tragedies. Maybe if we had known what was in store for us we would have been counting blessings instead of complaining.

IV

Fay Ann was married early in March on a brilliant Saturday afternoon. Alton's parents, at first violently opposed to the union, nevertheless had offered to help with the wedding expenses when they faced the inevitable. I think they were so appalled at the thought of being allied to a "gambling" family, and from the wrong side of town as well, that they merely wanted to get it over with.

Fay Ann politely refused their help; perhaps she hoped they would realize she wasn't marrying Alton for his money. Whether they did or not, it was a strained and uncomfortable time, relieved only by the loveliness of the bride, for she was indeed lovely, though terribly pale. She wore Mama's wedding dress from the thirties, the skirt bias cut, hanging gracefully from a yolk at the hips which Fay Ann had needed to let out only slightly since she was still as slim as ever. The back of the skirt just brushed the floor and the low vee neck was filled in with beaded net. The satin was ivory and almost darker in tone than Fay Ann's face.

Her sable hair was soft and curled and she wore a circlet of net instead of a veil. She let me sew some beads on it; they glimmered when they caught the light.

Fay Ann's best friend was maid of honor; I was bridesmaid in a peach colored dress of my sister's, altered to fit my flat shape, with a long skirt, which pleased me.

The brief ceremony was held in our front room, hardly conducive to a beautiful occasion, for though it was meticulously clean, the light green paint, always a color I considered unappealing, was faded and water marked. But the idea of a church wedding sent my sister into hysterics, so we decorated as best we could, creating a somewhat skimpy bower of daisies, picked from the field behind the house. The few friends who had been invited contributed a variety of food, everything from olives stuffed with cheese to tiny cream puffs filled with custard.

Mama had baked the wedding cake, two tiers, and bought a heart shaped arch with bride and groom from the grocery store for the top. I can only imagine what she was thinking, with the situation the same as hers had been almost exactly seventeen years before.

Daddy was morose. Mama had to threaten him to get him to walk Fay Ann down the aisle, improvised with borrowed folding chairs. When he answered the preacher's question about, "Who gives this woman…?"—he should have asked, "Who sacrifices this child?"—you could barely hear Daddy's response. ("Give away the bride." What a strange expression.) He barely smiled at anyone when he stood in the receiving line and avoided the guests as much as he was able.

Alton, finally out of uniform after four years in the army, wore a dark blue suit with a blue and gold tie and looked less chubby than he had the night he came to meet the family. He seemed happy with his child bride. Indeed, he wasn't that much more than a child himself. He was twenty-two, a somewhat pampered and spoiled rich man's son, slightly more sophisticated after his stint in service, just a little bewildered by the events and the prospect of becoming a father, though how many of his family and friends knew of that fact I have no idea.

Only Mama and I could see beneath the glittery smile and nervous warmth of Fay Ann's demeanor to the frightened little girl who would be leaving the only home she had ever known to become wife to a man she scarcely knew, and mother to a baby born too soon.

The Fawcett's wedding gift to the couple was, almost predictably, a home. It was small, but brand new and near them on the other side of town where speculators had developed a tract of land in the waning months of the war and were now stuck with mid-income housing which they were happy to sell for reasonable prices.

So, after a brief honeymoon in New York, Fay Ann, half a year from seventeen, became a housewife.

Which left me, for the first time ever, with a room all to myself. I hated it. Every time I woke, either in the middle of the night or when the sun rose, I looked for my sister and she wasn't there. A lump would form in my throat and I would struggle with the tears, refusing to let them fall, knowing, as I had for so long, that they wouldn't change a thing.

Mama took me to visit. There wasn't a lot of furniture but the house was neat and clean. Alton was at work in the new auto showroom he and his father had opened downtown and Fay Ann, her body now becoming thick and awkward, was trying to put up wallpaper in what would become the nursery.

She came to the door with a streak of paste on her face; by the time she finished greeting us her tears had washed it away.

"Oh, Mama, it's so good to see you. I felt like I was a million miles away."

She hugged me tight. "Do you miss school, Billie Jo? How was your last report card? You have to get good grades if you want to make anything of your life."

"It was okay. I'm glad it's summer; school got sorta boring."

"Don't ever say that! School is the whole answer," she burst out fiercely. "I'll go back just as soon as I can, or take correspondence courses or—well, somehow I'll graduate in spite of...." She broke off as a new trickle of tears spilled over. "I shouldn't fuss, Mama. I loved New York; we had a good time and Alton is already making good money at the agency. It's just...."

"I know, honey. It's just that you're too young." Mama was crying, too, so pretty soon my nose started to run. I wiped it on my shirtsleeve, which made both Mama and Fay Ann laugh.

"Go blow your nose, for crying out loud. Won't you ever grow up, Billie Jo?"

They were sitting on the couch, the only place to sit in the whole room, holding tightly to each other's hands, when I got back from the bathroom.

"When are you going to have the baby, Fay Ann? Can I hold it when it's born? Will it be a boy or a girl?"

"I don't know; you can't know before it gets here. Doesn't she know *anything*, Mama?"

"She's just eleven, honey. There's plenty of time."

"There's never plenty of time. She should know *everything*." She looked away, adding, "What does Daddy say about me?"

Mama shook her head and for the first time I could remember, did not reply, simply shook her head.

"Never mind, Mama. I understand. Maybe someday he'll forgive me." She sighed and pressed lightly on her stomach. "Is he...? I mean, I have a little extra money, if it would help?"

The question hung there waiting for a response. Mama's hand went to her mouth, then doubled into a fist. "No, darling, thank you." She paused, then continued, "It is a small miracle that I can see you financially comfortable. If you can make a good marriage with Alton then maybe this has happened for the best. I want you to be happy and that's all that really matters, even though it's come about in the wrong way."

I was watching Fay Ann as our mother spoke. Her eyes shifted, she looked at the wall, not at us, just nodded her head without answering and leaned over to hug us both.

Mama looked sadder than ever and even without Fay Ann to explain, I reasoned that it had as much to do with Dad's continuing gambling as my sister's abrupt departure. He was gone at least as much as ever, perhaps more.

Sometimes he would get home early and I would hear him saying, "Sweetheart, I have a little money for you." But other times he would be silent, and the only indication that he had returned was the squeak of the third step from the top as he climbed the stairs.

The weeks passed sluggishly, the world plodded on. By the time school rolled around in September I had grown used to the heartache surrounding me. School was simply a way to pass the day, play time equally so. Only Saturday matinees weren't dull. I remember them all: *Something for the Boys*—I got a chuckle out of Carmen Miranda and her bizarre headdresses; *Yankee Doodle Dandy* for the third time. They kept bringing it back; our town loved James Cagney; and my favorite for that whole year, *Ninotchka*, with the taciturn but spectacular Garbo.

As her due date approached we saw little of Fay Ann. Those few occasions we visited or she came to us she was pale and listless. Her body was misshapen but not terribly large; the maternity dresses she wore looked like she had slept in them, which always made me glance at my denim skirt to be sure it had been ironed.

My sister let me feel the baby kick and laughed at me. "Your eyes about bugged out of your head, Billie Jo. Are you going to come baby-sit for me when he gets here?"

"He? Do you know now?"

"No, I told you we have to wait 'til it's born. But Alton wants a boy, so I call it that. I'd as soon have a girl."

"Have you talked to the principal yet, honey?" Mama asked.

Ever too curious for my own good, I broke in, "What for? Are you back in school?"

They exchanged glances that immediately intrigued me more.

"Hush, Billie Jo. I'm just trying to get my teachers to let me take last semester's final exams so I can work on my senior year by correspondence school. But don't tell. It's a secret."

"Sure. I won't tell. But who'm I supposed to not tell?"

"Oh, you're hopeless. Just don't tell anyone. You promise?"

I nodded, not understanding why it was so secret. If I could quit school and just take a test to prove I'd been there, I'd have done it in a shot and been proud of it.

"Tell me why it's a secret."

Mama laughed and got up. "I want to start dinner. I'll be back in a few minutes. You rest, Fay Ann. And don't go bothering your sister with so many questions, Billie Jo."

"No, Ma'am," I said, and immediately turned back to my sister and asked again, "Why is it a secret?"

She sighed. "It just is. It might not work out and I'd rather not have everyone know about it."

Satisfied for the moment, I wriggled myself into the worn cushion of our second-hand couch. "What's it like being married?"

"It's.... Well, it's strange."

"Is it fun?"

"Sometimes," she said. "Don't ever be in a hurry, do you hear? Don't waste your life..." the unspoken phrase, "...like I did," weighted the air between us.

"Why did you get married if you didn't really want to?"

"I got pregnant. You know that."

"But why?"

She looked so defeated that I was sorry I hadn't listened to Mama. Again her gaze fastened on the wall.

"He looked so good in his uniform and seemed so grown up. He was older and different from the high school boyfriends I had. And he wanted to. So I did."

"Wanted to what?"

She shook herself and winced. "Ask Mama," she answered wearily. "I'm too tired to talk anymore."

Johnny arrived November fifth, three weeks early. He had a crop of curly black hair and eyes that certainly would stay blue. His face was broad and flat, his tongue thick, his chin small, his neck short. He was born a Down Syndrome child, what we then called a Mongoloid. The doctors limited their information to the simplistic: Johnny would never be normal. The extra chromosome had limited his brain function and malformed his heart. There was no way to predict how severe the retardation would be or whether his heart would beat for a day, a month or many years. Fay Ann was trapped in a tragedy not of her making but only of her desire to please, and Alton, hating her from the moment the doctors told him, accused her of having tricked him into the marriage. It was as if he thought it was her fault, that Johnny's birth defect was something Fay Ann had planned.

~

It has taken a week to learn this much about Billie Jo's—Alana's—early life. It is apparent that the strain on her is intense, that the memories are painful. I know her mother died several years ago, in this very house.

But I didn't know about the child, John, nor do I know what happened to him or his mother and father. It is difficult not to ask questions, not to push for information, to allow Alana to continue at her own pace.

Her mind is sharp as a razor, her memory astonishing, also her ability to put together events of the past, and there are times when her descriptions are so vivid that I have copied them verbatim and can take no credit for being creative in writing them down.

We consume gallons of tea and a little brandy along the way. Occasionally I talk her into allowing me to bring food and we sit companionably, discarding the tape recorder's imperatives, simply chatting like old friends as we eat.

I enjoy these moments, feel no need to hurry her. She will lean back in the old satin covered chair when she finishes talking, relax and wave a languid hand, still slim and beautiful, in spite of prominent veins. We speak of the world's events, of movies, past and present, and sometimes she asks, almost slyly, about my life and family. It seems unfair to avoid her questions when she so unselfishly shares her life with me. But my childhood would be of little interest and my current crisis—if indeed it is that—well, why should I burden her with my troubles? Occasionally I tell about episodes that might amuse her. Of course she knows there are things I keep to myself.

I'm comfortable wearing jeans and an old shirt; it doesn't seem to bother Alana that I'm so informal. She continues to wear old fashioned but exquisite clothing, dresses most often but sometimes slack suits with well known labels, as if she is on her way to a luncheon or afternoon tea.

On rare days she calls to postpone our morning talks to afternoon, yet I sense some urgency and wonder if her health is worse than she claims or if she simply doesn't wish to talk.

If it's a long day, to alleviate the intensity of Alana's story we go for a ride in my rental car. We drive through town and out to the country road where the table of West Texas stretches to infinity, broken only by the steel skeletons of oil derricks, like prehistoric monsters pecking for food in the arid earth.

Then we return to the house and get back to work.

V

In the weeks just before Johnny was born, and increasingly afterwards, with the shock of his physical problems, there were earthquake sized rumblings in my home.

Blithe and apparently unconcerned I continued the pattern established in happier days, but my parents' arguments grew in volume and frequency; there was less warmth in my father's greetings to Mama and her responses were monosyllabic when not totally silent. It was only a matter of time before divorce became inevitable.

My father moved out in December, just before Christmas. Dearly though I loved him, I was glad to see him go. It wasn't so much that I understood the emotions involved as that I sensed there would be no peace if he remained. I felt diminished somehow by his absence while the relief made me lighter, as if I had sweat away excess weight.

So we were two, with not much income to speak of and very little laughter. The Saturday matinees were no longer available unless I managed to baby-sit for a neighbor or my helpless little nephew, to give Fay Ann a break from her endless job of caring for him and for which I was paid the going rate of twenty-five cents an hour. But getting to her house was a problem. Mama's friends were generous about loaning their cars on occasion, but she was working full time at Woolworth's now, with little time for anything else. Also, since dedicated Fay Ann would leave Johnny only for a couple of hours and there was usually someone nearby to help out, Alton didn't like coming to pick me up for such a short stay.

Actually, I'm not sure Alton liked anything those days. He didn't say much but he looked disheveled, like a child in a tantrum, and wore a perpetual expression of anger. He smoked endlessly and occasionally smelled of alcohol.

As bad as he looked, Fay Ann looked worse. She had lost weight and her hair straggled down her back in an unkempt tangle. She rarely used makeup, which was the tip-off to me that she was in very bad shape. But she never gave up—the gutsy youngster with the rifle.

The only blessing in our lives then was that Mama was so worried about earning a living that she had no time to worry about her grandchild and his mother.

My eleventh year had come and gone, our small universe managing to survive in spite of everything.

Still reading headlines, I'd been vaguely aware of the world around me if anything caught my imagination: a saintly man by the strange name of Mahatma Gandhi was murdered; somewhere I couldn't find on the map, a state called Israel, came into existence; the Olympic Games were held for the first time since before the war; and oh, wonderful! for women a brand new look with full skirts and hems dropped almost to the ankles, courtesy of a designer in Paris named Christian Dior.

The memories of my twelfth year are rather vague. Yes, my body began to change, though we had no idea it would evolve into a figure that would have Hollywood gasping a few years later.

I saw few movies, but my interest in them never abated and when Mama went to have her hair done I went along to read fan magazines. So I knew all about Rita Hayworth divorcing Orson Wells for an Arab, and the scandal over Ingrid Bergman, who ran off with an important director in Italy. I carefully followed the Academy Award winners, from Jane Wyman in *Johnny Belinda* and Olivia de Havilland in *The Heiress* to Broderick Crawford in *All the King's Men* and Lawrence Olivier in *Hamlet*, my first encounter with Shakespeare.

When I did manage to save enough money for the theater I was very careful to choose a film I really wanted to see. I missed a lot I've since watched on television or tape, unless, of course, I had arranged for private screenings in those days when my status allowed it.

Of all I managed to see at that time, my favorite was *The Red Shoes*. Dancing would never be my forte as I certainly proved in *Hoofin' It* , but watching Moira Shearer introduced me to ballet and an art form that I hadn't discovered previously.

It wasn't until early in 1951, after a dismal Christmas, that life had another twist for us that eventually changed everything.

Exactly when or how Mama met Howard Rodinski isn't really important. That she seemed to brighten and become more like her old self was. It was a sort of awakening for me to watch her begin to smile again, to dress with more care, to experiment a little with makeup in an effort to keep up with changing fashion. She was happier than she had been for years, I guess, and it showed.

Howard began coming over for dinner. When he arrived it was usually with a small gift of some sort: flowers, a package of candy bars and sometimes, joy! three tickets to the Saturday matinee. I was back in business.

Classes were easy, perhaps too easy. I was thirteen years old, just getting my balance as a freshman in High School, newly aware of boys and pondering my changing shape with awe.

On the few occasions we visited Fay Ann—I no longer baby-sat for Johnny at all—she warned me repeatedly about being careful, telling me over and over that above all, I must not repeat Mama's and her own mistake; that I must forget my notions about Hollywood. That kind of success, she told me, happened only on the screen, never in real life; I must be the one in the family with an education, must become a professional.

I would nod, my heart aching for my sister, who cared for her son with total devotion, feeding him, encouraging him, trying to teach him to walk, which he was not yet able to do, though he was now almost three years old. She constantly talked to him with, I know, the unspoken hope that the doctors would magically wave away the malformed face and say his heart was now strong; that though he rarely spoke even a word, he would someday astonish everyone by getting up, running to the window and crying out, "When is Daddy coming home?"

~

Alana pauses in her narrative. With a sad smile she asks me what I know about Down Syndrome children. When I admit my ignorance, she tells me of the difference today from the days when children so afflicted were viewed as hopeless idiots and stuck away in a closet somewhere as if they were a disgrace. Today, it seems, doctors know how to treat a child born with those problems; and most defective hearts can be cured with surgery. Down Syndrome children are almost always happy and loving and many of them are able to lead full, productive lives.

"Yes," I agree with Alana, my tone reflecting my sympathy, "everything is different now."

~

Fay Ann spoke of Alton rarely, then with what began to seem like apprehension. And once, when I saw a bruise on her arm, so dark it was almost the color of eggplant, she quickly rolled down her sleeve before Mama noticed it, and said, "Just keep quiet, Billie Jo."

She had succeeded in persuading her teachers to allow her a chance to pass her final exams and had gone on with her education by correspondence. It was an agonizingly slow process but she did it; that alone was an accomplishment to keep her from despair.

Strangely, her diploma was never on display; on those few occasions we saw Fay Ann and Alton for dinner or some special event she always warned me not to speak of it.

We had some moments together and now it was Fay Ann asking the questions. They mostly concerned Mama.

"Is she happy, Billie Jo? Is Howard good for her? Do you think they'll get married?"

"Why would Mama get married again?" The thought had never occurred to me. "I don't want her to."

"Don't be so selfish; she's still young and she deserves some happiness. Howard seems to be a real nice man."

"Well, he is nice, but that doesn't mean she has to marry him. You aren't so very happy being married."

Fay Ann's hand pleated and smoothed the fabric of her blue skirt; she looked at me without saying anything for a long time. Then, too casually, "What makes you think that?"

"I just can tell. And anyhow, I bet I know how you got that bruise I saw on your arm."

"Don't you ever mention that again," she hissed, confirming what I had suspected. "I don't want anyone to know about it. Besides, it won't happen again; he promised."

While still another war surged in a place called Korea and a Senator by the name of McCarthy chased phantom Communists all across America, my life began to take shape in a very direct way.

First, Howard proposed to Mama and she accepted. They were married at City Hall. Mama wore a new, butter yellow dress and matching hat with a tiny veil. Howard looked uncomfortable in a too tight gray suit and too bright red tie.

We moved, not just around the corner but actually to the other side of town, not far from my sister, to a small house set behind a row of trees in a large corner lot. Howard was an oil rigger for Exxon; he made good, steady money and wonder of wonders! he didn't gamble.

The new house was pretty, with wood floors and bright rag rugs scattered around. The room that became mine had gables; the wallpaper was white with pink flowers.

I joined the High School Dramatic Club. Very quickly I began getting lead roles: it seemed I was a "natural." All my years of movie going were paying off. I played Mary Todd Lincoln in a purple satin hoop skirt, in an unmemorable one-act play, probably the only one the name of which I've forgotten. Then, in the January production of my sophomore year, Jo, in *Little Women* and in the late spring, Anna, in *Anna and the King of Siam*. It was heaven. There was never a question in my mind about what I would do with my life. The only thing I had no way of knowing then was just how soon that career would begin.

Howard brought us a television set. I was mesmerized. Right in our living room! And though those early days in black and white were not overloaded with quality presentations—a lot of comedy I really didn't enjoy and adventures like "The Lone Ranger," which I had outgrown—we laughed with Milton Berle, were introduced to future stars like Rosemary Clooney on the "Ed Sullivan Show," and faithfully watched, live, the "Pulitzer Prize Playhouse," which featured works by luminaries like Maxwell Anderson, Thorton Wilder and James

Michener. There was lighter fare, also: one evening there was a fire in a house down the street. We were so hypnotized by "The Hit Parade" that we didn't even know about it until the next day.

With all the warnings from Fay Ann and the example of the kind of tragedy that could occur, I was wary of boys. That didn't mean I was disinterested. I had my eye on one of the stage managers.

He was a senior, which meant we had no classes together so the only time I could talk to him was at rehearsals. We were backstage alone; everyone else had left.

I can feel it still, that first tentative sexual embrace. When Brian touched my breast I wanted to let him do whatever he wanted, to experience what had driven Mama into my father's arms and Alton to seduce my sister.

He was whispering, "Please," in my ear and Fay Ann was screaming, "No," in my head. I might not have stopped him if we had been someplace more conducive to experimenting. I needed more romance than the dusty floor backstage. The reality of our surroundings was most definitely a turnoff, at least to me.

The very best thing that could have happened did. I sneezed. I sneezed again. Then I started laughing.

Brian pulled away, angry. "What's so damn funny?"

I buttoned my blouse. "Come on, Brian. If I'm going to sneeze all evening we can't hope to…well, anything."

"Come to my house, then. No one's there."

"No. I'm going home. I don't want to do this anyhow."

"What do you mean? You were happy enough a few minutes ago. I didn't notice you objecting when I kissed you."

My thought was, a kiss does not a baby make. "That doesn't mean I want to go any further, Brian. I liked you kissing me. That's all." Oh, I sounded so sure of myself, so self-contained. But all the time my heart was racing and my hands were wet with nervous tension. It was close; fear saved me from making what could have been a serious mistake.

~

Alana laughs heartily, then sobers. She claims that though she's laughing now, then it didn't seem funny at all. What if she spent her whole life afraid of men? But it was a valuable lesson. Then, with a rueful shake of her head she adds an enigmatic, "Not that I heeded it later."

I am more intrigued than ever.

~

From then on I avoided Brian as much as possible, not too difficult since our paths seldom crossed on campus and I was onstage during most of the rehearsals. It was my favorite role so far, that of Eliza Doolittle in Shaw's *Pygmalion*, much too ambitious an undertaking for a high school drama club. But oh, how I loved playing it, dreaming that I, too, would blossom into a lady of gentle and dignified maturity, always knowing how to dress and which fork to use and how to behave at all the balls I would someday attend.

At home we had settled into a comfortable routine. Mama still worked at Woolworth's, though she was back to part time. She sang around the house, what a pleasure, and Howard continued to bring home a comfortable salary.

Fay Ann appeared with bruises on occasion, always with an excuse: "I fell; I twisted my arm lifting Johnny into his chair; I bumped my cheek when I got up in the dark." She still cared for Johnny with devotion, though Alton had begun a campaign to have him institutionalized, which horrified my mother. I thought it might become necessary; as Johnny grew larger tending him would become more and more difficult, not just emotionally but physically. How would tiny Fay Ann be able to cope with him when he was fully grown?

Does that sound cold? My heart ached more for my sister than for her stricken son.

We had a new car now, so Mama went to Fay Ann's to help out quite regularly, usually in the evening. If I wasn't at rehearsal I was busy with homework, or, on weekends, at a party or a movie.

Memory can be so vivid. The first time it happened I was at the dining room table, tearing out my hair over a report for history. Howard had been standing behind me for several minutes, a fact of which I was only dimly aware.

He cleared his throat. "Billie Jo, you have sure grown into a lovely young woman." He sounded strange and I looked up at him.

"Thank you, Howard."

"I've been watching you; you don't seem to have a boyfriend."

Puzzled and unsuspecting, I gestured unconcern with my shoulders.

He stepped close and his hands caressed my arms. "I think you need someone to show you what it's like to have a man care for you."

Riveted, I couldn't move. He couldn't mean what I thought he meant, he just couldn't.

He must have misread my expression of dismay and taken my silence for acquiescence; his hands slid to my breasts so that I was captive, him standing behind my chair reaching over my shoulders.

For one moment I was frozen; then I shoved the chair back so violently that he almost toppled; his first expression of astonishment gave way immediately to anger, but I didn't wait to listen to whatever he might say. I left my books on the table and flew up the stairs, screaming as I ran, "Don't you ever touch me again, never, do you hear?"

I threw myself on my bed, panting with panic. How could he have thought for one minute that his embrace would be welcome? What had I done to encourage such an obscene act? What sort of person was I?

As the panic subsided other, more rational thoughts rushed in to replace the self-abnegation: Mama. She was so happy, so trusting. How could I tell her and destroy that trust, take away all the comfort and pleasure she had found. Never for a minute did I doubt that she would believe me, or that she would do anything other than send Howard away. I couldn't tell her. This was a secret I must keep to myself and pray that there would never be a recurrence.

There was complete silence downstairs. It lulled me and I began to think that the whole incident was an aberration; it wouldn't happen again; perhaps Howard really assumed I needed that kind of affection. I supposed it was believable. It was what I wanted to believe.

Ah, then acting became a necessity. It was only slightly difficult when Mama and I were alone; when Howard was in the house and I had no excuse to go to my room, it required all my talent to pretend there was nothing wrong. But time truly does heal and as the weeks passed, the incident became just that: an incident. I almost forgot, too busy with life to pay much attention.

The last few weeks of spring semester were ahead. We were rehearsing another overly ambitious play, and I would soon be sixteen years old.

The mirror told me nothing about who I was; it told me encouraging things about how I appeared: the face that stared back at me was delicate, heart shaped, with high cheek bones, a straight nose, not too small, and big eyes. The skin was blessedly without blemishes, lightly tanned the shade of old ivory. Brows were arched naturally and required very little attention; teeth were white and even, mouth needed no filling out with lipstick; even when I was sad it was curved upward into a half smile. The little scar was an exclamation point, the cleft chin appealing. And in all but color, my hair imitated Rita Hayworth's red mop, cascading almost to my waist, blond, curly and luxurious.

The advantages of that image were obvious; what was important was that I had real talent. I don't know how I knew that, with my only experience a few appearances in a high school auditorium with no one but an English teacher and a prejudiced mother to encourage me. But somehow I knew and was willing to wait for the results, no matter how long it might take.

The corsage of carnations looked fresh and vibrant against the pink cotton of my strapless dress. We were off to a restaurant for celebration and I was thrilled. It was the best restaurant in Midland; I'd never been there before, nor had my Mother. Howard escorted us, one on each arm, like a knight, and seemed to be proud of his family.

They allowed me a sip from Mama's wine and I liked it. I had also liked having the waiter pull out my chair for me, shake out the napkin and lay it across my lap; nor was I intimidated by the array of silverware next to what Mama called a service plate.

Howard said, "Sixteen is very special. Order what you want." I ordered lobster thermidor, incredulous at the price. I loved him.

When dessert came I was amazed that in this dimly lit room with two wine glasses at every place on the starched white tablecloths, the waiters gathered at our table and sang "Happy Birthday." I knew I was glowing and the admiration in their eyes stimulated me just as applause after a performance always did. I wasn't embarrassed. In fact, I barely controlled the urge to rise from my chair and curtsy. The days of shyness were long gone.

Dreamy and floating, I pondered the evening as we drove home, too excited still to feel tired. We reached the house and Howard parked in the garage, leaving the wooden door open. We all walked to the front porch.

I said, "Mama, I'm going to sit out here for a while. I don't want to go to sleep yet."

"All right, honey. Happy birthday. Don't stay out too long."

She hugged me and went inside. I heard her heels on the stairs as she went up to their room.

I sat on my stole on the front step, looking up at a silver half moon, tipsy in the sky.

The June air was warm, dry, the breeze which sprang from the prairie beyond town a caress on my bare shoulders. I drifted, moonstruck, not really thinking of anything. I didn't hear him come across the yard; he had left through the back door. He lifted me in one abrupt gesture, pulling me close and bringing his lips down to mine before I had a moment to react.

"You're so beautiful," he muttered as I gasped, trying to bring my arms up, to push him away with all the strength I could summon.

"No," I breathed it out on a rush of air, trying to be quiet; their room was just above, the windows open. "Mama is upstairs; leave me alone."

"Your Mama is in the bathroom. Kiss me now."

"No, go away." I struggled but he still had me tight against his body and I could feel him, hard and erect against me.

"I will scream. I will."

"You won't. You don't want her to know. Now be a good girl. I won't hurt you."

He was forcing me back, step by step. I lost one shoe; my breath was rasping in rough, asthmatic gasps. My arms were imprisoned beneath his; his tightened around me until I could barely breathe. And all the time he was moving me farther and farther from the house.

We reached the car and I tried to grab a door handle but couldn't grasp it as he pushed me past and deeper into the small garage. Then he took my wrists in one tough hand and reached for the pull rope to let down the garage door. It didn't seem possible that with one hand he could control me; I twisted and kicked, but said nothing; I had no breath to speak.

"Stop it, Billie Jo. I won't hurt you. It's time you had a man."

"I don't want a man," I whispered through clenched teeth, stopping my struggle.

"Of course you do, a sweet, gorgeous thing like you. Don't you know how sexy you are?"

He was fumbling at his zipper and kissing my shoulder; then I felt him release me and for a moment thought he had relented. He hadn't. He ran a hand up my skirt and as he reached between my legs I brought up my knee as hard as I could.

He twisted so the blow was less effective than I hoped; but it stopped him. It stopped him cold.

"You little bitch." His hand raised to strike and I stared into his eyes. "How will I explain that to Mama?"

I locked the door to my room. The lock was stiff; it had never been turned before. I was too shocked to cry. There didn't seem to be anything to do about it. Who could I tell? Fay Ann had too many problems of her own; Mama's life would be destroyed; I had no friends close enough and besides, they were my age and would be as inexperienced as I. I hadn't been to church since I flatly refused to go back to Sunday school years before. In those days we had no clinics or counselors, no family therapy groups. There was no one.

I began the letter that night, though it took two weeks to finish it. Mama saved it and I found it among my clippings when I came back here. The writing is so faded that you wouldn't be able to read it but I remember it word for word. It said:

> My Dearest Mother,
>
> You know how much I love you and that hurting you is the last thing I want to do. That's why I can't face you and am leaving this for you to find instead of telling you in person. Yes, I'm young. But I've always known what I wanted and to be fair (and, I guess, defensive) you always encouraged me. I've saved some money and—please don't be mad—I took all the cash I could find in the house—$76—but I'll pay it back as soon as I can.

Tell Fay Ann not to worry. I pay attention to most of her advice. I hope she'll be O.K. Watch out for her, Mama.

I'm not afraid. I'll write as soon as I can.

You know where I'm going. I'm going to Hollywood.

Love,

Billie Jo

VI

And come to Hollywood she did, if not as a conqueror, at least not as the refugee she actually was.

A Greyhound bus carried her without incident across the last pancake stretch of the Great Staked Plains to the mountains of westernmost Texas, past El Paso and on into New Mexico, the night too dark to see more than outlines as they passed yet more mountains. After a short stop in Albuquerque, they sped on, through Gallup, then into Arizona.

The sun rose behind the jolting bus, following them with lambent light. It painted the landscape with watercolors bleeding together in pastel hues of orange, rose, lavender, aqua, lime. As Alana speaks I see Billie Jo straining at the window, too overwhelmed by the transient scenery to think of her grief and fear.

She tells me that her primary thought was of Midland, that dusty, flat and colorless town which was all she'd ever known. The landscape she was seeing for the first time was not a hammered together set created for the movies. It was real, with mountains and forests and deserts and more trees than she ever imagined could exist.

She says she spoke to no one and I would guess was unaware of the surreptitious glances the male passengers must have cast her way, sliding their eyes over her body appreciatively, always returning their gaze to her face to linger there in a sort of bemused wonderment at her unmistakable lack of conceit.

It was afternoon when they passed through the orange groves of

Pomona, Azuza and Cucamonga, names she knew well from the radio. She wanted to get out and pick the lush fruit, bury her face in the rich juice, knowing that she should not be so amazed—she knew California grew these crops—but seeing them on the trees as they zoomed by was another marvel to savor.

Then they began to cross the outskirts of the city. and I can sense how the expectations she had felt for so many miles slowly evaporated as the slums of East Los Angeles came into view. By the time the Greyhound arrived in Hollywood she was once more plunged into depression, wondering if she had done the right thing, wondering if her mother would understand, wondering what would happen to her, alone in a huge city with no resources, no education and no prospects.

The bus pulled into the terminal in early evening, sun still hanging over the distant horizon which Billie Jo knew was the ocean she had never seen.

The depot now is an occasional refuge for the increasing number of homeless in Los Angeles; crime is overt and frequent, sometimes violent. In 1953 it was safer and cleaner, still a place where wives arrived to join their husbands, home from Korea, and where servicemen began or ended their leaves.

Alana sighs and sips her tea; the printed silk of her dress falls gracefully to the floor, too old fashioned to be chic but somehow appropriate on her still slim frame.

She admits she was scared to death and had begun to think she should have stayed and let Howard "teach" her all those things he wanted her to learn.

A rueful smile crosses her lovely face as she explains that she simply didn't expect to reach Hollywood so young. Nineteen would have felt better.

It's full dark now and way past time to stop for the day. Before I rise to leave I ask if I may call her Alana. With the intimacy of the interviews, Miss Paige sounds so formal. She says she would prefer Billie.

I avoid her allusions to my marriage and family. She needn't know of the chaos my life is in at the moment; it has nothing to do with our job here. Strangely, she pushes—gently—but she pushes.

We went for a ride yesterday. Billie wanted to go to the cemetery. Of course I agreed to take her. I hesitated to ask why she wished to go there. For her mother I assumed; she took flowers.

We parked just outside the gate to a small but well tended graveyard and Billie asked, without turning her head towards me, "Would you like to come?"

It certainly wasn't my idea of a way to spend part of our too short excursion, but she apparently needed my company, so I nodded yes.

There were wilted roses at the simple tombstone when we arrived. Billie replaced them without comment about the new appearance of the marble, unblemished by wind or weather. It was not her mother's grave; to my surprise it had a name I'd never heard, yet was somehow strangely familiar; the carved message intrigued me:

JASON DAVID ELLIOT
1922—1995
FOR ALL THE YEARS YOU GAVE ME,
ETERNAL GRATITUDE AND LOVE.

I faced her, willing her to look at me. She met my gaze without flinching. "I don't know who this is. Are you going to tell me about him?" I asked.

There was another of her long silences. Then, "Yes, my dear, some day. But not now."

The long sessions tire Billie; it's clear they're very emotional. My curiosity never abates and I dislike the evenings I spend alone, organizing my notes, transcribing the tapes or watching television mindlessly while the other track in my head goes on to speculate what the next day's chapter of this story will be.

~

I collected my one suitcase and went immediately to the nearest phone booth, thinking, "Mary Lee has to be there still, she just has to."

For the first time I understood what "heart in my mouth" meant. My fingers trembled so that I could barely turn the pages of the directory. But as if it had been rehearsed, there was the name Farly and at the other end of the phone, Mary Lee, her voice so like it had been, it was as if the years since I'd seen her were wiped from the calendar.

When I told her who it was there was a silence so profound I was tempted to hang up; then the phone erupted with a shout so loud that I almost dropped the receiver.

"Billie Jo *Payner*? Is it really you? Where are you? How did you find me? What are you doing? Are you okay? Did you move to California?"

"Whoa, whoa. I'm here. At least I'm in Hollywood. I just got here."

"Is your mom okay? How's Fay Ann? Are you all here?"

"No. I mean we're not all here. I mean I'm here alone."

"Alone! But how? Why?"

"I'll tell you when I see you. I was hoping you could suggest a place for me to stay. I'm scared to just walk into any old place. And besides, I haven't much money."

"Wait a minute."

I could hear her talking and assumed it was to her mother. Her voice was crackling with excitement. She was back on the line in a couple of seconds. "This is what you do: find the next city bus that will bring you to Santa Monica. Get off at Yale. I'll check the schedule so I can meet you and you won't have to wait on the corner. We live right down the street from the bus stop. You can stay with us."

"Oh, you're wonderful. Just until I find a place of my own. Tell your Mom thanks; I'll tell her myself in a few minutes."

Mary Lee laughed. "It'll take you more than a few minutes, Billie Jo. It's a long way. But I'll be there. My God, I can't believe it! It's been what? Eight years?" She paused. "I don't guess any other sixteen-year-old will get off the bus, but just in case—what do you look like now?"

It was my turn to laugh. "Well, I'm taller. I'm still blond. And I'm wearing a navy blue cotton skirt and a white blouse."

"That'll do. I'll see you soon. Oh, I'm so excited."

The relief I felt at the warm welcome and hospitality lifted my exhaustion and depression. My mind raced with plans and ideas, all grandiose, of course—I knew the legend about Lana Turner and her discovery in Schwab's Drug Store as well as anyone.

But I was tired. After I asked directions to and found the bus for Santa Monica, I sat down and promptly fell asleep. How funny. To drive through the place I had been aching to see most of my life and then to sleep the whole way.

I didn't wake up until we were past what in those days was a village, West Los Angeles, filled with college students from UCLA. We passed the Veteran's Administration, Sawtelle, and not too long afterwards the driver called out, "Yale, Miss."

I grabbed my bag from the overhead and lurched towards the door, suddenly frightened again. So many things could go wrong. What if Mary Lee had met the wrong bus? What if her mother had changed her mind and didn't want a house guest, even for a few days? What if I couldn't find a job? Well, there was nothing I could do, so I got off the bus and was immediately smothered in a perfumed, bouffant skirted, shrieking embrace.

"I'd know you anywhere, Billie Jo. You haven't really changed a bit. You're still beautiful. Oh, God, I was always jealous and still will be, too."

I came as close to crying as I ever did as I hugged her and then stood away to look. She was tall, taller than I, and heavier; her chestnut brown hair was shoulder length, she wore mascara and eye shadow and a lipstick so light that I wasn't certain it was there. The bouffant skirt was held out with what seemed to be several petticoats and the blouse was off the shoulder. It didn't look like anything in the fashion magazines I'd seen at the beauty parlor in Midland, but then neither did my plain skirt and shirt.

Mary Lee shot questions at me all the way to her house, so fast that, mercifully, I had no chance to answer. I didn't want to say that I had run away and most especially the reason for it. I'd long since figured out what I wanted to tell the Farlys. The question was whether they would believe me. I wasn't confident, since they knew how old I was.

They lived in a duplex, on a quiet street three blocks from Wilshire Boulevard. Mr. Farly was there and when I said hello I called him Mayor; it just came naturally.

He chuckled. "Not anymore, young lady. That was years ago."

"You look wonderful," said Mrs. Farly, after offering coffee or coke. "Now tell us what you're doing here and how your family is."

I remembered the social chasm that had existed between our families and was grateful for her concern. "My father and mother were divorced and my mother has remarried. She's well. My sister. . . ." I couldn't. "She's all right."

Mary Lee looked sharply at me; I'd have to do a better job of acting than that.

"I'm only going to be here for a couple of months," I lied. "Mom wasn't happy about me coming but, you remember, Mary Lee, I've always wanted to be an actress, so I talked her into letting me come out just for the rest of the summer, to see what it's like. It's really only a vacation."

I didn't dare look at the Farlys to see if they were accepting all this nonsense. I simply kept on talking as if it were the most natural thing in the world for a sixteen-year-old girl to take a bus ride across half the country to a large city, a stranger with no place to stay and little in the way of financial resources to sustain her. I cursed myself for admitting to Mary Lee that I didn't have much money. Then I realized that her folks might have the idea I had counted on them to offer me refuge. But, of course I had no way to know they hadn't moved. It was mere luck that they were still in Santa Monica and in the phone book.

"You must be very tired if you took the bus all the way from Midland. Why don't you have a sandwich and then get some sleep. We can talk more in the morning."

I refused the food, though I was hungry, thanked the Farlys again and gratefully followed Mary Lee up the stairs to a small room with a single bed covered in a patchwork quilt that reminded me of Texas. My friend pointed to the bathroom and said to ask for anything I needed. We hugged each other again and she left me blessedly alone. I washed and collapsed into bed; I'd never been more tired in my life.

The two-hour time difference had me up early the next morning. The house was silent when I awoke, though the first light of morning was creeping into the room through the brightly curtained window. I was at the back of the house overlooking a small yard with bougainvillea and hibiscus edging the fence. I had to smile; I knew the flowers from a botany class; it did pay off to go to school.

Of course that thought sobered me in a hurry and started me wondering how I could ever complete my education which led me to wonder how I could support myself, since I had no skills; a little late to worry about that. I shook off the fear.

I decided to risk waking everyone and took a shower, dressed and went downstairs. Maybe there was a newspaper with want ads.

When Mrs. Farly came down and found me pouring over the

classified section of the paper she must have suspected something in my story was awry. She didn't say anything, much too southern well bred to question me. I wanted to ask her questions, though. I had no idea where anything was and it was obvious that I must work and have a bus stop close to whatever living space I could find.

It was a relief when Mary Lee appeared, wearing red striped pajamas and last night's makeup. We went to the living room where I was able to interrupt her incessant talking long enough to ask some questions of my own.

"I want a job, Mary Lee," I finally blurted. "Where should I look?"

This started another tirade about vacations and beaches that finally wore down, coming to a halt with an expectant look complete with raised eyebrows and pouting mouth.

"Just point me in the right direction for the bus and I'll call you as soon as I find a place to stay and a job." I had reached a point of desperation. "We aren't as well off financially as you. The only way I could come out is if I get a summer job."

Now the pout became an expression of disappointment but she said, "Wait a minute," disappeared into the kitchen and returned in thirty seconds with a newspaper so thick that it intimidated me.

"The paper you were looking at is the *Santa Monica Outlook.* This is the *L.A.Times.* It's got lots more stuff."

"It sure does," I said doubtfully. "Do you know how to find an area I could live in?"

We spent the next half-hour marking off help wanted ads and rooms for rent.

"This is silly," Mary Lee said suddenly. "Let's ask Mom if she knows of a job for you." And she once more dashed towards the kitchen where Mrs. Farly was fixing breakfast.

"Wait a minute," I called. "I haven't any experience doing anything special. Probably the only jobs I can handle are waiting tables or housekeeping. What kind of work does your Mom do, anyhow?"

"Oh, she's a bookkeeper at 20th Century Fox Studio."

VII

They might have called me a runner. I was never sure exactly what the definition of the job was. And I sure didn't care. I was actually on the lot of a major studio, amidst the frenetic activities of film production. It was sorcery.

Mrs. Farly had dutifully responded to her daughter's demands that she find a place for me; that same morning I floated into the gray passenger seat of her 1951 Chevy coupe and we drove down Olympic Boulevard to West Los Angeles where the studio occupied an area that looked as large to my wondering eyes as the whole town of Midland.

As we checked in through the gates, awestruck, I tried to grasp that I actually was passing over the same ground as some of the brightest stars ever to grace the screen. Names rolled across the windshield as if on a marquee: Loretta Young, Claudette Colbert, oh, my God, my heart banged against the cage of my chest: Gregory Peck; the directors: Hathaway, Preminger, even John Ford.

I didn't really notice when we parked or feel myself get out of the car. Following Mrs. Farly, my head oscillating like a metronome, either stumbling over my own feet or tripping over unseen obstacles, we arrived at the office of the head of accounting. I was terrified that they would put me to work in that department—my math was pitifully poor—but Miss Turell said, "Good. I just talked to Marge in personnel. She was moaning about needing someone in the costume department; go on over, honey. And don't tell them how old you are."

As I turned away, trying to fix in my mind her instructions on how to get where I was going in this huge city of a business, I heard her say, "That young lady won't be wasting her time running around the lot if one of the bigwigs gets a look at her."

A shiver ran across my shoulders and goose flesh rose on my arms. Could it happen?

The first day I was too busy to care. The costume department needed someone to rush articles to various sound stages; often changes were needed if something happened to a costume on the set; the usual person to handle that job had called in with the flu this particular day; I couldn't believe my luck.

I was enthralled with the huge stages several stories high, the sets, everything from cities to ancient Roman amphitheaters, the thick coiled lines running every which way, cameras on dollies moving through spaces crowded with actors, directors, extras, technicians and dozens of people whose function I couldn't even imagine.

Each time I arrived on a set I first would deliver whatever I carried to the wardrobe mistress, then stand in as dark and inconspicuous a place as I could find and watch as long as I dared.

The Robe was just finishing the last takes; *Three Coins in a Fountain* was well into production. *Desiree* was an incredible spectacle, with a majestic Brando as Napoleon and Merle Oberon a regal Josephine in the massive coronation scene; *Gentlemen Prefer Blonds* gave me my first cognizance of the magic of Marilyn.

The director's faces were new to me as were many of the character actors; but the stars were out, too many to name. Was I star struck? No, I was poleaxed.

At the end of the day I tried to calculate the mileage I had put on feet, shod, thank goodness and Mrs. Farly, in low comfortable sneakers, which she had insisted I wear. There was no way to figure it. The stages are so huge, the distances between so wide, I might have walked all the way from Midland. I fell asleep going out the front gate, slept all the way back to Santa Monica, and fell into bed without dinner or saying more than a mumbled, "What a day," to Mary Lee.

And that's the way it was for three weeks.

I wrote to Mama to tell her I was healthy and working and sent five dollars, the first installment on my debt. I didn't tell her where my job was and, for fear she would contact them, couldn't tell her about the kindness of the Farlys, or send a return address either; as much as I longed for news of her and Fay Ann I was afraid she would call the police or even come to California to get me.

I was aware that my welcome as Mary Lee's guest was rapidly wearing out, since I was not able to spend time shopping or going to the movies during the day and was too tired to be sociable in the evenings. I even was too tired to look at a newspaper on the weekends, let alone go out to track down any rooms which might have been available.

The only time I stirred from resting was when Mary Lee talked me into going to the beach. The idea energized me enough to move. The Pacific Ocean! And here I was only a mile or so away. Tired or not, this was too much of a temptation. I couldn't miss it.

Mrs. Farly packed a picnic lunch, loaded it and us into her car and dropped us off at the end of Wilshire Boulevard with an admonition to be careful of the waves.

"I'll pick you up here at two o'clock. Don't make me wait for you."

We were on a palisade overlooking a wide expanse of sand stretching to the sea where it broke in foaming white surf like some frothy brew whipped by a giant's hand. I was so enchanted that it took me a moment to realize that the gentle breeze smelled of the sun; fresh, clean and welcoming; salty yet strangely sweet. I closed my eyes, inhaled slowly, barely heard Mary Lee's, "Come on this way. There are stairs." She grabbed my arm and pulled me along.

We walked down and I stepped onto golden sand for the first time in my life, didn't notice anyone around me, didn't stop to help spread the blanket, didn't think to take off my shoes, simply kept walking until I stood at the edge of the world, transfixed.

When the ax fell near the end of summer, as it surely had to, not even one mogul had spotted me and I was still running like a train, taking mislaid or forgotten articles all over the lot. But I had learned. Oh, yes, quite a bit.

Now it was back to the want ads, since Mrs. Farly had no other suggestions as to employment.

The paper was not encouraging, but one ad caught my eye. It seemed far removed from the movie world I wanted to inhabit. And yet it was an intriguing anachronism: Whoever called for an "upstairs maid" those days? It read:

DOMESTIC HELP WANTED. UPSTAIRS MAID
GOOD SALARY. CALL CR 3769.

The number turned out to be that of an agent in Beverly Hills who refused to reveal so much as a word about the client other than that the duties would entail caring for an extensive wardrobe; it was a live-in position—perfect—and I must go there for an interview. Probably I was too young but—here the man sighed—it had been difficult to fill the job and he would send me there on the chance I would please the lady of the house.

As to references, when I explained—mentally apologizing to my mother—that I was an orphan from the south, new in town, inexperienced and desperate for work, he sighed again and said it was still worth a try. He immediately sent me to a place I'd never heard of, Brentwood, 426 No. Bristol Circle, in a taxi for which he paid. It seemed I was not the only one desperate; I wondered what kind of a scrape I had gotten myself into.

After a drive down streets with immense, beautifully landscaped homes the cab pulled up in front of a fenced property where several women waited, as if aimlessly. They looked at me curiously as I rang a bell, announced my name and was admitted through the gate.

The house was large, one wing almost separate from the rest; there was a swimming pool of course, and a pool house, plus what I later discovered was a theater, all within the extensive, manicured grounds.

The interview was conducted by the housekeeper, Mrs.Milligan, who led me straight into the kitchen and seated me at a formica table without once mentioning the name of my prospective employer. More and more nervous, I pictured some sort of ogre and wondered if I had somehow time warped into a contemporary Manderlay, complete with a Mrs. Danvers and appropriate ghosts. I wasn't too enthused about playing Joan Fontaine's role but if it came to that I hoped there would be a Lawrence Olivier to rescue me.

With constant references to my age—which I'd given as eighteen and received skeptical glances—I was hired conditionally, starting immediately. The last person had left abruptly without notice and I was the first even remotely plausible applicant.

Another taxi ride—I'd ridden more cabs in this day than in my whole life before—and I was back in Santa Monica. I left an apologetic and profuse thank you note to the Farly's with a promise to call as soon as I had time from my new job.

My room was small, off the back stairs, cheerful,with yellow walls and my own bathroom! Never, never before. Whatever the job, it would be a first I'd not forget.

Mrs. Milligan conducted me to a sitting room upstairs next to a large bedroom and more closets than had been in our whole house in Midland, including one filled entirely with cleansing lotions. There was a dressing room and office, also, though I had only a glimpse of them and the two giant poster beds in the bedroom.

In the closets, hung, racked or tucked into niches, were no less than two hundred outfits, everything from simple silk day dresses to elaborate evening gowns, each with matching shoes, bags, hats and accessories. My mouth hung open and I heard an appreciative chuckle from Mrs. Milligan.

"Yes, it does sort of take one by surprise, doesn't it? You have to keep everything picked up and put away, make sure everything is clean, with no drooping hems or split seams, no run down heels or loose buckles on the ankle straps. There can be no damage of any kind and if that doesn't keep you busy enough you must do the same for the children."

"Do they all have this many closets?" If she'd said yes, I'd have left, bathroom or no bathroom.

"No. They have a fair amount of clothes, though. And they must be perfectly dressed at all times. Of course Christina is away at boarding school so its only Chris and the twins."

That was the clue. "Who's house is this?" I asked finally, faintly.

"Joan Crawford's," she said with a surprised look. "I thought you knew that."

Bemused, I only shook my head. "I had no idea." When I recovered from the shock, I asked, "Who were all those women outside the gate?"

"Those are some of Miss Crawford's fans. They volunteer to work here, just to be near her. She doesn't like them coming into the house though."

Amazing. Miss Crawford still believed what she had said in the late twenties: A star should live like a star.

It wasn't until I'd been there almost two weeks that I met Miss Crawford. She swept imperiously into her sitting room one afternoon after one of her frequent showers, as I was mending a hem on an evening gown—a broad shouldered Adrian in spectacular coral silk, slashed almost to the waist in front. I was learning a lot about style.

She stopped short when she saw me, then laughed that throaty laugh and said, "You must be the new upstairs maid. My, you are young."

"Eighteen, ma'am," I lied.

"Humm. Well, get on with it. And when you finish that, I need this dress tonight. There is a snap coming off."

She went to the second closet and pulled down a black cocktail dress with beads sweeping across the front. The snap was barely loose; how she could have known I can't imagine.

"Yes, ma'am. I'll fix it."

"Let me look at you," she said, suddenly, and pulled me towards the window. "You're not bad looking. Stay upstairs tonight. I don't want to see you near the dining room. Do you understand?"

I sure understood. She was having a dinner party and Mrs. Milligan said all kinds of important people were coming, including Michael Curtiz, who directed Joan in her Academy Award-winner *Mildred Pierce* in 1945, and an unknown, therefore strange addition to a distinguished gathering, by the name of Clint Eastwood.

I was miffed to think that I must hide. Where better to be noticed than at Joan Crawford's home, even if I was a maid. I felt like the child relegated to looking through the banister. And I didn't dare do even that. I needed the job.

The next meeting between us was more tempestuous. I hadn't pressed Cathy's dress the way Joan wanted it. She threw it on the floor and stamped on it.

"Now," she screamed, "do it right."

I lasted three months which was surely some sort of record. Almost every penny went into the bank account, my first, established with my earnings from 20th. It was growing nicely, so nicely that it was possible to look for some sort of apartment. The question was where. For I was more determined than ever to crash the gates of Hollywood. I decided that the first priority would be to choose the studio I'd most like to work for. Then I'd locate nearby, get a night job and start trying to meet people who might be able to help.

How? I'd no idea.

~

One would think, looking back on that time in Alana's life, there could be no chance of her ever breaking into a Hollywood just beginning to recover from the trauma of the Communist witch hunt by Senator McCarthy, plus the breakdown of the star-studio tradition.

And yet it shouldn't be surprising. She had the looks and talent and more important, the guts and tenacity.

She found a job near Paramount Studio in Hollywood, rented a tiny guest house in back of someone's home and began her campaign.

When we drive into the flat, dry, almost featureless country around Midland it seems difficult to believe that Alana Paige could return here to live after the lush tropical Southern California landscape and the luxury which she must have enjoyed there. But she appears perfectly content with her surroundings.

She is more comfortable with me now; her reminiscences are coming with less hesitation. And she is leaving the childhood memories behind as she gains confidence.

Whatever she tells me now, I will accept her version of the evolution of her career. I like her; I hope she feels it.

So many times interviews will be plagued with subtle attempts to color or improvise, to add little touches of fantasy for appearance's sake, rather than simply sticking to reality. Not so with this indomitable lady. Everything she says has the ring of truth about it, every detail seems as crystal clear as if it had happened this morning.

She is a wonder.

I find her looking at me in a searching, troubled way as if there were a need to get inside my brain. It is I who should be feeling that, not she. But perhaps it's my imagination. It could be that she simply wants to be sure, after the long time spent on her early days, that I'm still interested.

I am.

VIII

Why did I pick Paramount Studio?

I suppose the real reason was location: MGM was in Culver City, Universal in Burbank and 20th difficult to reach without a car; Hollywood had always been my destination, so that's where I gravitated.

I'd like to sound more esoteric and say it was the list of distinguished directors or at least that I felt some community with the stars associated with that particular studio; names like Gary Cooper, Montgomery Clift, both Fairbanks, William Holden, Barbara Stanwyck and now that charmer, Audrey Hepburn, whose *Roman Holiday* had just been released.

But the stars moved around anyhow, and someone who was with MGM or Columbia today well might be with Universal or RKO tomorrow. Hitchcock had moved to Paramount from Warner Brothers. Anyhow, I had to start somewhere.

Walking down Santa Monica Boulevard from the tiny guest house I'd rented behind what must have been the last bungalow left, amidst the various shops and restaurants on the street, I spotted a sign in a drive-in window and an hour later I was employed again. It was close to my new home; things seemed to be going my way.

I somehow weathered a lonely Thanksgiving. But now Christmas was around the corner. I was so homesick I felt ill. So I went to the nearest phone booth, took a deep breath, dropped at least a million coins into the slot, and placed a call to Mama, the first since leaving Texas.

"Billie Jo? Is it really you?"

Mama's tears started the moment she heard my voice. "It's me, Mama. I miss you so much I had to talk to you."

"It's been almost six months, Billie Jo. I got your letters. Are you really all right? Where are you? Do you have enough money? If I send some will you come home? Honey, you're too young to be on your own out there."

I started laughing."Whoa, one question at a time. First, I'm fine. Second, yes, I have enough money. I have a job...well, it's not very glamorous, but at least I'm working. I have a little place of my own and.... Oh, I miss you so much."

"Please come home, Billie Jo. We talked about going to look for you but Howard said it's too big; we'd never find you. We all miss you; even Howard."

That gave me pause. I certainly never wanted to see *him* again. I was sure he'd talked Mama out of looking for me because, of course, he would be afraid I'd tell her why I left.

"I can't come home, Mama."

"Whyever not?"

"It's just something I have to do."

"Are you really in Hollywood, Billie Jo?" Mama's voice became stern, like it always did when she got mad. It was better for me than the tears. I didn't answer.

"Are you going to school?"

"No, not yet. But I will when I can. Right now I have to work."

"You aren't...you haven't...."

"No, Mama, I'm not with a man." There seemed little point to telling her how many propositions I'd fended off already. It had become so routine that I answered almost by rote and didn't even notice whether there was a reaction.

I could hear her sigh of relief through a thousand miles of phone line.

"How is Fay Ann?"

"Oh, honey, it's so hard. Poor Johnny. But he's a happy child, for all his problems. It's just so difficult to care for him and Alton is...well, I shouldn't be unkind but he's...I just don't know what she's going to do."

"Give her my love," I said, thinking how inadequate that was.

"Please come home, honey. You could get here by Christmas if you left tomorrow."

"I can't, Mama. Please don't ask me. I'll call you again soon. Have a happy Christmas. I love you."

I hung up, not waiting for the respondent, "I love you, too."

Since I hadn't contacted the Farlys except for a thank-you note I couldn't call them and, truth to tell, I wouldn't have been too happy to spend the holiday with Mary Lee anyhow. There was a flightiness, a superficiality about her I couldn't identify but which made me wary.

I didn't know anyone else except another waitress where I was working, so Christmas was a dreary, miserable day—serving hamburgers and cokes to kids who could be home with their families but were either too rebellious to care or too oblivious to know what they were missing.

1954 rolled around, lumbered on, and I hadn't made any progress at all. Sometimes when I called home Mama had bad news to relate. My grandmother and then my grandfather died during that first frenzied year I spent in Hollywood. My father had left Midland after the divorce; we had only seen him a few times and my grandparents only once, but the loss made me feel somehow adrift: part of my past was gone.

When I asked about Fay Ann and Johnny Mama would get very quiet which told me more than I wanted to know. Often she would say simply, "Not well." Occasionally she would add, "Alton is useless." Then, if I asked for an explanation, she would change the subject. Too involved with myself, I didn't try very hard to find out more.

The summer was long, hot and unproductive; work seemed more pointless and frustrating than ever. I hadn't mentioned my seventeenth birthday to anyone; too risky since I was still underage, even though tucked in my purse was the doctored copy of my birth certificate; so far I'd scraped through without using it. It hadn't been too hard to change the 1937 into 1935, but it still made me nervous, knowing I had altered it.

I was so tired that the world seemed to slip by without my noticing any event that didn't reach up and hit me in the face. I didn't know 'til later that a so far unknown by the name of Elvis Presley had made a record that would skyrocket him to fame, that the Supreme Court of the United States ordered school integration—or that a makeup artist, eating a quick bite after leaving work, would see me and remember my face when a few weeks later a cattle call went out for extras for a De Mille epic called *The Ten Commandments.*

"I've been eating drive-in meals for three days," the man said, "waiting for you. No one knows exactly where you live. All I could find out is your name: Billie."

"Billie Jo," I corrected, absently, wary as always of a man I didn't know—or did know, for that matter.

"Whatever," said the stranger. "I'm Nat Reinhold. I'm a makeup artist at Paramount. I saw you here a while ago. You shouldn't be waiting cars, you should be in films."

As hard as I tried not to react to this statement, my insides just did clench a little; arrogantly, I believed it to be true.

"Right. And I'm Debbie Reynolds. What's your order?"

"You're much too sophisticated looking to be Debbie Reynolds. I mean it; I'm not on the make." He paused, then reached into his pocket and pulled out a leather card case.

"Look," he said, extricating one card from the case, "bring this to the studio Monday. I'll get you an appointment with the casting director. You don't even have to see me. By the way, with your looks it doesn't matter much, but do you think you can act?"

Could I act? So well that I didn't blink an eye as I looked at the card, thanked Nat Reinhold and placidly said, "Yes, I can act, but now I have to take your order or I'm going to get fired."

"I can't face another hamburger." He laughed, handed me a five, said, "Break a leg Monday," backed his car from the restaurant and drove off, waving out the window. I stared after him, disbelieving. Could it really happen? Was this the break I'd been waiting for?

The manager put an abrupt end to my reverie. "Get back to work, Billie. Guys in that Buick been waiting ten minutes."

"Okay."

I don't remember anything else about that day.

Monday morning!

My hands were shaking so hard that on the third try to put on makeup I gave up. Mascara and a little lipstick would have to do. One last glance in the small mirror—oh, how I longed for one of Crawford's full length ones—and my face was as ready as it ever would be.

What to wear!

After trying on everything in my meager collection I ended up in a full skirt of red wool and a white long sleeve blouse. If I couldn't afford designer clothes I wouldn't pretend. I snapped a wide black belt around my waist and pulled my only coat out of the closet.

Across the yard to the sidewalk, down Santa Monica Boulevard and around the corner to Gower to the studio gate, then a full ninety seconds to gather my courage. I walked to the guard station, handed him Mr. Reinhold's card with a trembling hand and held my breath.

"I have a Billie Jo on the list. No last name." The guard looked up with wise eyes, close together in a round, red face. "Unless your last name is Jo."

I gave him my best smile. "It is today. Where do I go?"

He pointed the way and I passed under the Paramount arch and through the gate.

The three weeks at 20th had educated me. I understood the workings and the logistics of a large studio. It didn't take me long to find the office to which I'd been directed.

What did take long was getting through the dozens of people waiting. The men were handsome and many of the women were beautiful. They wore everything from some kind of skin-tight knitted stuff to Chanel, all of them made up for the camera. My courage began to seep away. It did no good to tell myself that I was an actress, that I had talent. How would I ever get the opportunity to show it?

Slowly the crowd diminished until there were, perhaps, two dozen of us left. When "Billie Jo" was called out there were snickers from some of the others; it did sound funny but I was in no mood to laugh. I followed the secretary into an office where a harried looking woman sat behind a cluttered desk.

"You're Billie Jo? How old are you?"

"Eighteen."

"Right. Well, I'm not gonna ask for your birth certificate. Turn around."

I pivoted.

Then she closes the book and asks me to wait for her to catch up with the narrative before I look any further. She could ask or tell me to do anything and I'd agree. She continues to amaze and beguile me; I'm growing truly fond of her.

We have tea and some of the butter cookies I brought from the local bakery. She looks at me, head cocked in the same way she has done in movies since the fifties and for the first time since we began asks a direct question.

"You never tell me anything about yourself, your family; do you know...." She falters, an uncharacteristic hesitation. "Where do you live?"

I'm so surprised that I stammer, then scurry to tell her I live in northern California, which she surely knows since she called me there. She shakes her head and grimaces and asks where I was born. Why would she care? I tell her that also. I just want to follow her career and say so. She sighs and continues.

~

Just when I was beginning to worry, Mr. Grovin had his secretary call me into his office. He had another screenplay, this time with a lead for me. Disbelieving, I sat in one of the plush pale green chairs in front of a desk of mahogany as large as our dining room table in Midland. Nat was talking about publicity, finally interrupted by Mr. Grovin.

"She isn't there yet, Mr. Reinhold. I think you're jumping the gun."

"This is the time for PR. She...."

As he had with me, Mr. Grovin simply kept on talking. "The studio will do right by Miss Paige, Mr. Reinhold. I think we have the makings of a star if we give her the best vehicles and don't get in too much of a hurry."

"But...."

"That's it, Mr. Reinhold. MGM owns Miss Paige now; she is a contract player, you know."

"But...."

I had to break in before this got to be some kind of comedy. Nat was as new to managing as I was to movie making.

"Tell me about the script, please, Mr. Grovin."

They run all the old movies on TV now. Perhaps you've seen it: *Without Love.* That was my first starring role. It sounds immodest to say I think I surprised everyone. Nat kept repeating, "I knew you'd photograph like a dream; but you really can act."

And I kept saying, "I told you."

Without Love was just what Mr. Grovin called it: the right vehicle. It catapulted me to a dizzying level in the business. Now all I had to do was stay there. Quite a challenge for a youngster from the sticks.

Well, at least I would no longer have to lie about my age, though since I'd lied to get my Social Security and to join SAG, I couldn't figure out how to get back those two years.

Salaries weren't as insanely high as they are now, even for independents; a contract player, however, was really the lowest of the low. Still, it was a great deal more money than I had ever had before. It was feasible to find a slightly larger apartment than my tiny guesthouse; then I took driving lessons and bought a car. Imagine! My very own car—and new, too. I was so excited I took it on the Pasadena Freeway as soon as I got my license.

My apartment was on the second floor of a duplex on Sycamore Avenue just south of the Hollywood-Los Angeles border. It had two bedrooms, a fireplace, and a balcony that looked out over a back yard fragrant with orange blossoms and riotous with the magenta of bougainvillea.

Nat would come there to visit, throw his compact frame onto my second-hand couch and regale me with hilarious tales about Mae West's antics or Will Hays and the chaotic days of censorship, or incidents about stars and their gaffes on screen, like the time Ronald Reagan, shooting *Bedtime for Bonzo,* couldn't get his fly zipped.

Sometimes, depending on his mood, he'd relate Hollywood secrets and rumors. He knew about bizarre suicides, like Peg Entwistle jumping off the Hollywoodland sign and John Bowers walking into the ocean at Malibu—the basis for the screenplay of *A Star Is Born*—plus too many other sad tales of disillusioned people, using as many methods of self destruction as one could possibly imagine.

He revealed more than I wanted to know about the Black Dahlia murder and introduced me to a Hollywood I hadn't dreamed existed, with glimpses into a scandalous, dissolute profession. I was getting my first taste of what fame could mean and Nat was making me wonder if I really wanted to be a part of it.

He was an encyclopedia of Hollywood history, but whichever type of story he was telling, he always ended with, "Don't ever take yourself too seriously."

Nat was a remarkable man. He was nice looking, with sandy hair too long for my taste, inquisitive brown eyes and broad shoulders on a medium tall frame. He always kept his word to me, learned to handle my business affairs—and some other people's, also—never stole from me, never stepped over the line of a hug and a kiss, sometimes knowing when I most needed them.

He loved his wife and child—as I came to—and as far as I know never cheated on them. A far cry from the majority of personnel in the movie business where almost anything seemed permissible.

God knows I had my share of men—and women, too, for that matter—trying to seduce me. I quickly got the reputation of ice woman, which, I chuckle to admit, suited me just fine. I continued to maintain the mystery of my beginnings, though I never bothered to analyze why. I had long since, and with amazing ease, learned to switch accents, so Texas never showed up in my speech unless called for.

As for romance, somehow Fay Ann's voice continued to echo, and the sorrow of her life constantly reminded me of what could happen. I was afraid of any entanglement. Besides, I was so busy that I would hardly have had time for a man in my life. It was all I could do to read the many books I began to buy, determined that if I couldn't go to school formally, I'd educate myself, by correspondence course, if necessary. My sister had done it; I could, too.

The studio planned to cast me in another starring role and Nat had convinced them that I deserved a higher salary. I went to I. Magnin on Wilshire Boulevard and spent what to me then was a fortune on clothes: starting from the skin out, I bought lingerie, shoes, bags, dresses and suits. Plus an evening gown, another first, a pale turquoise strapless, bouffant skirted, heavy silk Givenchy with a darker turquoise coat over it; simple and elegant.

I needed it. A premiere! My first. The excitement was almost suffocating. In my new gown, my hair pulled on top of my head and fastened with a clip, small studs in my ears, Nat, Teri and I drove up Hollywood Boulevard in a rented limo, to the red carpet in front of Grauman's Chinese Theater.

The driver opened the door, Nat stepped out and offered me his hand. I took a deep breath, smiled falsely at him, too scared for sincerity, and put my foot on the curb. A cheer rang out and I glanced around to see who had arrived. Nat whispered in my ear, "It's for you."

There's a picture in this album of the way I looked that evening but nothing could show how I felt.

X

There are many pictures from that exciting time in Billie's life. Her second leading role was received even more enthusiastically than the first so there was increasing publicity, over which Nat Reinhold somehow succeeded in keeping a measure of control.

Not that there was any particular gossip. Alana Paige's life was monastic, frustrating, I'm sure, to the reporters, like Hedda Hopper and Louella Parsons, who loved to exacerbate the slightest rumor into thundering reality.

The studio sent Alana on manufactured "dates" with a gaggle of up and coming male leads, from Tab Hunter to Leslie Nielsen to Sal Mineo, none of whom interested Billie in the least. Going out with them to Ciros or the Coconut Grove at the Ambassador Hotel was simply part of the job, though she relished the parties and enjoyed dining in restaurants from Musso and Frank's or the Brown Derby, to Perino's or Scandia.

She confesses, with a grin, that her favorite was an occasional sneak to Dolores' Drive-In for a hot dog, when she could get Nat to take her there.

Meeting more Hollywood VIPs, visiting in the opulent homes and shopping in the best stores were benefits, also, all a part of the life of a rising star.

It was later, she tells me, that she began to tire of the constant crowds of autograph hunters, reporters and photographers who surrounded her each time she appeared in public. She made a conscious decision to maintain as much privacy in her life as possible, and soon she rarely left home unless her profession called for it.

Frequently she asked the stores to send garments for her approval so she could avoid well-meaning fans, then felt guilty, knowing she owed her career to them.

She soared to the top of her profession in two years, managing to balance the intoxicating thrill of fame with an extraordinary measure of common sense.

She moved again, this time into a rented house, secluded behind eucalyptus trees and bougainvillea gone wild, above the Sunset Strip not far from the Trocadero, that famous—or infamous—playground of the best known names of the era.

Now she was able to invite her mother to visit, anxious to introduce her to Los Angeles and the excitement of her new life.

~

Mama told me she couldn't come to California. Fay Ann was sick and needed her. When I asked what the doctors said she began to cry again. That was all I needed to make up my mind.

I was finished shooting *Ridin' High* and exhausted; rehearsals scheduled for the next production wouldn't begin for two weeks and I wanted some sort of change while I waited. I called Nat and told him what I planned to do.

He said, "You'll never get away with it, Billie. Your face is too well known now. Anyway why do you keep trying to hide it? There's nothing wrong with being from Texas and going back to visit your family."

The intense need for secrecy was an extension of my growing desire for privacy; I was unsure about the cause but amused that speculation about my wish for seclusion only seemed to increase my popularity. If the need was a presentment of things to come I was unaware of it.

In any case, it was a challenge and I was determined to make the visit without anyone finding out. I bought a brown, shapeless wig, a dress two sizes too large, some theatrical putty, and started experimenting with makeup. It took a few days to get it right.

I swore Maria, my housekeeper—imagine! a housekeeper!—to secrecy, telling her if anyone called, to say I was ill and couldn't be

made a record that would skyrocket him to fame, that the Supreme Court of the United States ordered school integration—or that a makeup artist, eating a quick bite after leaving work, would see me and remember my face when a few weeks later a cattle call went out for extras for a De Mille epic called *The Ten Commandments.*

"I've been eating drive-in meals for three days," the man said, "waiting for you. No one knows exactly where you live. All I could find out is your name: Billie."

"Billie Jo," I corrected, absently, wary as always of a man I didn't know—or did know, for that matter.

"Whatever," said the stranger. "I'm Nat Reinhold. I'm a makeup artist at Paramount. I saw you here a while ago. You shouldn't be waiting cars, you should be in films."

As hard as I tried not to react to this statement, my insides just did clench a little; arrogantly, I believed it to be true.

"Right. And I'm Debbie Reynolds. What's your order?"

"You're much too sophisticated looking to be Debbie Reynolds. I mean it; I'm not on the make." He paused, then reached into his pocket and pulled out a leather card case.

"Look," he said, extricating one card from the case, "bring this to the studio Monday. I'll get you an appointment with the casting director. You don't even have to see me. By the way, with your looks it doesn't matter much, but do you think you can act?"

Could I act? So well that I didn't blink an eye as I looked at the card, thanked Nat Reinhold and placidly said, "Yes, I can act, but now I have to take your order or I'm going to get fired."

"I can't face another hamburger." He laughed, handed me a five, said, "Break a leg Monday," backed his car from the restaurant and drove off, waving out the window. I stared after him, disbelieving. Could it really happen? Was this the break I'd been waiting for?

The manager put an abrupt end to my reverie. "Get back to work, Billie. Guys in that Buick been waiting ten minutes."

"Okay."

I don't remember anything else about that day.

Monday morning!

My hands were shaking so hard that on the third try to put on makeup I gave up. Mascara and a little lipstick would have to do. One

last glance in the small mirror—oh, how I longed for one of Crawford's full length ones—and my face was as ready as it ever would be.

What to wear!

After trying on everything in my meager collection I ended up in a full skirt of red wool and a white long sleeve blouse. If I couldn't afford designer clothes I wouldn't pretend. I snapped a wide black belt around my waist and pulled my only coat out of the closet.

Across the yard to the sidewalk, down Santa Monica Boulevard and around the corner to Gower to the studio gate, then a full ninety seconds to gather my courage. I walked to the guard station, handed him Mr. Reinhold's card with a trembling hand and held my breath.

"I have a Billie Jo on the list. No last name." The guard looked up with wise eyes, close together in a round, red face. "Unless your last name is Jo."

I gave him my best smile. "It is today. Where do I go?"

He pointed the way and I passed under the Paramount arch and through the gate.

The three weeks at 20th had educated me. I understood the workings and the logistics of a large studio. It didn't take me long to find the office to which I'd been directed.

What did take long was getting through the dozens of people waiting. The men were handsome and many of the women were beautiful. They wore everything from some kind of skin-tight knitted stuff to Chanel, all of them made up for the camera. My courage began to seep away. It did no good to tell myself that I was an actress, that I had talent. How would I ever get the opportunity to show it?

Slowly the crowd diminished until there were, perhaps, two dozen of us left. When "Billie Jo" was called out there were snickers from some of the others; it did sound funny but I was in no mood to laugh. I followed the secretary into an office where a harried looking woman sat behind a cluttered desk.

"You're Billie Jo? How old are you?"

"Eighteen."

"Right. Well, I'm not gonna ask for your birth certificate. Turn around."

I pivoted.

"Humm. You are a beauty." She rose from her chair and walked over to me. She took my chin in two fingers and turned my face back and forth. "No makeup? I'll be damned. Nat said I'd like you. He's right. You're gonna be wasted in this DeMille thing. But we're short about twelve bodies."

She went back to her desk, leaving me astounded. Did this mean I'd get a chance?

~

So somewhere in the back of the crowd Billie waved a fan, dressed in a robe of scratchy muslin, her shining hair covered by an unbecoming brown scarf. It wasn't much of an opportunity. But it got her into Actor's Equity.

She laughs now when she talks of that first exhilarating experience in front of the camera, even in the back row behind a huge crowd of extras. She tells me it didn't discourage her that after The Ten Commandments *she didn't see Nat Reinhold again or that the casting director ignored her calls for weeks.*

She talked to her mother several times, always depressed about Fay Ann and angry about Alton when their conversation was finished. She sent money and continued to do so after her small debt was paid, until her mother said to stop; there was no need.

When guilt got the better of her she called Mary Lee who was her usual ebullient self, prattling on about a new boyfriend and then asking probing questions about Billie Jo's job.

Billie Jo's antenna went up. She tells me it was obvious that Mary Lee thought there was a man involved somewhere and it didn't take long to realize that, assuming she was the success she was determined to be, Mary Lee would be a threat to any desire for privacy. Billie Jo says, with a self-mocking smile, that I would soon see she could be ruthless if necessary.

She stayed on at the drive-in, fending off lewd comments and weird propositions with the poise of a woman twice her age.

She looked in the paper for any upcoming productions that might need extras or walk-ons: futility; there wasn't a single cattle-call. And she waited, knowing in her heart that something would happen, something was standing in the wings for her—and that it would be great when it came.

IX

Several of us were talking about Bogart in *Caine Mutiny*, which we'd all seen recently, when a brand-new bright red Thunderbird pulled up to the restaurant. It was another girl's station so I was surprised when she came back and said, "He wants to talk to you."

"Who?"

"I don't know but he asked if you were still working here."

I went over and Nat Reinhold stuck his head out of the window.

"Hi, Billie. Remember me?"

"Of course I remember you. Did you know I got to be in *Ten Commandments*? I never did thank you."

"So what have you done since?"

"Nothing. I keep calling but. . . ."

"I've moved over to MGM so I'm not around here much anymore. Say, listen, *Guys and Dolls* is just starting to shoot. There might be a spot for you. Want me to try?"

"Are you kidding? What do you mean a spot? Why would you bother, anyhow? You don't even know me."

"Well," he began, "I know how hard it is to get going. The first time I saw you I thought you'd photograph like a dream. I don't mean I could get you a screen test or anything. But I like to check out my judgment sometimes, see if I'm right about people." He blushed, added, "Besides, I'm looking to change my job. I'd rather be an agent than a makeup artist any day. I have to start work at four A.M. some-

times. My wife's not happy." He laughed. "I'm not so great at makeup, anyhow."

"I'd take anything. And Mr. Reinhold, if I ever get the chance, I'll show you what kind of an actress I am."

He laughed again. "Sometimes I wonder if it even matters as long as you look good and have the right connections. But that's just my jaded point of view. It couldn't hurt if you can act. Do you have a phone? I'll call you."

"I don't. I could call you."

"Okay. Here's another card. Call me next week."

"The last time you gave me a card it brought me luck. Maybe this one will too."

Brando! Sinatra! I couldn't believe I was actually on the set with them and Vivian Blaine and gorgeous Jean Simmons. Again I was relegated to the background, reasonably, of course. And a good thing too. If I'd been asked to dance, even Michael Kidd couldn't have saved me. It encouraged me a little that Brando couldn't sing. Maybe my reedy soprano wouldn't be as big a liability as I'd feared.

So there I was, in a mob scene, dressed in a New York looking outfit two inches too big around the waist. And it was really the beginning for me; the dream of "a mogul" spotting me that I had hoped for when I was a runner at 20th Century Fox, came true in a way so classic that it defies belief.

Walking across the set after the scene had been shot, the heel came off my pump. I stumbled and would have fallen if a small man with frizzy gray hair had not thrust out an arm to catch me.

Embarrassed, I started to apologize, looked at his face and was struck dumb. It was Harold Grovin, one of the finest directors at MGM. His face was parchment white, as if he never had so much as seen the sun, and his hand, which now held my elbow, was long and bony, too large for his petit frame.

"I'm so sorry, Mr. Grovin," I finally managed. "It's my shoe. The heel came off."

"So I see, young lady. Is it from our wardrobe department?"

"Yes, sir."

"That figures. Are you hurt?" And without waiting for an answer, "Were you in the scene they just shot?"

"Yes, sir, I was," I smiled at him, "but I doubt you could see me." I began to relax. He wouldn't bite.

"What else have you done?"

"Nothing, sir. I mean I was an extra in *Ten Commandments* but that doesn't count."

"How did you get this job?"

"A makeup artist, Nat Reinhold, found me." I didn't like the way that sounded but before I had a chance to clarify, he had continued as if talking to a mannequin.

"I don't know him. Have you ever had a screen test?"

Breathless, my hand in front of my mouth, I could only shake my head.

"I don't suppose you know anything about acting."

"Oh, but I do, sir."

"Stop calling me sir. Come here," and he dragged me, limping on one shoe, over to the cameraman. "George, run me a few feet of film on this young woman, just enough to see how she photographs." He turned me towards the light. "How old are you, anyhow?"

"I'm eighteen." The lie came easily now. Besides I was getting close.

"Umm." With one scant eyebrow raised he continued to turn my head back and forth as the casting director had done.

"You don't have a bad side. Everybody has one bad side but you don't."

It seemed to amaze him.

"There's a script I like. . . ."

I waited for him to continue but he stopped.

"What's your name?"

I told him.

"Well, that will have to change. Call me tomorrow." And he took off across the set like a rabbit.

I looked helplessly at George who laughed at my flabbergasted expression and said, "He wants you on film. Let's do it. I'll square it with Siegel." He pointed to a spot on the set. "Over there."

"What do I do?"

He said, "Stand still 'til I tell you to move."

The camera whirred as the film passed through it. It was the most wonderful sound I'd ever heard.

He took me full front, then a left, then a right profile.

"Okay. That's it. He said call him tomorrow."

"I will," I said fervently, my poise deserting me entirely. I sounded like a kid let loose in a candy factory.

~

So the stories were true. She, in the best Lana Turner tradition, had been discovered, if not at Schwab's Drug Store, or wherever it really was, certainly in as unlikely a situation.

Billie laughs: A broken heel! she says, then adds that without Nat she wouldn't have been there at all which is why she asked him to be her agent/manager. What did she know about business?

The rest is history: the real screen test, the seven-year contract with the studio just when big stars were beginning to assert their independence; the name change, the ingenue role waiting for someone young with the right face and form to walk into it.

Texas Belle *could never be called a box office smash and Grovin suffered for that, but it was a vehicle for Alana Paige who out-acted the stars with a skill and subtlety that would have done Bernhardt justice. It was a part less than she hoped for, more than she expected. She was on her way.*

~

I called Mama to share the excitement of my first true film appearance. She was so astounded she could barely speak, which was exactly how I felt. I kept pinching myself—then reminding her that she had been the one to encourage me. When we hung up I realized that I'd not asked about Fay Ann or talked about anything other than myself. I did start to give Mama my address but something held me back so I just said I'd call soon again.

Most of the pre-production was finished; we started shooting almost immediately. It was all so new. Costumes, makeup, the hot lights, my overeager responses which caused Mr. Grovin to yell at me constantly.

Still stage struck, I sometimes missed lines since I was so rapt watching Kirk Douglas and Piper Laurie work, which only proved that while my acting might be good I was far from professional.

We were in production for five months; my skills grew; my awe began to diminish; Mr. Grovin liked my work.

Nat had agreed to act as my manager. He said the career change was probably going to save his marriage: Teri was tired of his ridiculous hours. We had no idea how the public would see me, though he never lost faith; he kept saying I'd make it "big time"; I was "going places." There were moments when I wasn't sure. So just in case, I squirreled away my salary, made no changes in my life style and held my breath.

When *Texas Belle* was finally in the can there was a sneak preview in Burbank. In the true tradition of Hollywood movie land, I stood in the lobby in as out of sight a corner as possible, to listen. What I heard about the production didn't thrill me. What I heard about "that young actress who played Miranda," broke me out in goose flesh and sent my pulse racing.

I clipped every review I could find, gathered them together with publicity stills and mailed them home. How long it would be before Midland would get a print to screen I'd no idea. But no matter. Mama could take the pictures to show Fay Ann in the meanwhile.

~

Those old clippings, yellowed and beginning to crumble, are in the heavy albums Billie brings for me to see. Her mother, predictably, had put everything she could find into scrapbooks, from the first article, Alana as Miranda, to the last, her finest role, in The Velvet Glove *as Mrs. Bottinger, the aging matriarch of a politically powerful family;* The Velvet Glove *was not only critically acclaimed but also immensely popular with viewing audiences everywhere.*

She leans forward as I turn pages, laughing at some of the articles, shaking her head at others with comments that indicate her displeasure. When I ask why, she tells me she wasn't satisfied with her performance or she didn't like what makeup had done or that the reporter made up the whole story. She kept her life so secret no one even knew where she was from.

Occasionally she points a derisive finger at a costume and says something like, "Did you ever see such an outlandish outfit? I could have done a better job of designing myself."

disturbed. I thanked whatever force had warned me all those months ago to be careful of Mary Lee. I'm ashamed to admit that when she told me she was going to Florida with her boyfriend I was pleased to be rid of the obligation I felt towards her and her parents for taking me in when I arrived in town. Our childhood friendship had not rekindled; there was no reason to pursue it. Somehow I knew that anything I told Mary Lee would appear someday in *Variety* or *The Inquirer.*

On a wet day in January, a mousy, poorly dressed woman boarded a Union Pacific train to Midland-Odessa, arrived in early morning, rented a Ford and drove through a town unchanged, to the house now surrounded with fully grown foliage, that Howard had bought for Mama six years earlier. When I knocked on the shellacked front door I heard her voice grumbling; then she opened it a crack and asked, "Yes? Can I help you?"

"I'm the Avon lady," I began, then couldn't maintain. I started laughing. "It's me, Mama, Billie Jo."

She stared at me, then her face lit up, she threw the door wide and her arms engulfed me so recklessly that I almost lost my balance.

"Billie Jo! What happened to you? You look like someone else. I didn't even know you."

"I'm a pretty good actress, huh?" I laughed and twirled around and gave her a big kiss. "I didn't want to tell anyone I was coming so I made up this disguise. It worked!"

"It certainly did. But how did you…?"

"This way." I pulled the tan putty from my nose and chin; that left me with a two-tone complexion. Then I wiped off the thick eyebrows and spit out the wadding which had made my face round. "Now?"

"You look wonderful, even half and half." Mama was so excited she was stuttering. I felt great.

"Tell me everything, Billie Jo. You've been gone so long it seems like forever. You're all grown up now and a big star. I was afraid we'd never see you again."

"I kept telling you I'd be back when I could. Didn't you believe me, Mama?"

"I wanted to. Howard kept saying you'd gone for good, that you were ashamed of us. He's at work; he'll be so happy to see you."

That brought me down with a bang. How could I have forgotten him? Occasionally ignoring reality was a serious problem for me. Well, I'd just have to tolerate Howard.

"How could you believe such a thing? I've called you every week; well, as soon as I had enough money to, I did. If I hadn't wanted to see you why would I have kept calling and asking you to come visit?" Something wasn't right and a wave of confusion washed over me. Was I ashamed? Was that why I kept my private life so closely guarded?

"It doesn't matter now, Billie Jo. You're here. I love you. You're here."

"Let me get my bag from the car. I need a shower."

"We don't have a shower, honey, just a bath tub."

"That's all right, Mama. I don't care. I just want to change clothes."

"While you do that I'll call Fay Ann."

"How is she, Mama?"

There was a long pause. Then Mama said, "Go get your things, honey."

I looked at her more carefully then. She had lines on her forehead and a downward slant to her mouth that never had been there before, even when my father was at his most difficult.

"What is it, Mama? Is it Fay Ann or Johnny?" Another thought struck me. "Or is Howard…?"

"No, not Howard; we've had a few problems but we get along pretty good. It's Fay Ann. You go get your things and have your bath. I'll make you some hot chocolate and we'll talk as soon as you've changed."

Sitting at the old kitchen table with a chipped, steaming mug clasped between my hands, dressed in blue jeans and an old shirt, feeling twelve years old again, I waited for Mama to tell me what was wrong. I expected the bad news to be about Johnny and his health.

She shook her head.

"No. Johnny is very weak and is in a wheelchair most of the time. But as hard as it is, we're all resigned to it. I haven't wanted to tell you. It's Alton. He's beating Fay Ann. She's just home from the hospital; he broke her collarbone."

I felt the blood drain from my head and a sinking in my whole body, as if the floor beneath me had dropped ten feet.

"I knew it," I whispered.

Mama asked what I meant.

"I think I always knew it; he was hurting her before I left. It started after Johnny was born."

"You never told me."

"Fay Ann wouldn't let me. Besides, I was just a kid. What did I know about it?"

We sat, silent. I had no idea what my mother's reactions were but I felt a rage so all consuming that I grew dizzy. I'm sure that if Alton had been in the room I would have attacked him.

Finally I was enough in control to ask, "What can we do?"

Mama shook her head wearily. "I've tried to talk her into leaving him but she refuses. I think she's afraid to."

"I'll talk to her. Maybe she can come out to California. I could take care of her." But even as I said it I realized how empty that suggestion was. How could I possibly take care of Fay Ann—and Johnny? What a mess.

Still in jeans, I drove Mama to Fay Ann's house. As we pulled into the circular driveway my sister opened the front door and waited, face pale, arm in a sling and her body so thin she was almost transparent.

I flew from the car wanting to wrap her in my arms but when I reached the door I was afraid my impetuosity would break her in two. Gently I hugged her and she hugged me back with fragile intensity. She was crying.

"Billie Jo. I thought I'd never see you again. Let me look at you, you a big star in Hollywood." She stared at me, then, as if shocked, "But you don't look any different."

I had to laugh. "I guess you've seen me on screen. But that's play-acting. I'm still me. I've missed you so much, Fay Ann. I've been trying to get back home for the longest time but either I was shooting a movie or studying for the next one. Never mind, I'm here now."

"Let's go inside. Come on, Mama." She smiled a mechanical smile at our mother and we all went into the house.

When we were seated in the fastidiously clean living room and Fay Ann had brought us both drinks we didn't want, I pointed to her shoulder. "I know he did it. I want you to leave him now, this very minute. You can. . . ."

She interrupted me in mid-sentence.

"Don't start, Billie Jo. I can't leave. If I do, Alton will ask for custody and get it. His father has all the politicians in this town in his pocket. Johnny will end up in an institution." She snorted a brief, bitter laugh. "Not that Alton wouldn't rather have him in one anyhow. But as long as I stay here I can keep him safe."

"Safe? What do you mean safe? Is he in some kind of danger? From Alton, maybe?"

"I don't mean it that way. Alton wouldn't hurt him; he knows I'd kill him if he did." She paused and the fierce look on her face told me she meant exactly what she said. I shivered. No wonder my sister was so thin and tired. She looked forty—and she was only 6 years older than I.

"Is he…how is he?"

"Rosita will bring him down in a few minutes. You'll see for yourself."

I wasn't sure I wanted to see this ill-starred child. There was silence, heavy and morbidly expectant, though of course it was only my own feeling, one I could erase by walking out that front door and not coming back. I toyed with the idea for a fraction of a second, enjoying the illusion of freedom it gave me.

The sound of metal rasping against wood brought me back as a wheelchair bumped the door, then rolled into the room, pushed by a stocky Hispanic woman. In the chair was a young boy, large headed, with small nose and thick lips, his ears set low on his head under a mop of curly black hair.

"This is your Aunt Billie Jo, Johnny. She's the one in the movies."

"Hi, An' Bil," said the boy, a sunny smile lighting his misshapen face.

I couldn't judge how severe the retardation was. "Hi, Johnny," was all I could manage. I bent over to kiss him and he grabbed me, slobbering a kiss on my ear. My eyes grew hot.

We left Fay Ann to care for her son. When the door closed behind us I felt as if I carried the burden of Atlas on my shoulders. Neither Mama nor I uttered a word as we drove back to the house.

When we were inside I finally broke the silence. "Is there anything we can do? Should I talk to him?"

"He isn't very easy to talk to. He denies everything, says he's never touched her, that she's just clumsy. I think he's got a girlfriend. He keeps saying he has to make business trips, then he's gone for a day or two. What 'business trips'?" she asked rhetorically. "He has a Ford dealership. All his business is right here in town."

She shook her head, blew out a, "Ha! A girlfriend might be a blessing for Fay Ann. I wish he'd leave her. We could take care of her here. But he'd have to give her alimony and child support. I think he's having problems at the agency."

"If Fay Ann needs anything—anything at all—let me know. I'm making lots of money now, Mama. I can easily afford to help her."

"It's not money she needs. It's to get away from Alton. And she won't."

There didn't seem much to say after that.

Three days later, dispirited, and tired of dodging Howard after the few obligatory meetings, I replaced the putty and makeup and drove back to town to leave the car and catch the train for California. All the excitement I had felt on the eastward journey was gone and I was tired to the bone. The idea of beginning another shoot was almost too much.

But as we passed through the orange groves, not yet totally converted into concrete and stucco, my energy began to bubble and my thoughts to swirl. I decided to pull a Scarlett O'Hara: I'd think about Fay Ann and Johnny tomorrow.

I got back to Hollywood two days before we started rehearsals. Idiotically, they had cast me in a dancing role, maybe because it worked so well for Debbie Reynolds; she never had danced before *Singin' in the Rain*. Anyway it almost ruined my career. I told them I couldn't do it, but they wanted someone with my looks for *Hoofin' It*. Crazy! Working with Donald O'Conner was wonderful though. He tried so hard to get me limber enough not to look like a wood doll. Nothing helped. Of all my movies, that was the one I was most happy to finish. I hated it!

But then they cast me as Isis. The new role was different from the others, deeper and more intense, an opportunity to stretch myself and try for new heights in my crazy, obsessive profession.

~

The role of Isis in Pharaoh *was always one of Billie's favorites. Though she admits that her performances increased in power as the years passed, Isis gave her her first chance to do something other than ingenue, pretty, almost brainless roles. The fact that audiences loved her in those parts made her happy, but left her dissatisfied.*

Her salary increased exponentially and with it her wardrobe. She carefully added designer labels when she could: a Madame Gres, a Balenciaga, a Norman Norell, which she adored: a shimmering sheath of sequins, unadorned, fitting like a second skin in a bronze tone that made her look like a sculpture by Erté.

She was glorious, with her mane of blond hair, her brown eyes shining with youth and health, her perfect lips and white teeth, the enticing cleft in her chin, and—yes—her stunning figure and proud carriage; she was a shimmering, incandescent beauty.

Her schedule was hectic and almost without breaks. The studio still owned her though she had been spared the stormy encounters with the legendary Louis B. Mayer, who had left MGM in 1951.

Grovin continued to direct her, but Alana Paige also worked under Minnelli and then Charles Waters, in his first picture after High Society, *possibly the best and brightest movie of 1956 and the last movie Grace Kelly made before becoming a princess.*

Alana used what little spare time she could wrest from her turbulent days to study: literature and art, history, languages, even some science and math, not ever her best subjects. She explored music, from Charlie Parker to Ravel, from Sarah Vaughn to Gian Carlo Menotti. She was embarrassed by her lack of formal education, remembered Fay Ann's heroic struggle to win a high school diploma and was determined that she, Alana, not be considered "an airhead"—her words—if she were lucky enough to encounter someone "brainy."

Much later, when she was awarded an honorary degree from the film department at UCLA, she was ecstatic, almost euphoric, claiming it was more important to her than an Oscar.

With work and study, what little social life she pursued continued to be restricted to Nat and Teri, to empty dating, and an occasional meeting with one of the few women from work with whom she felt comfortable, some of them with names at least as big as her own. Eva Marie Saint became a close friend—as close as Billie would let anyone become—and

Billie enjoyed visiting her quiet home at the end of Mandeville Canyon or meeting her for a rare luncheon at one of the less visible restaurants.

She laughs when she tells me how sterile her life was at that time, saying that Fay Ann's story kept her pure; she simply was scared to death. I can't imagine Billie Jo afraid of anything.

XI

Those were very busy, exciting years. But there were some tragedies, too. I heard from my father. He had been in Mexico, came back because he was sick; he said the doctors didn't give him very long and he wanted to see me before he died. When he came to the door, frayed cuffs showing beneath the sleeves of a worn tweed jacket, he was so thin and pale that I would hardly have known him. He looked at me for a long time, nodding his head, and finally said, "You told us you'd do it when you were just a little girl."

He gazed around the living room where I had brought iced tea and slices of Maria's orange cake, taking his time, examining the white Berber rugs on the polished wood floor, the white couch and raspberry chairs and the framed posters from my movies. Then he looked back at me and I was embarrassed to be wearing a pale Dior dress that probably cost more than my father earned in a month.

"You look the part, too. I'm happy for you."

I felt childish and speechless.

He had called Mama to get my number, and knew about Johnny and Alton.

"I hope you're smarter than your sister. She was so stupid. . . ." He stopped to think about what he'd just said. "I mean. . .well you're already older than she was when. . .what I mean to say is, just be careful. . . ."

I didn't know whether to respond with outrage at the manner in which he spoke about Fay Ann, or assurance that I wasn't interested in anyone and didn't have time in any case. Then I looked at his wasted face and just smiled instead, and told him I'd be careful.

He didn't stay long after that. We talked briefly about Texas and world conditions and other subjects that neither of us cared a lot about, trying to dispel the awkwardness I know we both felt.

When I asked where I could call him, he gestured vaguely and said he'd call me next time he got back to L.A., that he was returning to Mexico for a while; he had unfinished business there. He didn't say what and I didn't ask.

I never saw him again.

~

Billie made two more incognito trips to Midland and shot an astounding seven more films between 1957 and 1960, all successful. She claims they weren't much to be proud of but I've seen them and, though the plots were perhaps vapid and superficial, you couldn't criticize Alana Paige's performances.

Late that year Billie flatly refused to be loaned to United Artists (and dye her hair) for West Side Story *and got away without suspension by reminding the powers that be of the near disaster of* Hoofin' It. *With a mischievous grin, she says they would never have gotten the Academy Award if she had danced; UA didn't know how lucky they were she wouldn't do it.*

~

They were lucky but I was luckier. I was available for the princess in *Royal Interlude*, a role I really wanted. When I found out that MGM was willing to loan me to Universal I was thrilled. It was already known around town that the studio intended an all-out publicity campaign, complete with an opening in London in May, hopefully with the royal family in attendance. In all the years I'd dreamed of being an actress I'd never imagined it would lead to an opportunity to meet the Queen of England.

My knees were shaking so hard standing in the receiving line at the opening that my earrings jangled; I thought I'd be stuck in that curtsy to the Queen until the evening was over. Or fall down, can you imagine? She was so gracious and Prince Phillip so handsome. Of course I lost the Oscar I dreamed of to Sophia Loren, which was a disappointment. I hate to admit how masterful Sophia was that year.

When I called Mama from England she was so excited she was yelling into the phone. "Tell me, tell me." I told her if she didn't calm down she'd have a stroke, but she only lowered her voice a little and kept on shouting. I guess she thought an overseas call required a louder voice.

I called Fay Ann, too. I'd been talking to her regularly, trying to time my calls for when I knew Alton would be away from home. I could hear the strain in her voice, though she tried to be thrilled for me.

Johnny was almost twelve by then. He was able to walk a little, and communicated with his mother and grandmother. His father mostly left him alone. When I asked if Alton also was leaving Fay Ann alone, she mumbled something, then asked about my gown. Coward that I was, I described my jade green chiffon Mainbocher and Queen Elizabeth's jewels, then every other dress from that wonderful evening that I could remember.

But when we hung up I knew I would always feel guilty, knew it was a forlorn hope that she would ever find happiness, that my only sister was miserable and that I hadn't the slightest idea how to help her.

I'd been well paid for *Royal Interlude* so I had plenty of money. Nat wasn't too happy with me staying in Europe, since my contract was about to expire and he was negotiating for my next film. But I felt I deserved a vacation so I went on to Paris, spent three weeks at the Ritz, wandering around the streets in disguise, feeling free. I had discovered that it wasn't the adulation I needed, it was the knowledge that I'd achieved what I'd dreamed of all those years. I was an actress—a damned good one, too.

Walking around the Place Vendome or up the Champs-Elysées, awed at the splendor of Sainte Chapelle, absorbing as much as I could at the Louvre, climbing the unending steps in Montmartre; I loved every minute of it. I got such a great laugh out of everyone thinking it terribly strange that I spent so much time alone in my hotel room, never guessing I wasn't even there. I greatly enjoyed the intrigue of getting away undiscovered.

Then, of course, I became Alana Paige again, and went shopping on the Rue de St. Honore and Rue de la Paix, doing what everyone expected, having a wonderful time spending money on jewelry and clothes and all the gifts I dragged home to send to Midland later. The restaurants were glamorous; the food was delectable and we had champagne at every meal; I loved Tour d'Argent and a bistro on the Seine but when I was in disguise I ate only from patisseries or at tiny cafés. It was glorious fun.

I appeared in a benefit at the Opera, met De Gaulle and President and Mrs. Kennedy, when she charmed the French by speaking their language and he charmed the world by saying he was merely her escort.

At an Embassy party, eavesdropping on the American diplomats I met, I heard veiled discussions of the stirring Civil Rights movement at home and concerns about violence in Alabama. This led to heated conversations between segregationists and integrationists, hushed by wives or Embassy personnel. There was gossip about Hemingway's suicide, Trujillo's assassination, and Krushchev, as well as joy over Shepard's space flight. I listened to it all and must have been wide-eyed if anyone noticed.

~

The image of Alana on the streets of Paris, buying designer clothing and jewelry by Cartier or Van Cleef and Arpels makes me smile. I can picture her glowing, ethereal face and graceful, slender body on the Rue de la Paix, her retinue following, admiring, and probably irritating the hell out of her, see her striding, fluid, smooth, down the avenue, head high and smile beaming.

But more interesting was her growing awareness of the world around her—not only in the "industry." She had mentioned earlier how devastated she had been when Clark Gable died and then, while she was in England, Gary Cooper, though she had never worked with either of them. But there is a different look about her when she speaks of what we still call "current events." There is no way yet to understand how—or even if—those events affected her; sometimes she answers my questions—before I even ask them—but occasionally, with a languid wave she says, "Later," as if we both have all the time in the world.

Those are the moments when I'm most tempted to start talking about myself. Something in the atmosphere is conducive to revelations; could it be that she is waiting for me to reveal the ghosts of my past before she opens a door to some dark closet?

XII

A week in conservative Switzerland was a respite after France, where I had finally tired of the bother of disguise. Then I moved on to Italy.

But after three weeks there I was homesick, in spite of being treated like a queen, with every dignitary I met kissing my hand and making a fuss. I missed Nat and the excitement of a new script, getting up at the crack of dawn for makeup, and the challenge of becoming another person while the lights were on. I missed Mama and Fay Ann. It was time to go home.

At Heathrow, a welcome three-hour layover in the boring, uncomfortable eleven and a half-hour flight to California, I deplaned to walk around before I became too stiff to move. I went to the Duty Free Shop to look for a bottle of Miss Dior for Teri that I'd forgotten to pick up in Paris.

Across the aisle was a figure that caught my attention. He was tall enough to stand above several other men in the store, and had narrow hips with broad shoulders enhanced by the American Air Force uniform he wore. I watched his quiet but self-assured manner with the cashier, watched him pick up a small package from the counter, watched him walk gracefully towards the door of the shop.

As if aware of my stare, he turned and I found myself gazing into smoky eyes under brows like wings, in a face chiseled as precisely as a statue by Michelangelo. There was an instant of recognition and then a slight frown, which creased his forehead above the straight nose. It was only after he had left the store that I realized his skin was the color of Kahlua laced with cream.

After all these years I was still cautious and seldom interested in any of the men I met, usually turned off by handsome ones, since that was all one saw in Hollywood. I suppose I should tell you about the two affairs I finally did have; at last I'd learned a little about sex and birth control—all the stuff Mama had been too shy or too repressed to explain.

One of my lovers was a pretty famous star—I won't tell who, and we were together for a while. Another was one of the set designers; it was brief but satisfying.

Nat, being my best buddy and confidant, had a fit; he already had serious problems with my obsessive desire for privacy; an affair just complicated his life more. It wasn't easy to keep secrets in such a gossipy town. On rare occasions my guard dropped and the remnant of a Texas accent slipped out, but by some miracle we kept my origins, family background and finally, my meager sex life, quiet. I'm positive it couldn't be done today, but somehow Nat managed it then, and I'll always be grateful to him. Without it…well, that part of my story comes later.

Anyway, I was discrete about everything and for a long while so indifferent to men in general that even Rona Barrett had difficulty keeping me in the columns. In current times I would have been rumored a lesbian. But I am not. Oh, no, not at all.

~

Billie Jo mentions the two affairs as if they were boring experiments; the description she gave of the stranger feels entirely different. I want to hear more about this man who obviously plays some part in Alana Paige's life, but she pauses in her story, gazing out towards the sere plains of West Texas. Her eyes have taken on that faraway look once more, a sort of haunted expression. I hold my breath, hoping this is the moment for revelations, secrets. When I think about it, I realize how little gossip I've ever heard about her early life, how chaste she has always seemed—a Garboesque character. So I'm surprised about the affairs.

But then I'm constantly being surprised by this remarkable woman who, with no apparent resentment, relinquished fame and fortune to return to her childhood home and anonymity.

We sip tea, eat cookies that I brought again this morning. We haven't gone for a ride in a few days. It's hot outside but quite comfortable where we sit, and I suddenly realize, at some point in the past, air conditioning has been added to this small home.

Billie Jo is wearing one of her silk dresses, Balmain, I think, and looks like royalty from some fictitious European country. She seems less upset than nostalgic.

She recovers, looks at me and smiles a warm, self-deprecating smile, but remains enigmatic; my frustration suddenly blossoms and I'm angry. What am I doing here if all Alana wants is to reminisce about her childhood and a few sordid affairs?

She recognizes my anger and puts her hand on mine. She asks for patience; how can I refuse? In the short time I've spent in this woman's company I've begun to respect and care for her. If she needs my patience, I'll try to supply it.

I sigh and ask if she wants to continue.

~

The flight from London was every bit as boring as I had expected, flying by night over the ocean, then crossing the continent with the sun chasing us over the clouds. I did manage to get a little sleep before we landed all those hours later at LAX.

Getting home was heaven, and starting back to work the same exciting challenge it had been more than six years before. It was very strange that I dreamed of the man from the airport, trying to get to him, always thwarted by the wall the Communists had just erected in Berlin.

When *A Day in May* finished shooting I went on one of my incognito trips to Texas, finally to take all the gifts I'd brought from Europe. Mama was overwhelmed with the Parisian clothes and perfume; Fay Ann loved the book from the Louvre but the dress I brought was too large; she had lost even more weight and looked careworn and weary. Johnny's condition was unchanged; he was still confined to his wheelchair most of the time, his muscle tone poor, his heart diseased. His eyes, a beautiful, almost turquoise blue, were up-slanted at a sharp angle, his nose small, lips and tongue large. He said hello in a thick, guttural voice, smiling, though I'm not sure he truly remembered me; he seemed pleased with the gifts I'd gotten him, especially a puppet from Italy, with brightly striped pantaloons and a red jacket.

Alton was spending more and more time away from home; that meant Fay Ann had fewer bruises than in the past, certainly something to be grateful for. I asked her to come to Hollywood with me for a few weeks but, predictably, she refused. As usual I felt frustrated and helpless.

For the first time in my visits from California, I spent an hour or so alone with Howard. He was deferential, almost frightened. It was a lovely revenge and I took great pleasure in making him uncomfortable. When Mama came back from whatever errand she had been pursuing, I smiled sweetly at Howard and said, "How nice! It's been years since we had any time alone, and I remember the last few times so well."

He harrumphed, cleared his throat and beat a hasty retreat to the garage to finish some sort of project. Mama looked at me apologetically. "That's not like him at all. I wonder what's on his mind."

"Doesn't matter, Mama," I said, managing somehow to smother my giggles. "Let's make some hot chocolate."

Nat talked me into doing some personal appearances for our armed forces. It wasn't at all what I wanted, but when I'd told him my first choice was to ride the buses in Alabama, he almost had a heart attack. I'd never seen him so upset.

"You can't do that, Billie," he yelled, "unless you want to say goodbye to your career—not to mention maybe your life. I'm with you in sentiment, but it just isn't a good idea." He'd calmed down by the time he got to the end of his sentence. "I'll get you appearances at some bases. Maybe you can do an overseas with Jack Benny."

"Don't be silly, Nat. I can't dance and my singing is strictly 'if necessary.'"

"That's all right, Billie. Just stand there and let 'em look at you."

That was the most insensitive remark I'd ever heard from Nat; I let him know I was displeased. But I wanted to do something "extra" now, and short of serving at canteens—somehow too reminiscent of my early days in Hollywood—I couldn't think of anything.

So there I was on my second personal appearance, this time at

Norton Air Force Base in a pale gold satin Jimmy Galanos gown, standing next to Rita Moreno—who most certainly could dance—feeling like an idiot. I was introduced amid cat calls and whistles, said a few words, waved, and turned away.

Swearing I'd never put myself in such a humiliating position again, I almost blindly rushed towards the limo waiting sedately behind the stage. I smashed into a body clad in olive drab, medals on its chest, epaulets with two silver bars on its shoulders.

Knowing before I looked, I lifted my head and gazed into the smoky eyes, wordless. The arched brows were high, the mouth quirked upwards. A blush started in my feet and traveled with the speed of light to my face. My lips parted; no sound emerged.

"I wouldn't want you to apologize, Miss Paige. I've never had a more welcome collision."

"You...you...."

"The name is Andrew. My friends call me Drew. I hope you will, too." He paused, looked bemused for a moment. "Sorry. I'm not much of a poet, am I?"

He had, whether deliberately or purely by accident, given me a little time to recover my wits, if not my dignity.

I had to laugh. "Still, I am sorry. I wasn't looking where I was going."

"You were in a pretty big hurry. I hope nothing's wrong."

"No. Well, yes. I'm just not any good at these personal appearances." Now why in the world was I telling him that? "I mean, I can't dance, like Rita, and I can't sing like anyone. So why am I here?"

"If I told you you're so beautiful it's a pleasure just to look at you, you'd probably walk away."

"Yes. But thank you." That was such a disappointing thing for him to say. Was he shallow? Were his wonderful looks a shell, empty of character? His milk chocolate skin glowed like amber; the uniform fit perfectly, enhancing the breadth of shoulder; his bearing was military and proud. And the eyes, those startling, gray, lazy eyes stared into mine with an intensity that belied his casual manner.

I didn't want to walk away. This stranger, this man I had glimpsed so briefly in an airport, halfway around the world and almost twelve months ago, made my heart accelerate; *say* something, Drew whatever your name is. Rescue me.

He did. "Miss Paige, would you join me for a drink at the Officer's Club?"

"I'd be delighted."

We sat at a corner table, nursing one drink, then another, making them last. Officers of all rank and both genders arrived and left, but I was only dimly aware of them, and for the most part they left us alone, only one or two asking for an autograph. I was learning about this intriguing man, who was not the least bit shallow, who shared my philosophies and enjoyed my pleasures. It sounds so trite to say we were soul mates. But that was how I saw it then, and I still do.

We talked far into the night, neither of us willing to leave, until it was closing time and there was no choice.

"Billie, I have to be in Washington tomorrow. It isn't anything I can cancel or change. May I call you as soon as I get back?"

What a question. "Of course." I gave him my private number, and in a gesture totally foreign to me, put my hand over his. "I knew when I saw you at Heathrow that we'd meet again; that we'd be friends."

"I'd almost given up hope," he said, "and I had no idea you'd be here tonight."

"I'll have to thank Nat; it was he who arranged it."

"Thank him for me, too," he smiled, and I fell into his eyes.

As it turned out, it was more than a month before we met again. Drew had some mysterious business that took him somewhere overseas, then back to Washington, before he returned to California.

I tried to concentrate on the new script Nat had brought, finally throwing it into the corner in a fit of temper that raised Maria's eyebrows. She was a gem, Maria, more friend than housekeeper, though my home was immaculate and I'd never eaten better.

Luck truly had been with me when I hired her, more impressed with her independent demeanor than concerned with her one short leg. Her coppery flat face with it's flashing black eyes was usually smiling; her squat body was constantly in motion, keeping time to whatever popular song played on her radio as she sang with it, mostly off key.

I'd bought a new house the preceding year, actually a new *old* house. It was a rambling Spanish, tiled roof building, tucked away in Bel Air, as inaccessible as I could get it. Palm trees and eucalyptus screened it from the hills above, and it was protected by the long sharp thorns of intertwined bougainvillea on three sides, with a small pool and fruit trees in back, a driveway and gate in front.

Inside it was cool, with planked floors where I'd scattered cream-colored Berber rugs. Again I chose white for my walls, except in my bedroom, which was a pale coral with a glorious Aubusson on the polished wood. Chocolate brown sofas with bright pillows softened the stark surroundings of my living room. My bookshelves were filling up; also, I was beginning to collect art; what joy!

Then Nat brought me a puppy. I tried to refuse, since I was so often away from home. But I took one look at that adorable face and couldn't give her up. We named her Shadow, a good name for a black Labrador.

Shadow and I went for walks around my property, she swam in the pool more than I did, and if anyone managed to get near the house, she let me know immediately.

Shadow sat at my feet; I fondled her ears and got back to the screenplay that Maria had handed me, finished reading, and decided I must accept it. It was an excellent script if I could just keep focused. The problem was I had no desire to tie up all my time, pretty silly, since I had no idea when Drew would be free, or indeed *if* he would be free.

Ah, Drew. Andrew Scott Westerly, born in Virginia thirty-two years ago, to the president of a black college and a Jamaican beauty fleeing upheaval and riots in her native land, graduate of the United States Air Force Academy, captain in the Air Force, once married, no children, all man. He obsessed my thoughts, kept me awake nights, inhabited my dreams when I did sleep.

Nat knew something was different in my life but I wasn't ready to share Drew with him yet. I would, when the time was right. He kept asking what was going on.

"Billie, you've been a nervous wreck for weeks. Are you going to tell me what's wrong?"

"Nothing's wrong, everything's right. Well, it will be soon. I'll tell you then."

He shook his head, but had known me long enough to know that if I'd made up my mind about something I wouldn't change it.

I tried to keep up with what was happening in the world. I knew, with satisfaction, that the Supreme Court had overturned the conviction of some Freedom Riders, that, in my own profession, Marilyn Monroe, that beautiful, lost girl, had died, perhaps by her own hand, and, of course, that Kennedy had backed Khrushchev down over the missiles in Cuba.

The truth was, I was trying to keep my mind busy enough to forget why I was waiting. Half the time, breath held, I found myself listening for the phone to ring, then frantic when the call wasn't Drew's soft voice with the slight lilt he must have inherited from his Jamaican mother.

I signed the contract for *Some Kind of Magic* without realizing it was a remake of the Cary Grant, Katherine Hepburn *Bringing Up Baby*, a big success, which *Some Kind of Magic* never was. In fact, it was the biggest flop of my career. I didn't care—that might have been part of the problem—but it promised to be a fairly quick shoot and kept me busy.

I want to know about Drew but Billie digresses; I'm nearly crazy with frustration. It's almost as if it's deliberate, as if she delays to extend my time with her as much as possible. I'm ready to start writing this story—but the most exciting parts of it are still a mystery. Westerly is not the name on the gravestone in the cemetery we visited. Who are these people? How did they shape Billie's life? And why is she procrastinating about telling me?

~

The next time we were together was so brief that it almost doesn't bear mentioning, except for what I learned. Drew was again heading abroad. Early one morning we spent a couple of hours uncomfortably ensconced in a waiting room at some sort of small military base in downtown Los Angeles, to which I had driven, still sleepy from long hours in front of the camera. Aware that I would be late for the day's shoot, angry and upset at the situation and my apparent inability to say no, when I arrived I was less than congenial.

Then I saw him and all the anger drained away. He greeted me with a reserve I didn't expect, shaking my hand when all I wanted to do was throw myself into his arms, wherever we were, whoever was watching.

"What a terrible thing to ask you to do, to drive down here at this ungodly hour. I promise the next time will be more conventional and a real visit. Thank you so much for coming."

"I wanted to see you. I'm glad I came. Where are you going? Is it a secret?"

"I'm going to Saigon, but that's really all I can tell you."

Saigon! My whole body crawled when I realized what he was telling me. They were fighting a war in Vietnam. Americans were being killed there. Would he be in danger? I barely knew him; he couldn't be snatched away before we even had time to love each other.

"Don't look so scared," he laughed. "I'm just a liaison, nowhere near the fighting."

That helped; so did the fact that he had read me so easily. I tried to relax. We had a good time, just sitting with heavy mugs of awful coffee, talking about anything that occurred to us.

But the time melted like snow in the sunshine and he had to leave me. He glanced around the barren room; no one; he took me in his arms; those sculpted lips met mine; I dissolved.

"I'll be back, Billie; keep the faith." He was gone.

This time a few weeks separated us. It was becoming obvious that if I were to have any relationship at all with this man who seemed to have bewitched me, I must reconcile myself to infrequent meetings of very short duration. Damn. I wasn't happy.

But each time his soft voice responded to my hello on the telephone, I melted; he could have asked for anything; I would have given it to him.

Once more we met in a setting that was barren of any redeeming qualities; it was becoming very strange indeed.

"I won't do this again. It might be your idea of more conventional, and it might be longer. But it's depressing—and the coffee is terrible." I tried to smile at him, but found my effort extremely weak. Where was the actress when I needed her?

"Billie, I'm at a loss. I have no idea what to do." He took my hand, turned it palm up and traced my lifeline with a slender finger. A shiver ran down my spine.

"Do about what?"

He gazed at me for a long moment before answering. Then, "I

want to spend every available minute with you. I want to know you, love you." He puffed his cheeks and blew out a breath. "But there are problems."

What was he talking about? "What problems? Don't you see I want the same?"

"Have you ever really looked at me, Billie?"

"What a strange question. I love looking at you."

"What color am I, Alana Paige?"

I stared at him, at the gray eyes, a gene from some ancestor, perhaps a slave owner; at the arched wings of his brows, the mouth I so wanted to kiss, the broad shoulders under the olive drab wool of his uniform, and then at the smooth milk chocolate of his skin. "I love the color of your skin!"

"Do you realize what would happen to your career if we're seen together? This is 1962 but it might as well still be the dark ages. Yes, things are changing, but very slowly; there were riots in September when James Meredith enrolled in the University of Mississippi.

"Why do you think I've met you in these godawful places? Because I know how deserted they usually are, how out of the way. We can't go anywhere public; your face is public property: everyone recognizes it."

He released my hand at last but it remained on the table, without will. He was right, of course. The press would be ecstatic. I tried to think of any recent biracial alliances in Hollywood or, indeed, anywhere; my brain refused all activity. I couldn't think of any at all.

He watched me as I juggled my desires with the obvious truth of what he had said. It took me a minute or two to reason out what I wanted to tell him. It came out more egocentric than I had intended but, mercifully, he understood what I was trying to say.

"It's too soon to make the kind of commitment I'd like to make. We don't know each other well enough for me to risk my career—yet. But," I smiled at him, "if we both end up wanting the same thing...."

"So I guess that means we have to keep meeting in these out of the way places," he said, with both brows raised.

"Why?"

"What?"

"I have a perfectly good home; it's at least as private as this," I looked around, "and Maria I trust with my life."

That's how it happened that on his way back from wherever he had been this time, Drew drove from Norton to Bel Air, up the wooded roads to my driveway, where Shadow barked frantically, then dashed over to him wagging her tail like mad and slobbering all over his uniform. Some watchdog. He scratched her head, looked into her eyes and talked to her quietly, without letting me hear a word. Then he looked at me and said, "It's our secret. Hello, Billie Jo."

His arms went around me, his head bent to mine, and my knees went rubbery as he kissed me, ever so gently. Breathless, I took his hand and led him into the house. He looked around appreciatively. "You have beautiful taste. Your home is lovely."

It was a compliment that warmed my heart and colored my face. After all, my physical beauty was a lucky accident; taste was something I'd worked for.

We settled on one of the brown couches; soon Maria brought tea. Her eyebrows flew up when she met Drew but she maintained her composure; it was more surprise than disapproval. I remembered then that I'd never mentioned that Drew was a black man; in spite of the conversation Drew and I had had some weeks before, it had seemed superfluous to me.

XIII

It's difficult for me to believe that the Alana Paige I know could have been so naive. Obviously she was, at the very least, infatuated with Drew. Did she expect to marry him? There were few interracial marriages in those days; I think only about one half of one percent.

In the scrapbooks I've not seen anyone who resembles her description of him; perhaps the fascination with him only lasted for a short while. But why, if that were true, would she even bother to tell so much about their meetings? I'm baffled but I'll just have to wait.

The day is over and I'm at my laptop in my hotel room.

Reviewing the time with Billie I've come to the conclusion that there is an underlying reason I don't yet understand for her to be so detailed in her storytelling. She keeps looking at me quizzically, as if she's waiting for something, though what it could be is a real puzzle.

Tomorrow is halfway into the third week I've been here. At the beginning, when I asked how long Billie thought the interviews would take she was vague; I didn't press her. I'm glad—relieved is a better word—to be away from home right now. But my curiosity is so strong I'm constantly stressed and my neck hurts! I have to laugh. A stiff neck is a small price to pay for the truth about Alana Paige's life; no one else has been granted an interview since she left Hollywood, though I know a few have tried over the years.

In spite of my curiosity, if Billie will, tomorrow I'd like to take her for a drive, get her out of the house for a few hours, do something nice for her—I don't know what yet, but I'll think of something.

My editor has sent me a large fat envelope but I'm too tired to look at it tonight. It can wait.

~

Liz Taylor was throwing a big Valentine's Day party at the Beverly Hills Hotel. Nat and Teri were picking me up, though I had no desire to go. I'd not seen or heard from Drew since his last visit and I was frantic. Did it mean I had been wrong about his feelings for me? Was he capable of deceit, stringing me along for some reason of his own? It certainly had nothing to do with my fame or Hollywood, since we'd never been seen together. He couldn't have lied about his divorce. Could he?

I reluctantly went through the closet looking for an appropriate gown for the evening. The white silk, long sleeved and almost backless Nan Goodman seemed as good a choice as any, so I tossed it on the bed and started the shower. The phone for the gate rang; I cursed under my breath. Nat was very early. Well, he'd just have to wait. I stepped into the shower; Maria would take care of Nat for me. She would probably scold him for going out on a holiday evening, since she was convinced that the accident risk escalated threefold those nights. She might very well be right.

Shadow dashed into the bedroom, scrabbling for a foothold on the wood floor. She was panting, her tongue hanging like a man's necktie, all excited about something. I caught my breath in a gasp; she was rarely that excited.

I turned off the shower, threw on a terrycloth robe, shook out my hair, and started from the room. But the doorway was filled with a form clad in jeans, a navy blue shirt and tweed jacket, and loafers without socks. I'd never seen him out of uniform before. He was still gorgeous!

Drew stood there, absently scratching Shadow's head. "Is it all right, Billie?" he asked. "I didn't call, just wanted to get here as soon as possible."

"I haven't heard from you in three months," I exaggerated. "I almost decided I was wrong about everything…about us."

"Sit, Shadow," he ordered, and to my amazement she did. He walked the few steps to me as I stood, frozen…with longing? with fear? His arms wrapped around me; I laid my head on his chest, my eyes hot and stinging.

"You're not wrong about anything, Billie. I love you and would be here always, if only I could," he whispered into my tousled hair.

"Where were you; why couldn't you call?"

"Traveling; I can't tell you more than that. I'm sorry."

I looked up into his eyes. They were clouded with something I couldn't read, distant, sorrowful, perhaps even frightened, some of the unexpressed emotion communicating itself to me as if by osmosis. Then he was aware of me and his arms tightened. I clung to him; some instinct told me not to ask what was wrong, so I was silent, waiting.

"Terrible things are happening in the world again, Billie. I've become a part of them and I hate it."

"You've been back to Vietnam, haven't you?"

His smile was strained. "Let's forget the world tonight." His eyes strayed to the white dress tossed carelessly on the bed. "But you were dressing to go somewhere. My timing is appallingly bad."

"Do you really think I'd rather go out than stay here with you? But Nat will be by for me in a few minutes. I'll have to tell him. I can't ask Maria to do that for me."

Reluctantly, I freed myself from his arms just as the gate phone rang again. "Come on. You and Nat will like each other."

So instead of telling Nat earlier, when I had the time, that I had a genuine love interest in my life, I simply introduced them.

Nat shook Drew's hand and surprised me by saying, "I think you're the one who's been putting sparkle in Billie's eyes lately. I'm glad to meet you." And I had thought I was an actress!

He couldn't have started the relationship with Drew in a more compelling way. They liked each other from the beginning, which was a blessing; if I'd had any flak from Nat my life would have become unbearable.

"Would you like to join us at the Beverly Hills Hotel this evening?" he asked Drew slyly. "Teri's waiting in the car. We can make it a foursome."

"Ignoring the fact that you're in a tuxedo and I'm in Levis, I'd refuse anyhow. But thank you for the invitation. I hope this isn't the kind of affair that Billie is obligated to attend?"

"I'll make her excuses. Teri will be disappointed." Then he grew serious. "I won't say why she couldn't come. And I think discretion is called for. I hope you don't misconstrue my meaning."

"It's something we've talked about before. You're right, unfortunately. We have been and will continue to be discrete."

Nat smiled at him and I knew we were safe, not only from gossip but also from disapproval. I was surprised at how relieved I felt. I hugged Nat and whispered, "Thank you."

"You deserve some happiness, Billie." He smiled at Drew again. "Take care of her."

Drew nodded. "I'll do my best."

We were alone. Suddenly I was shy though my body gravitated towards Drew even as I tried to retreat. Fay Ann's voice clamored in my head. This was no experimental affair, indulged in to add experience or satisfy curiosity. This was obsession, witchery, perhaps even madness.

~

Her voice, never loud, grows softer still. As I watch, fascinated, Billie's eyelids half close, and her mouth parts slightly as the hand holding her teacup ever so gently puts it in its saucer. She becomes younger looking, radiant. As beautiful as she always has looked to me, this nevertheless is an astounding transformation. I wonder if she is having some sort of attack, until she gazes at me so appealingly that my heart turns over. I'm aware that this part of her story has never been told before, that in a secretive life, this is the beginning of the ultimate secret. My pulse beats in the hollow of my throat. As if it could all be told in the time it takes to exhale, I hold my breath.

~

Drew kissed me and warnings faded to non-existence; I heard only the pounding of blood as it raced through my veins, the murmur of Drew's words in my ear as he repeated, "You, Billie, I need you, you're the only sanity in my life and I'll never make it without you. Promise you'll be here for me. Promise!"

"I promise, Drew. Whenever you need me I'll be here. I love you; the rest is only…things."

He carried me into the bedroom, sat on the bed with me in his arms.

"You know we can't go back after this, Billie. Are you sure?"

It was the most right thing I had ever done. I laughed at him.

XIV

Billie is too much of a lady—or perhaps I should say too much of her generation—to describe her sexual experiences with Drew in detail. She has left that to my discretion and my writer's imagination, which conjures up a sublime love scene.

I picture Drew sitting on the bed holding Billie in his arms, her laughing, exquisite face turned up to his. He laughs with her, then bends his head to touch her lips with his own, trying for some measure of restraint, but succumbing to desire as her passion soars.

The terrycloth robe falls away, leaving Alana's full breasts exposed to Drew's hands and mouth. She sighs and arches her back, aching for his touch, so rapt her own hands seem paralyzed. She is absorbing, storing.

Drew rolls sideways, places Alana on the bed, caressing the length of her body as he does so. He kicks off his shoes, sits beside her.

Finally Alana's hands recover their mobility and she begins to unbutton Drew's shirt; he straightens his arms to help as she reaches behind him to drag the shirt away, her eyes marveling at the breadth of his shoulders, the muscular definition of his rib cage and upper abdomen. She unbuckles his belt, then, suddenly shy, fumbles with the zipper of his jeans. He reaches down to help, laughs shakily, slides the Levis and jockey shorts down his long runner's legs, kicks them aside.

Alana's gaze roams the length of his body, stopping for a fraction of a second to wonder at his erection, so virile, so proud. He makes no effort to cover himself under her scrutiny, instead remains still for a moment, meeting her brown eyes with his own, now darkened to charcoal.

"I want you," their voices collide.

"It seems fairly apparent, doesn't it?" Drew asks with some irony, his voice hoarse with longing.

She reaches for him, enfolds him in her arms and clings, breathing in the scent of soap and sweat, faint traces of after-shave and, somehow, leather.

He finds her hardened nipples; sucks gently, savoring the taste of her skin as her hands mindlessly stroke his back.

"Oh," she exclaims in surprise, as he begins to travel down her body, trailing tiny electrical charges as he goes that threaten to light her up like a flash bulb, then, "Oh, my God," as his tongue finds its way between her legs, to flick the cleft and search inside for the sweet essence of her.

She is vibrating like a tuning fork; Drew, pleased, begins his journey back, reaching her mouth at last, kissing it, touching the tiny scar on her lip with his tongue.

Billie runs suddenly hot fingers through the hair on his chest, following it downward until it meets the denser hair at his groin and the satin smoothness of his penis; he gasps, whispers, "Yes," so she glides her hand up and down, grateful to bring him this pleasure.

Their breathing grows labored as they descend deeper into the magic of their love until there is no distinction between them, as Drew finds his way to the core of Billie, and the ripples of pleasure spread outward from the center of her being.

Her head tilts back; her mouth opens wide, her breath held, then released in ragged gusts. Aflame, Drew joins her, his body jerking in spasms of release until they both collapse, his welcome weight resting on her welcoming body.

~

Afterwards, as I waited for my heartbeat to slow to merely racing, I thought of Mama. Finally I understood why she couldn't resist my father, why Fay Ann succumbed to what must have been the same urgency on Alton's part, though her relationship with Alton bore no resemblance to mine with Drew. My toes still tingled and I had learned about nerve endings, and what the novels meant when they described two people carried away by passion. I was awestruck.

Drew's arm held me comfortably against his body, my head resting snuggled into his neck. We lay quietly, satiated. I would have been content to stay there forever, just feeling him beside me.

He became restless though; I could tell by the tightening of his muscles, his shoulders tensing, biceps swelling. I raised my head. "What is it, Drew?" His face again wore the look I had come to dread: distant, sad, afraid.

"Tell me!"

For the first time he revealed just a little of what was gnawing at him.

"If you knew what my job has become, you might feel differently about me, Billie."

I waited, smiling inwardly, wondering what he could possibly do that would change my feelings for this man I adored with all my heart and soul.

"I'm a...messenger...sent to extract information from high ranking captive Vietcong." He hesitated. "Our methods are less than humane."

I saw the clenching of his jaws, pulled myself upright, more disturbed by this revelation than I cared to show.

"Have you a choice, my love?"

"Whatever you hear on the news or read in the papers to the contrary, we're in a war. Not a good time to resign my commission. I've put in for a transfer but been refused."

"Then you've answered my question. You have no choice. There's no use tormenting yourself."

"That sounds so simple. But of course it isn't." He laughed bitterly. "When this is all over, I'll be a different man. And maybe not one I can live with."

My blood seemed to freeze. "Don't, Drew. You can't control everything. It might all be over soon."

"I don't think so, Billie. I think this conflict is going to be around for a long time." He paused, almost seemed to shake himself loose from some horrific thought.

I had no answers for him. I couldn't do anything except hold him in my arms, and pray to a God about whose existence I had serious doubts to keep him safe.

We finally rose from the bed when our appetites demanded something in addition to love. I knew Maria was sound asleep since it was only four A.M. My cooking skills were a little weak, but I managed some eggs and toast with a wonderful raspberry jam I'd found at Jurgenson's. We ate at the kitchen table, Drew in my terry robe, I in an old shirt, just long enough to cover me, just short enough to cause Drew to say with a lopsided grin, "You're teasing me, Billie. You have no right to look that good in the middle of the night."

I ate the last bite of egg and rose to cross to his side of the table. When I bent to kiss him, he groaned and pulled me down. I felt him growing hard beneath me, took his hand, leading him back to bed. We didn't talk for a long time after that.

When we awoke the sun was already high overhead. Drew looked at his watch, sitting accusingly on the nightstand.

"Christ, I have to go. I have a plane to catch."

He kissed me briefly, as my mood plunged into something not quite despair. I didn't follow him into the shower, afraid that he'd sense my withdrawal, and misinterpret it.

The sound of running water became voices in my head, predicting disaster. All the doubts we'd discussed and dismissed coalesced: what would happen to my career if some reporter discovered our relationship; would it be a repeat of the scandal when Ingrid Bergman ran off with Rossellini? If so, as an American, could I simply escape to Italy or somewhere and continue working? If I had to give up my career would I just fade away like Gail Russell; how would I manage to support myself? Well, I could handle it all if I had Drew. But I'd no idea what plans he had for us. Could we marry, settle down somewhere without society making our life as a biracial couple miserable?

All these half-formed, semi-rational ideas chased themselves around in my head while I waited, tense and frightened, for Drew to finish his shower. When the water abruptly shut off, all the activity in my brain seemed to cease with it; I was left with the one overriding thought I had been avoiding: that Drew soon would be gone again.

Saying goodbye to Drew was one of the most difficult moments of my life. Again he had been unable to tell me where he was going: "I've told you much too much already," which made it obvious that he was on his way back to Vietnam, where the fighting had expanded and more casualties were reported in the news.

I joined the ranks of all the women seeing the men they loved off to war—declared or not. There was no predicting when he would be back, though he continued to say he was nowhere near combat and therefore not in any danger. I tried to believe him.

He was gone for four months. We finished shooting *Some Kind of Magic* during that time, the strain of doing comedy almost more than I could manage. What salvaged my sanity were the letters, not very many, not very informative, but always loving. I received five during that time, wrote volumes back, though I sent only some of them, and rarely received acknowledgment. That meant he was traveling again.

When *Some Kind of Magic* was complete I told Nat I needed a vacation, that I would take some time off before signing another contract. Dear Nat. He understood and didn't pressure me. We had one conversation about Drew but it was so traumatic for me that he never asked again.

The Reinholds had a cottage at Lake Arrowhead, small, rustic, just what I needed to remove me from the Hollywood scene. It was Teri who suggested I drive there and stay as long as necessary to "feel better." She didn't know that I couldn't feel better until Drew returned from whatever mission he was currently assigned.

I left detailed instructions with Maria, and after she stocked the most innocuous car I could borrow with food and warm clothes, Shadow and I drove up the mountain to a cabin even more secluded than my home.

I settled in to read, take walks in the woods, breathe in the crisp mountain air, and just be lazy, an unknown luxury. I ate sparingly, had a glass of wine each evening and tried to sleep without nightmares about jungles and Vietcong soldiers.

After two weeks I was ready to face my normally chaotic world again, so I packed up, loaded an obviously reluctant Shadow into the car and returned to Bel Air where Maria did a rapid, squint-eyed examination of my face and pronounced me, "Better."

When I called to thank Nat and Teri for their generosity, Nat told me to look at the new script he had dropped off; he knew I'd like it, and Universal wanted me for the part. There was nothing for me to do but wait, anyhow, so I was happy to sign on for *Better You Than Me*, which was a huge success, somehow, though my heart was never in it. I spent more time scouring the newspapers than rehearsing.

As much as was going on during that period—the phenomenon of Martin Luther King, the shocking tragedy of Kennedy's death, and, comic relief, the Beatles, my daily, frantic inspection of the newspapers was in fruitless search for some reassurance that Vietnam was quieting down, that our servicemen were coming home.

Each time he landed in California, Drew managed somehow to see me, whether for a few days, only a few hours or an abbreviated overnight. One visit, in a cold and windy February, was less than satisfactory; too strained since we both were aware of its brevity. But as he went towards the shower, he called over his shoulder, "I have some good news."

I followed him, hoping. I kept it light. "That you've known all night and not shared with me? What a rat! Tell."

"I have two weeks leave in May. What do you think?"

"What do I think? Are you crazy?" I jumped into the shower with my robe on, to hug Drew and tell him how thrilled I was at the prospect of two whole weeks alone together.

"I think it's wonderful." Immediately, I pictured Nat's cottage. "How would you like to spend it in an isolated cabin at Lake Arrowhead?"

I warned Nat that I'd be gone, whether or not the studio needed me, and that he'd have to say I was sick with some dread disease, unable to see anyone or take any calls, whatever was necessary to allow me a getaway. Then I begged for the use of the cabin, to which he replied, "Only if you promise to put on a little weight. Thin is good, but you're overdoing it, Billie."

"I promise. I'll buy ice cream and have some every day; I'll eat so much I'll be a balloon; you'll ask me to diet. Oh, Nat, I can't contain myself." I was a five-year-old, hopping from foot to foot, waiting for Christmas.

It was the most wonderful two weeks of my life. I was happy, deliriously happy. The air was fresh and cool this early in May, the forest surrounding us green and lush. We took Shadow with us, walked in the pine scented woods, decided against swimming in the frigid lake, read neglected books and talked endlessly, our discussions as intimate as our acts of love.

For the first time I told about Howard and why I'd escaped to Hollywood so young, about my father and his gambling, which destroyed his marriage, about Fay Ann and Johnny, his Down Syndrome, and mindless, retarded smile.

Drew told me of his mother's discontent as the wife of a college president, her exotic beauty a handicap among the other wives, and the consequent isolation she endured. Drew was her consolation; he, too, had to escape from home before his personality was smothered by his mother's love. We shared our secrets and hopes, saw no one, knew nothing of the world's events.

Still cold enough for fires at night, we would have a simple dinner, then take our wine, sit on the floor in front of the fireplace listening to the crackle of the logs and the "whoo" of an owl somewhere in the trees outside, until our need for each other was too great to resist. Sometimes we would make love there, in the flickering glow of the burning logs, sometimes retreat to the bedroom under the warmth of the down quilt and always, always, we devoured each other with a hunger that never seemed to diminish.

Two weeks vanished like a magician's trick; we were faced with still another parting. It was too much to bear.

XV

Bless Nat for covering me the two weeks I was away. He had the studio so convinced I was ill that they told the press I was on leave with a bad attack of the flu, sent me flowers and a message that they would shoot around me, and I could have another two weeks off to recuperate.

We had a few problems at the house with some reporters who tried to crash the gate; Maria put a stop to that in a hurry. I'd never want to cross Maria when she's angry; she's a tiger.

As unexpectedly generous as it was of the studio, I was too nervous to enjoy the leisure. I felt guilty that it had been several months since I'd visited Mama and Fay Ann; I knew it was a diminished desire to be there, exposed to the trauma of Fay Ann's life.

I would go to Midland; this time I decided to drive.

Nat bought me a used gray Chevy Impala, so nondescript that no one would look at it twice. I put on dark glasses, tied a scarf around my hair, which I'd pinned up, wore a plaid shirt with a tan cotton skirt and flat heels. I looked as nondescript as my car.

It took almost three days to get to Midland. Once or twice people at the motels where I stayed looked at me strangely as I checked in with a name like Mary Strane or Helen Parker, depositing cash in lieu of a credit card. I could hear their thoughts: That looks like Alana Paige; no, not in those clothes. Besides, she'd never be staying in a motel; she'd be flying first class wherever she wanted to go. As miserable as I felt without Drew, I enjoyed the charade and the knowledge that it would be a wonderful story to tell him when we were together again.

In Midland there were few changes since I'd left a century or so before. But Mama was under a strain; it showed in the new lines around her mouth and between her eyes. She blamed it on old age; she was only fifty-two so that didn't wash. Unless she was hiding something like a health problem, I suspected it was the constant worry about Fay Ann and Johnny. It certainly wasn't financial; I offered money occasionally but she always refused, saying they didn't need anything. Howard was nearing retirement but they never had been extravagant, and he had invested wisely.

What she told me about Alton was a different story. She had been right: the dealership was in trouble. Mama thought he was skimming money off the top. If that were true and he was found out, he could go to prison. I had never before seen Mama vindictive.

"I hope he does. Serve him right." She said it with venom.

"You seem awfully mad at him," I said, casually.

"Don't like him; never did as a matter of fact."

"Well," I sighed, "we share that feeling. Trouble is there's nothing we can do about it."

"I been telling Fay Ann to leave him for years. Howard and I could take care of her and Johnny. But she just glares at me and shakes her head. I don't know what's wrong with that girl."

"She has to live her own life," I told Mama gently, "just like the rest of us."

Mama hugged me. "What about you? You haven't told me anything about yourself."

My eyes shifted away from hers. "My next movie is. . . ."

"I already know about your next movie," she interrupted tartly. "I'm asking about *you.* Something's going on."

I hadn't mentioned Drew to Mama. She must always have wondered why I never talked about any special man in my life. I didn't know whether to be more surprised that she was asking now—for she was—or that she had never asked before.

"Yes, there is someone. But it's too soon and too complicated to talk about yet."

"Is he married, Billie Jo?" she asked, severely, eyes narrowed, the old disciplinarian displaying herself, making me giggle.

"No, Mama, he's not married."

She watched me as if I were going to say more, or at least she wanted me to, but somehow I just couldn't. With her innate wisdom she didn't insist; I felt relieved. How would this southern lady—even adopted southern—feel when her daughter brought home a black man? And if his parents felt the same way about me? It had never occurred to me before that they might have the same resistance. This was the first tangible evidence I had experienced of the discomfort Drew and I might face as a couple.

We drove to Fay Ann's in my Impala. The house needed a coat of paint and some repair work on the exterior. It looked as if Mama was right about money, confirmed when I discovered that there was no longer a Rosita to help Fay Ann. That meant she had all the care of Johnny as well as what housekeeping she could manage.

"Why didn't you tell me?" I asked, outraged. "I would have sent you what you need. You shouldn't be doing all of this by yourself."

"Johnny really isn't much trouble. I just don't have the time or the heart for keeping the house neat. It's clean; that's enough."

"But, Fay Ann, I'd be so happy to help."

"Thank you, Billie Jo." She looked at me for a long time. "I'm in better shape than you think. Less money, but Alton has been real nice lately."

"You can't possibly have anything good to say about that man."

"He's my husband. He's Johnny's father. That all counts for something," she chided, softly.

"I swear I can't figure out what," I said, angrily. "You can't be all that forgiving."

"He's my husband," she repeated. "He even helps with Johnny sometimes."

"Big deal," I muttered under my breath. Mama was taking it all in, shaking her head, brows raised, mouth pursed in wonder, the breath escaping in a long exhale.

It had been ages since I'd seen Alton. When he arrived home from the office, ostensibly to welcome me—he'd never done that before—I was startled at how different he looked. Gone was the boyish, slightly pudgy young man I remembered. Instead he was slim, well dressed, smooth looking. His sandy hair had receded, but was somehow becoming, and his blue eyes had intensified in color. I realized he must be wearing tinted contact lenses.

And he was charming. He greeted me with a brotherly kiss on the cheek and a warm, "It's really good to see you again, Billie Jo."

We sat at the dining room table, sipping iced tea in the already hot Texas spring. Alton lit a cigarette, held it casually in his left hand. His voice flowed easily, briefly discussing politics, telling amusing stories about his work, asking casual questions about Hollywood and more specific questions about my career.

It wasn't until Mama and I were alone that I recognized what I'd subtly felt, sitting across the table from him. He was a con-man. And good at it, too. I wondered what he wanted from me.

~

The script for Goin' Home *was waiting for Alana when she arrived back in Bel Air, tired and lonely, again anxious to work while she waited for Drew. She was enthralled with it and half convinced that it would be her second chance for an Oscar. An extra advantage was the salary—more than she had made in the last four films together. She finished the retakes of* Better You Than Me, *wondering why she was so much more tired than normal after a day on the set, attributing it to the drive from Texas plus the usual worries after she had been there.*

It wasn't until she missed her period and began vomiting in the mornings that she realized the cause. She told herself that there was a different reason, that she had better see a doctor. Her thoughts were all on Drew. If it were true would he be happy? She was alternately ecstatic and terrified.

She signed the Goin' Home *contract immediately, risky since the shooting schedule could well extend into her sixth month if she were pregnant. But she was still so slim—too thin, Nat told her again—that she had no fear of being discovered, at least for a long time.*

She shopped for a dress to wear to the Academy Awards, figuring she'd have no time to do it later. An elegant white chiffon St. Laurent with beading swirling down the skirt, it was a gorgeous gown that would do justice to her figure, which she was determined to have regained in time to wear it. The baby would be about six weeks old by early April.

~

I mused about the history of our family. First my mother, then Fay Ann and now me, all pregnant out of wedlock. These thoughts always upset me because they led to images of Johnny. How much chance was there that Down Syndrome would repeat itself? If it did would I be able to cope? Would Drew?

Or on a more spiritual level, was it punishment for sin? And if so, why had Fay Ann and I escaped some equally debilitating birth defect? Anyway I rejected the idea as irrational; how had Johnny sinned?

Goin' Home was entirely different from so much of the fluff the studios gave me. It was a wonderful script and the film was a beautiful production, each person involved doing his part to make the whole movie shine that year. We started immediately.

I enjoyed working with talented Anne Bancroft and the suave, handsome Cary Grant, always an idol. We were making good progress and promised to finish on schedule, a good thing.

I did get nominated for an Oscar that year. I never made the awards ceremony.

When I was in my third month I knew I should have medical evaluation. Well, there was nothing unusual about a woman going to a gynecologist. Teri would know of one I could see.

I liked Dr. Mauser. A gentle, soft spoken man, sixty-something, with salt and pepper hair and kind brown eyes under thick, gold-rimmed lenses, he greeted me with normal warmth, did not fawn as so many might have, and seemed trustworthy. I had to hope so; if he were inclined to talk, my life would split open like a ripe tomato. I asked about confidentiality; he surprised me. I had not known that patient/doctor information was legally protected. That was a great relief.

He confirmed my pregnancy, said everything looked fine, predicted a delivery date, the month and week I knew it would be.

"So anything I tell you will stay in this room?"

He smiled at me. "I'm not inclined to talk about my patients anyway, Miss Paige. And you aren't the first Hollywood personality to come to me in this situation. I'm just glad you aren't asking me for an abortion, which I would refuse to do. Personal feelings aside, I have no desire to lose my license."

"Of course. Besides, an abortion is the last thing I want. I already love this baby."

"May I ask? Are you…I mean have you plans…?"

"Am I going to get married? Yes, just as soon as he gets back from Vietnam."

"I see. Well, that's good news. I'm pleased for you."

Was I crazy? Maybe Drew had no intention of marrying me. We hadn't spoken of the future much, too immersed in our present. No, as soon as he found out he would insist; if my career were to suffer from our relationship, so be it. In any case, I wanted the baby with all my heart, wished there weren't so many months to wait.

I floated from the doctor's office on a cloud of dreams; if only Drew would hurry!

Maria found me on my knees by the toilet a few mornings later. She nodded her head like one of those toys on springs, helped me into bed and asked when I was expecting.

I told her the date. There was no point trying to fool her; she was as wise as Mama, probably why I loved her so much.

"Saltines," I begged.

She brought the crackers on a tray with tea and honey.

The only other question she asked was, "Does Mr. Drew know?"

"Not yet."

"You'll get married." It was a statement of fact, not a query. My heart seemed to swell with gratitude. If Maria knew this, how could I ever doubt?

Nat said he had a story for me to look at, a good part that would intrigue me.

When I refused he was mystified.

"It's the kind of role you love, Billie. If the producer knows you'll do it he'll be able to get the financing without any trouble."

"I said no, Nat. I meant it. I don't intend to do another movie for a year or more."

"Why? Are you sick? Is something wrong?"

Morning sickness and my sore and tender breasts were the only indication that there were remarkable changes going on in my body. As it began to swell minutely I chose my clothes with great care and no one remarked on my fuller bosom or the slight convexity of my abdomen. But this was temporary.

It was time to tell him.

"You can't mean this, Billie," he whispered, as if someone were in the next room listening.

"Please don't scold, Nat. I'm so happy."

"Your career just ate it, *Alana.*"

"Not if we can keep it a secret for long enough to finish shooting *Goin' Home,*" I tried to reason. "By that time, when I really start to show I won't leave the house. As soon as Drew gets back; we can marry quietly and...well..." I faltered.

"Does he know about this?"

"No, but he'll be as thrilled as I am."

"Billie. Billie. Have you talked about marriage?"

"Not specifically," I dodged, "but we don't have to talk about it. We love each other."

"You're out of your mind."

How could he be so cruel? "Why?"

"First," he ticked off on an index finger, "the minute you show up at a maternity ward with a *very* premature baby the gossip will hit this town like a hurricane. Second, you might love each other but that doesn't automatically mean Drew wants to get married. Third, the public isn't ready for a mixed marriage anyway."

"Lena is married to a white man," I protested, "and it hasn't hurt her career. Besides, I don't give a damn about my career if I have Drew."

"Lena Horne is married to a white doctor and *she's* the star, so he needn't be concerned. Reverse it and they'd have just as much of a problem. You don't think you care about your career now, but you will. And it will be gone."

My hand covered my mouth. Nat, always there for me since the beginning had just delivered a knockout punch to my joy and hopes.

"You're wrong, Nat," I shouted at him in desperation.

"Jesus, Billie, sometimes you act like you haven't a brain cell in your head. Half of Hollywood has affairs; they don't toss their careers away because of them."

"If the public won't accept Drew as my husband I'll just leave."

Nat took my hands in his. As always, his volatile anger had evaporated quickly and he was calm. I knew it wasn't his own business he was protecting; he had grown with me, and now had many important clients. He was trying to help.

He sighed. "All right, honey," he said gently. "I know how much Drew means to you. If it comes to that I'll do everything in my power to help."

He paused to think. "Where is he now?" he asked. "Is there any way you can contact him?"

The heat exploded behind my eyes. "I usually get letters when he's gone but I haven't heard from him for weeks. I only know he's over there somewhere," I gestured west with my head.

"Write to him; ask him what he wants to do. It's not too late. If he doesn't want to get married, then you can. . . ."

"Can what? I won't have an abortion; it's almost too late anyhow. Put it up for adoption? You don't seem to understand; I want the baby; I'm not going to give it away like an old dress!" I could feel my face flushing; I grew hot then cold, at the idea of giving up my child—Drew's child. "I wouldn't. I couldn't!"

There was a long silence. Then Nat leaned over and put his arms around me, held me as I struggled with the tears I never shed, still knowing they wouldn't change a damn thing.

"Okay, Billie. I'll help with the baby and the career. We'll see it through, try to do whatever damage control is necessary. I love you, honey. We're a team; we'll handle it."

"Oh, Nat, thank you. I've always depended on you and you've always come through for me. I love you, too."

We sat there, not moving, for what seemed like an eon. I was so relieved; Nat would take care of everything for me.

~

What a shock this last hour has been! Again I'm made aware of how little I had known about the life of Alana Paige beyond her illustrious name.

If she had a baby, what happened to it? Or did she abort after all or perhaps miscarry, like her mother. That could be why she has paled, why she has begun to speak as if talking about someone else. Defense? My heart goes out to her.

Perhaps we should call this whole thing off. I'd give it up gladly to spare her this pain.

She is sitting quietly, watching my expression, probably reading my thoughts. She touches my hand and says it's all right; she wants me to know. I listen.

As she tells me of her faith in Nat's ability to smooth the rocky path she had chosen, I am amazed again at her naiveté. Billie is an intelligent woman. How could she have been so blind to the mores of a society that, in those years, still raised eyebrows at a woman having a child out of wedlock or even one born two months early—weighing seven pounds?

From my research on Clark Gable, I remember that Loretta Young adopted a child after retiring from the screen for a year. It was rumored to be hers and Gable's; it was so frowned on that the truth was never revealed.

Abortions were still illegal when Billie was pregnant, but there were doctors who would perform them—for a price. I'm sure there was more than one star in Hollywood who managed to terminate an unwanted pregnancy.

Billie was determined to have the baby, though. I'm so surprised at the information she has just shared with me that my brain is addled. She has started to crack open that closet; the secrets she has begun to tell explain a lot about her disappearance from Hollywood. She might have a son or daughter in the next town; maybe even grandchildren.

Then why is she so sad?

XVI

Goin' Home was finishing up and the last day of shooting was celebrated with the traditional wrap party. I was relieved to put on comfortable slacks and a sweater, since my costumes were becoming very tight, though wardrobe had done a great job of camouflage, looking at me suspiciously as I tried to convince them I was simply gaining a little weight.

Earlier, in the middle of the last take, with Cary, Anne and I on a set crowded with extras and technicians, I suddenly felt the baby move. I managed somehow to finish the scene, then went to a phone and called Nat. I told him he had to come over immediately. Of course he thought something was wrong; he came flying from Beverly Hills. It was scandalous of me to frighten him, but he and Maria were the only ones I could tell. Nat said I glowed like polished silver and finally looked larger than a pencil, so he forgave me.

At home, exhausted from emotional stress plus the last difficult days in front of sometimes uncooperative cameras, I put Mozart on the stereo, tossed my clothes on the bed, pulled on a wooly robe, and dropped onto the chaise.

Maria brought me a tray with crackers, brie and a tiny dab of caviar, but I only wanted tea. Too tired to eat, too tense to sleep, I scratched idly at Shadow's head as I stared into the fireplace where small flames danced like miniature acrobats in flamboyant costumes.

My thoughts were on Drew, missing him, wondering where he was, and why it had been so long since I'd heard from him.

The phone shattered my reverie.

Mama's voice, thick with tears, said, "Honey, is there any way you could come? Johnny's critical in the hospital and Fay Ann is near to collapse. I don't know what to do for her."

I felt the heat behind my eyes. It didn't matter that we'd known since birth that Johnny had a limited life span. Fay Ann had given him her whole heart and mind since the day he was born. If he were dying now she would be desolated, perhaps for always.

"Mama, I'll come tomorrow. Tell her I'm on my way."

"I know it's a sacrifice, but we really need you."

"I'll be there, Mama. Now tell me what happened."

There was a silence so long and so heavy I thought Mama had fainted.

"Mother?"

"Yes, Billie Jo. I'm here. I just don't want to say anything over the phone. I'll tell you when you get here."

She hung up without even waiting for a goodbye; I was left holding a dead receiver and an unanswered question.

Nat got tickets for me under a fictitious name; the next afternoon I boarded a small plane bound for Midland-Odessa, a gray haired, tired looking, badly dressed woman in her early fifties, met at the airport by her equally tired looking mother—of the same age. Under different circumstances it would have delighted us both.

In the car, as I took off the wig and shook out my hair, I asked, "How is he? Did he have a heart attack?"

"It's not his heart…it's…some complications."

"Well, tell me. No, tell me about Fay Ann first."

"Fay Ann is threatening to kill Alton."

"What!"

"Yes. But it's his fault Johnny's in the hospital and she says if Johnny dies she's going to kill him. I'm scared she means it."

"I thought they…tell me what happened."

"Johnny was in his chair on the porch, playing with that old puppet you brought him. Alton told him to put it down but he wouldn't. Alton grabbed it out of his hand. He was yelling something about 'too old for it'. Johnny tried to get it back and Alton hit him so hard that he tumbled out of his chair and fell off the porch. He hit his head on the edge of the step." She stopped to wipe her eyes. "It didn't look too bad.

Fay Ann called me and when we got him to the doctor he said it was…I think he called it something like a sub…I don't know…his brain swelled up." She wiped away more tears.

Grinding my teeth, I asked, "Do they think he'll die?"

"They don't know yet."

It sounded bad. "Let's go straight to the hospital," I decided. "I'd better put my wig back on."

The rails were down on one side; Fay Ann was sitting on the edge of Johnny's bed, holding his hand. Black curls framed his face, white except at the left temple which had turned a livid blue and green.

I walked up to my sister and put my arms around her. She felt as fragile as fine crystal.

She tried to smile at my wig and makeup. "Mama shouldn't have called you. There isn't anything to do but wait."

My wry thought was, I'm good at that. "Then I'll wait with you," I said

We kept a vigil until the end. Johnny never regained consciousness. When it was over, Fay Ann said, in a voice as quiet and controlled as I'd ever heard, "Alton belongs in jail but his father will keep him out, so I'm going to kill him."

"Please, Fay Ann, no matter how responsible Alton is for this tragedy, you don't want to end up in jail yourself."

She didn't hear me.

"I have a gun. I intend to use it, for Johnny and for all the misery he's put me through."

"You can leave him now. There's no reason to stay any longer."

She looked at me, suddenly wild-eyed, as if I were there to trap her. "I won't stay. I'll be gone as soon as he's dead. I…" Her mouth snapped shut, her hand across it.

"Let's go home now. We'll talk about this after you get some rest."

She came with me without resistance, moving as if hypnotized.

Mama put Fay Ann to bed in my old room. When I left her she was staring blankly at the wall. I wondered what, if anything, she saw there.

My sister was still in shock at the funeral. Mama said she asked where I was but seemed satisfied when told I was ill. Alton stood with his own family, slightly apart from Fay Ann, as if he were afraid she would carry out her threat right there at the cemetery.

Not ill at all, I took advantage of the time everyone was gone to hunt for the gun she had told me about. I found the .22 in a box high in her closet, where Johnny couldn't possibly have reached. I locked it in my suitcase.

Bringing food of all sorts, callers gathered in the living room to pay their respects. A few of them looked familiar to me but they seemed hesitant to approach. Maybe they thought I was too "Hollywood" for them. I didn't care; it was my sister who concerned me.

Alton was talking to Fay Ann, wringing his hands like an old woman. There were tears in his eyes. I heard only a part of what he said, enough to know he was pleading with her to believe how sorry he was, that it was a terrible accident, that he never had intended harm, that he only wanted her back.

She stared at him. "You are a dead man, Alton."

A shiver crawled up my spine.

I spent a week in Midland, mourning with Mama and even Howard, who had cared for Johnny more than anyone realized. Fay Ann began to awaken from her stony silence, to be aware of others around her. I hoped it was a sign of healing.

When she finally began to cry, the tears didn't stop. She cried constantly, her grief alarming in its intensity.

For five days Alton almost never left her side. He seemed devastated, his remorse so genuine I began to believe I had misjudged him. He held Fay Ann's hand, brushed her hair, brought her food and drink. She began to respond; it seemed she had forgotten her threat. I was keeping the gun though, just in case.

The police concluded that Johnny's death was an accident, which I suppose, in a way, it was. The legalities eluded me, though I sensed Mr. Fawcett's hand in it somewhere.

The day before I was to leave, Alton came to me with a plea, his eyes glassy with unshed tears.

"Billie, Fay Ann needs you. Please stay a while longer."

My hands clenched; I exhaled a gusty breath. He was right about my sister needing me. But soon my pregnancy would be obvious to everyone. I didn't want that to happen here, for Mama to bear the scandal, though there would be fallout enough later, even here in Midland.

"I can't do that, Alton. I have...commitments at home."

"Then would you consider taking her with you to California?"

"Of course I'll take her home with me; I've tried to many times. Do you think she will?"

"I don't know. I don't know how I'll manage without her, either. But I think she has a better chance to recover there than here. Johnny was her life." His face was raw with pain. "I was a bad husband; I see that now." He turned away, his shoulders shaking. I put my hand on his arm, all my misgivings submerged in the face of his loss.

"Why don't you bring her?"

His head swiveled towards me. A gleam lit his eyes for a microsecond, then vanished. "What?"

"It would be good for you both. I have plenty of room; you could stay for a while, until you feel better. It would give Fay Ann a chance to heal and it would give you a chance to make up for past...failures."

He looked at me in amazement.

"Would you mind? It would be wonderful for us both; I could easily be away from the dealership for a while."

"I'd be glad to have you," I said, half truthfully.

That easily I made my fatal mistake.

It was a week after I arrived home that Mama called to say Fay Ann and Alton had decided to drive; they were on their way and would take their time, getting to Los Angeles in six or seven days. I had hoped Mama would come too, but she refused, saying she wouldn't be happy cooped up in a car with Alton; she was glad he was out of her sight for a while, though of course she'd miss Fay Ann.

I decided it would be a good break for Mama, who had devoted so much of her life trying to help with Johnny. She hadn't had any real time to herself for years.

Maria made sure the guestroom was clean, with fresh linens and all the comforts we could provide.

I shuddered when I thought of Fay Ann's reaction to my pregnancy. I'm the third, third strike you're out, I thought, giggling hysterically at the knowledge of her horror, unless of course Drew made it back in the next couple of weeks. By that time I'd be so obvious no clothes would be able to disguise it. The giggles became a heavy lump in my chest: where was he?

~

Billie wilts and gradually even her voice is faded. As much as I need to know what happened to her sister and Alton, to Drew and the baby, she has exhausted us both telling me about the death of her nephew. I want her to stop; this is taking too much out of her; I think we should wait for another day. I suggest tea or brandy.

She smiles wanly, tells me I'm kind, slowly rises to go for glasses and a bottle of Courvoisier. It's late, almost time to stop for the evening in any case.

I am inspired and ask if she would consider going to dinner with me.

The slightest smile crosses her face so briefly I think perhaps it is imagination, then she agrees; I find myself inordinately pleased. When I ask where, she names a restaurant, so we finish our drinks and make the short trip to Odessa, a good respite, time out for both of us to regain some equilibrium.

She has recovered her poise on the drive; whether genuine or feigned, her good spirits are revived. An attendant takes my car; we enter a very nice room, each table softly lit with candles in ceramic holders on glossy white tablecloths, leather-bound menus standing like sentinels at each place setting.

Billie has deliberately chosen a restaurant where she is known, for they call her by her given name or Mrs. Elliot. This is shocking: it's the name of the man buried in the small cemetery on the outskirts of town. Perhaps she did marry, but when?

Her eyes twinkle with mischief as we wait to be seated. She says that not all things are as they seem. Well, of course not! What is she holding back now? She refuses to be hurried, speaks at her own pace, no matter how impatient I get.

Where did the name Elliot come from?

New mysteries.

XVII

I just rediscovered the envelope my editor sent, carelessly buried under notes and magazines on the seat of a chair; I'd forgotten all about it. Tomorrow I must take the time to look, though my guess is it will only be more suggestions as to how I should write this story. She is a very good editor but I have no intention of letting her write Billie's history for me.

For now I toss it aside, too tired after the emotional day and a lovely dinner with perhaps more wine than I should have had after the brandy earlier.

Listening to Billie is like waiting for news of a loved one in surgery. You want to hurry the doctors but know you have to be patient, no matter how difficult. Billie isn't the only one who knows what waiting feels like. I'm about to start smoking again.

I suspect she has a great deal to tell me about her sister and Alton. Especially Alton. It was in reference to him that she said something about a fatal mistake. Was she being facetious? We all make comments that we don't intend to be taken seriously. It's on tape but I have no desire to listen for it now; it's too late; I promised to be early in the morning; Billie wants to cook me breakfast.

I need to sleep. Trouble is, I dream, and though I can't remember the details—they all involve Billie and an unseen Drew—they frighten me, and I awake as tired as when I went to bed.

Breakfast? I'm really pleased.

~

"I'll get it Maria," I called as I walked to the front door, my heels clacking on the parquet floor, the emerald green silk of a voluminous caftan effectively hiding my swelling belly. Fay Ann had called from the gate; they had arrived, probably tired from the accumulated stress plus the drive from Texas, no matter how unhurried the trip.

When I opened the door my immediate thought was, Who are these waifs? Fay Ann was wispy thin in torn jeans and an old tee shirt; Alton no longer looked like a suave businessman, more like a somewhat shabby professor. He wore glasses, and I wondered briefly what had happened to his contact lenses.

I hugged my sister, carefully standing to the side to prevent contact, gave a more reserved greeting to Alton and led them into the house.

Fay Ann looked around, taking in the beautifully proportioned rooms, the huge oak beams, the arched doorways, the comfortable furniture placed casually, colors cheerful and welcoming. She seemed overwhelmed.

Shadow came dashing into the hall from the kitchen, Maria shouting at her to behave. I laughed and grabbed Shadow as she went by, almost pulled off my feet. She struggled briefly, then began wagging her tail, and subsided next to me while I made introductions. She licked my sister's outstretched hand. But when Alton tried to pet her she growled and backed away. We all laughed uneasily; spouted platitudes: she would grow to like him in time.

Maria appeared, apologizing for Shadow's escape; I made human introductions; she asked if she could bring in luggage. She and Alton went outside to get the bags from the Galaxie; Fay Ann and I sat in the living room, a few brief moments of privacy.

"Are you all right?"

"Better than I expected," she replied. "We always knew we'd lose Johnny. I just didn't think it would be in such a…violent way. Alton has been wonderful to me. He's truly sorry."

"I thought you were going to kill him," I ventured, testing.

"He hasn't lost his temper with me once since…" Her fingers played with the pillow she clutched. "I have to give him a chance."

As relieved as I was at her change of heart, I retained a slight doubt that anyone could turn around as completely as this. True, he seemed better and who was I to say it was impossible? Yes, he had to be given a chance. I would still be wary.

I was silent as my sister examined the room item by item. She turned wondering eyes to me.

"Did you have an interior decorator? This place is beautiful."

As I bit my tongue against the wry question, Why do you think I couldn't have done it myself?, Alton and Maria returned with the bags. I heard Maria say, "I'll put them in your room," some unintelligible answer from Alton, then he came in to join us.

"Isn't it beautiful, Alton?" Fay Ann smoothed the nubby aqua raw silk of the pillow. "Aren't the colors wonderful?"

"They are indeed," he drawled, scanning the furniture and the art on the walls.

There was a strange, uncomfortable silence for a moment, then, disconcerted and confused, I asked what they would like to drink or if they would prefer to go to their room and rest.

Alton opted for rest, so I led them to the guest room, kissed Fay Ann, said, "Consider this your home for now and let me or Maria know if there's anything you want."

As I walked away from them I took note that it was he, not she, who made the decision. Then I shook off the ungenerous suspicion; someone had to decide.

For several days my sister and brother-in-law chose to remain at home, relaxing, recuperating, wandering around the garden or swimming desultorily in the heated pool. The weather was Southern California at its best: crystal clear and warm by day, just crisp enough for a fire at night. The scent of lemon blossoms wafted from the orchard, and the roses, ever blooming in Southern California, made bright splashes of color against the white stucco walls of the house.

We had delicious dinners at the oval table, by candlelight, Maria at her best, then spent the evenings talking, reminiscing, once even playing Monopoly.

Nat came by to meet Fay Ann, liked her immediately and suggested he and Teri would like to get together with us. When I walked him out to the driveway he said, "Be careful of that man, Billie. I don't know what it is but there's something...not quite right about him."

"You have no idea how much he's improved. I guess it took a tragedy for him to wake up. Anyhow he's my brother-in-law. I can't tell Fay Ann what to do with her life."

Nat just grunted.

In a couple of weeks Fay Ann began to gain a little weight; her color improved; she no longer looked bleached, like a sheet fresh from the laundry.

We called Mama whose joy at her older daughter's improvement was palpable. She and Howard were well; "...stay and have a wonderful time."

It wasn't until Fay Ann knocked on my door and entered without waiting for my, "Come in," that the trouble started. I was caught, arms outstretched in the act of putting on my robe, frozen there like a Giacometti statue. She glanced from my body to my face and back to my stomach.

"Oh, no, you aren't!"

I finished putting on the robe.

"Yes, I am." I forestalled her next comment. "I'm happier than I've ever been in my life. Well, I will be when he gets home."

"Home," she said, scornfully, sitting on the bed. "Does that mean you're living with him, or that you're married and we never knew about it?"

I could see the anger begin to overcome the shock.

"No," I confessed, stung by her scorn. "I followed in the family footsteps." I turned away, ashamed of the unintended cruelty.

"How could you, after...?"

"The same as Mama. The same as you...except I'm so in love. Don't be mad, Fay Ann; all the years 'til now I heard you in my head. They laugh and call me ice lady in Hollywood. I confess to a couple of affairs—after all, I'm way over twenty-one—but I was always careful. Then Drew...."

She interrupted. "Who is Drew? *Where* is Drew? If you love him so much why isn't he here? Why aren't you married? Or doesn't he want to marry you?"

"He's in Vietnam."

"And you don't know when he'll be back, right? Alton and I were bad enough. This will kill Mama."

Panic sank me onto the bed next to her. I took her hand. "Please,

please don't say anything until he gets back. I don't want to tell her 'til then, when everything is ...." I trailed off, wondering when everything would be all right again. "Then we can tell her."

"Oh Billie Jo, why is the world so hard?" she cried. "I would have been so happy not to get married, but it was a disgrace to have a baby without a husband; it would have been such a scandal. And now you want to get married and there's no groom." She started to laugh, slightly hysterical.

"There will be soon." I put my arms around her. "You can be my matron-of-honor. It will all be fine, you'll see."

~

Billie calmed her sister with her own conviction that the world would turn properly. Love conquers all, etc, etc.

Her sister promised to say nothing to their mother but there was no way to keep it a secret from Alton. Billie says when she told him he began to laugh. She quotes him, "Caught like us, huh? What kind of a man is this Drew?"

"A wonderful man," she told him.

"Yeah? Well, he'd better get back here soon or your career's going down the toilet."

In a rare moment alone, Fay Ann told Billie that Mr. Fawcett had long since turned the agency over to his son. Run mostly by the assistant manager, now it was almost bankrupt, a fact she revealed without emotion. Alton never had discussed business with her. She knew nothing about it, or indeed the potential repercussions of its failure, especially if Alton were caught embezzling.

So, aware of how proud Fay Ann was, Billie was careful to find Alton by himself at the pool one morning. Maria had just served him breakfast; he was drinking coffee, looking pleased with himself. She handed him several credit cards, telling him not to say anything to her sister. Since she no longer wished to be seen in public, she couldn't be a real hostess and take them out; that didn't mean they couldn't start sight-seeing. She knew they were beginning to feel homebound.

Though she was disappointed not to be accompanied by the glamorous Alana Paige, Fay Ann understood, and was excited at the prospect of discovering Hollywood, the color flushing her cheeks and sparkling her eyes for the first time in years.

That day the United States Post Office was good to Billie. At last it brought a letter from Drew.

~

The baby kicked wildly, which was what I wanted to do: kick up my heels, shout for joy, share my happiness with the world. A letter from Drew, the first in more than four months. I couldn't wait to open it, tore the envelope as I walked clumsily across the parquet floor, flopped onto the couch, Shadow jumping up next to me, infected with my elation.

It was a wonderful letter, full of love and reassurance that he would soon be home. He was being transferred at last, stationed in Washington D.C. He wanted me to join him there and get married, asking, foolish man, if I would consider moving and what it might do to my career—as if I cared.

I was suddenly lighthearted; we would be together. I would win Mama's approval, charm his parents, be a good Air Force wife, learn to cook his favorite dishes.

I'd better be sure I had records of his favorite music, get him some casual clothes for D.C. weather, remember to buy some flattering maternity clothes and...would he still want me, with my growing belly and my increasingly ungainly walk?

Yes, I was convinced he would.

He wrote that he had been upcountry—he didn't explain that—and had been unable to receive or send letters. He had managed to give this one to a pilot heading back, so at least I would know he was safe and loved me. Madly, he said. His mail would be waiting for him when he got to Saigon.

I shared the news with Maria, who nodded in her quiet way, and patted me on the back. "Mr. Drew will be a good daddy," she said. "A good husband, too, not like Mr. Alton."

"What do you mean, Maria," I asked, startled out of my euphoria.

She studied me for a long moment. "He's not a good man, Miss Billie. You be careful of him. Miss Fay Ann should send him away."

"I don't think she will. But once Drew is back, he can handle Alton if there are any problems."

She made a noncommittal sound and went back to rolling dough for a pie crust.

My guests had spent the afternoon shopping in Beverly Hills and the evening dining at Perino's. They got home around nine o'clock, Alton once more dapper in a sharkskin suit and red Countess Mara tie. When I got close enough to him I could smell the alcohol.

Fay Ann wore a new pale blue dress from I. Magnin's that draped gracefully, adding much needed bulk to her still overly thin body.

I read all the pertinent parts of my letter to her; she hugged me and asked how soon Drew would be back. That was the only question I couldn't answer; it diminished my happiness, though it couldn't erase it completely.

"As soon as they let him, Fay Ann. He'll be here as soon as they let him. I just hope it's before the baby comes."

Thanksgiving was behind us, Christmas looming, my anxiety over more silence from Drew growing as my hopes diminished, seeping from me like moisture through limestone.

Seven months since I'd seen him; seven months of alternating terror and exhilaration, complacency and uncertainty.

Dr. Mauser reported baby and mother healthy.

Rolling and kicking, a constant delight, I loved picturing little elbows and knees pushing against the wall of my abdomen. Soothing it with little pats and caresses, I whispered words of encouragement to it, "It won't be long now, darling. I'll be able to hold you in my arms."

Nat came to me with questions about phone and credit card bills. He was appalled when I told him I'd given the cards to Alton.

"What was in your mind, Billie?" he raged. "You have astronomical charges for clothes and food and strange things like jewelry I don't see Fay Ann wearing. Your phone bills have two really long calls to El Paso. Do you know anyone in El Paso?"

"No," I said doubtfully. "Could it be a mistake?"

"From your phone? Hardly. You have to put a stop to this, Billie or I won't be responsible for paying these bills anymore."

"I guess I'd better talk to him," I said with reluctance. "I can think of more pleasant things to do with my time."

I intended to discuss the situation with Alton but continually got sidetracked, as my mind seemed permanently stuck in second gear, unable to concentrate on mundane things while I waited for whichever would come first, my baby or my lover.

I called Dr. Mauser to ask if I could give birth at home; I didn't want to go to the hospital without Drew, and I knew the public reaction I would get.

The doctor said it could be done, but he would prefer the hospital in case of any emergency. That frightened me, but he quickly put me at ease. "You and the baby are fine," he said. "I don't expect any problems. Hospitals are simply more practical; it's where we have all the facilities to care for mother and child."

As the year came to a close Nat started bringing me new screenplays to explore. Considerations about my career began to intrude into my jumbled thoughts. I might need the money my work provided, especially, I thought in a moment of clarity, if I continued to support Fay Ann and Alton. Nat said my expenses had gotten out of control.

I would never burden Drew with my family, but I still hadn't spoken to Alton.

Maria brought the mail to me; I was lethargic. I could hear Fay Ann in the garden, saying something to her husband that caused him to raise his voice; I couldn't make out the words. I threw aside the large envelope from Nat's office that contained fan mail—I tried to answer those myself—and scanned the letters; Drew's distinctive writing didn't appear on any of the envelopes. There was one, however, from a Captain James Cassidy. I didn't know a Captain James Cassidy.

Suddenly the breath left my body; I felt dizzy, the heavy scent of gardenias outside the windows suffocating. With trembling fingers I opened the envelope; a single sheet of paper and another envelope fell into my hands. I have no idea how long I sat there before making the monumentally difficult decision as to which I should look at first. I put the second envelope beside me on the sofa and raised the letter to eyes that at first refused to focus.

Jan. 4, 1965

Dear Miss Paige,

Drew asked me to hold the enclosed letter for him and mail it if he were unable to mail it himself.

It is with great sorrow that I tell you of Captain Weatherly's death in an attack on the Bienhoa air base near Saigon. He did not suffer; it was too fast.

He had just flown a helicopter back from a dangerous mission near the Cambodian border and was due to report to headquarters about the information he had learned from a high-ranking Vietcong officer.

The base was bombed on November 19. I apologize for my delay in telling you. I was injured and have only just returned to duty in the last few days.

He spoke often of you, Miss Paige, and it was obvious that he loved you deeply.

You have my deepest sympathy. If there is anything I can do for you, please contact me at the address above.

Very sincerely yours,

James Cassidy

I folded my hands protectively over the baby in my body. My blood had turned to ice and felt as if it were draining from me, leaving me weak and dislocated. I sat motionless, waiting to scream, waiting to faint, waiting for the roof to fall or an earthquake to swallow me. Nothing happened.

The room steadied, the furniture remained stationary. Shadow slept on a corner of the Berber rug. Voices still echoed from outside. Maria's familiar soprano still echoed from the kitchen, a Latin rhythm.

I heard myself moan, not loud, just an echo as I visualized a life empty of Drew. How would I go on without him? A glimmer of thought was there somewhere if I could only grasp it. Later, I told myself, like Scarlett.

Another eon passed as I sat, unable to move. What could I do? How could I fill this sudden void that left me a hollow vessel, brittle and fragile as an eggshell. Surely I would crumble into fragments.

"What are you doing in here in the dark?" came Fay Ann's

unfamiliar voice, from a great distance. "I thought you were in your room, napping."

Dark? It had somehow become evening.

Fay Ann turned on a lamp, came to me, concerned. "Are you all right, Billie Jo? What's wrong? You look terrible. You're white as a ghost."

I handed her the letter.

"Oh, my God," she said, and sank down beside me, gathering me into her arms. "Oh, Billie, oh, honey, I'm so sorry."

The tears started from her eyes and I felt a stab of jealousy that she could cry. My eyes felt dry, hot and burning. As always the relief of tears was denied me.

"Is there anything.... Do you want me to call Mama? No, no, of course not. What can I do?"

Maria, a tray of drinks and hors d'oeuvres in her hands, limped into the room, stopped short. She put the tray down, knelt beside me.

"Is it Mr. Drew?" she asked.

I nodded.

"Oh, Miss Alana," and her kind face, too, was wet with tears as she took my hands in hers and held them to her face.

She rose then; dimly I heard her on the telephone; she had called Nat.

Alton came in at some point; I was aware of his presence and the hushed voices telling him what had happened. Then Fay Ann asked if I wanted her to read me Drew's letter.

Why did I say yes? I'll never be able to answer that question.

She read,

> My Dearest Billie,
>
> This is a letter I hope you never receive.
>
> There's little I can say to ease what I know will be your pain. But there are some things I want said for you to remember for as long as you have memory.
>
> I want to thank you. You gave your love to me generously, without hesitation, without restraint. I think that love would have carried us through any adversity, illness, poverty, all the words in the marriage ceremony that I wanted to say to you. It would have gotten us through the difficulties of liv-

ing biracial in a racist world; all our enemies would have been conquered in the face of our love.

By itself I'm not sure my love for you would have been strong enough to do that. Though you know I love you—madly, as I've told you before.

Hold that, my darling, and go forward with your life; you don't think so now, but in time you *will* find someone else. I just hope he will deserve you.

Your,

Drew

XVIII

A knife enters my heart. I double over under the force of it. As if this were an event that happened yesterday I wish to express condolences, and can find absolutely no words.

Billie looks at me sympathetically, tells me, "It was a very long time ago, my dear. One carries that pain forever but the sharp edges of it dull eventually. One learns to think of all losses without becoming despondent."

She shows me the letters, now faded with age of course, tied with ribbon among a small stack of other envelopes, each with the handwriting she had described as distinctive.

Billie is calm, waiting for me to recover my equilibrium. We had a large breakfast—fortification?—and have been sitting in the living room with our coffee cups, a half-full pot on the table. I'm still at a loss so I remain silent, waiting for some understanding of how Billie survived this blow.

~

Recall from the next weeks is a tangled skein, some echoing in my own head, some told me afterwards by the people who lived it. I was trapped somewhere between reality and my need to implode: a black hole.

At first Maria fed me broth and sat by my side, holding my hand.

Fay Ann hovered anxiously, but didn't call Mama, a mixed blessing, for I dimly thought Mama might make the hurt go away, at the same time I was aware there was something I didn't want her to know.

Nat came many times, and he must have answered Alton's questions about Drew. He forced me to get out of bed to walk around the house, Shadow padding beside us quietly, as if she knew I had no strength to play with her. Teri, sworn to secrecy about my pregnancy, wanted to help. How could anyone help?

I grew more lucid but cared about nothing, except to wish my baby—Drew's baby—would soon be more than a shifting weight inside me. Yes, eventually I had to feel again, no matter how difficult. For now it was all I could do to think rationally; I certainly didn't trust my mind's ability to make decisions.

I spent a lot of time sitting in front of a television set without the least idea what was on the screen. I slept a great deal, but as often as I seemed to be sleeping, I was awake, eyes closed, wanting only solitude.

I heard Maria asking if Mr. Nat thought I should go to the hospital, to which he answered rightly, "I think that would be the last thing she would want."

Then I heard Alton arguing with my sister. "You don't seem to get it, Fay Ann. She might need her career to get well, but when she has this baby she won't have a career to go back to. Nothing the press loves more than a scandal."

"That's ridiculous, Alton. It's not like it was when I got pregnant. More and more women are having babies without being married."

"Yeah, but none of them are Alana Paige. I'm telling you, her career will go down the tubes. Think if the baby is black."

Her Southern upbringing silenced Fay Ann. Finally, so quietly I barely heard her, she said, "That's racist, Alton; I should expect it from you." But she sounded doubtful. Then, "We need to get her to the doctor, to make sure she's all right."

"She'll be all right. She just needs to get over the shock. You don't see any signs of the baby coming do you?"

"No, she's not having contractions, if that's what you mean. She's not due for another three weeks."

The voices faded, hushed by Maria's crisp orders. I went back to sleep, too weary to care if my career was finished.

The next time I woke, Alton was beside me in a dark room. He was speaking quietly, brushing back my hair, all solicitude. "Billie Jo, I'm going to take you someplace safe, someplace you can have your baby and get on your feet again. You need time to pull yourself together. Then you'll come back here and Nat will have all those movies for you. You'll keep on making movies, Billie, making lots of movies, lots of money. I'll take care of it all. Don't you worry about a thing."

I dreamed of Drew: he was coming to take me away. We would go someplace safe and I would have a beautiful baby boy who looked just like his father.

If Drew were coming for me why did I need Alton?

Alton called Dr. Mauser and told him he was my fiancé returned from Vietnam, we were getting married secretly; he was reassigned to another state, so we would be moving immediately. He thanked him for the expert care and promised to inform him when the baby was born.

Then he told Maria that I had decided to go to Texas to be with my mother; we were leaving as soon as practical since I was so near delivery time. She asked me if I was sure but I only nodded, yes, I wanted to go. What I wanted, of course, was to go with Drew, but that was too difficult to explain. She cried, not at all sure what Alton was up to but convinced it was no good. Alton pleaded with her to stay, to take care of the house.

Indignant, she informed him she had no intention of leaving the house empty; she and Shadow would manage nicely, thank you.

Nat was more difficult. He wanted to talk to me. He was told I was sleeping; he said I was sleeping entirely too much. He asked that I call him; was told yes, if there were time. Then he insisted that he be kept informed of my progress. He demanded Mama's number. The number he was given, I found out later, was not related to Mama or anyone I knew, simply a friend of Alton's who had been warned to contact Fay Ann when necessary. When Nat asked how soon we were going, Alton told him as soon as Maria finished packing for me.

All of this was done from my office phone while Fay Ann, the innocent, was throwing their clothes into a suitcase, trying to figure out why I had changed my mind about telling Mama and why she shouldn't phone her to say we were coming.

Alton made one other call that day. I found out about that one much, much later.

On a bleak afternoon in late January, I was tucked into the back seat of the Galaxie with pillows and blankets. Alton, careful and considerate, suggested I might rest better there. Fay Ann sat beside him in the front. We drove away, leaving Maria waving anxiously from the driveway, Shadow panting beside her.

We stopped only for food, drink and bathroom breaks, traveling straight through the night, passing by Palm Springs, through Blythe, and into Arizona, crossing the desert before full daylight. Outside Phoenix I grew curious enough to wonder where we were, then decided it didn't matter, so I went back to sleep.

Alton drove like one pursued, on to Tucson where he finally relinquished the wheel to Fay Ann so he could rest. She drove to the New Mexico border, then woke him, as instructed. When she protested that they should stop at least for a few hours, his response was, "We don't want Billie going into labor in the car, do we?"

In Las Cruces Alton stopped to get drinks; he told Fay Ann to stay in the car with me, he'd bring them to us. It was an unseasonable, blistering, New Mexico style hot outside; I drank the heavily sweetened iced tea greedily.

We turned south towards El Paso; it was then I heard Alton tell Fay Ann he wasn't going to Midland; he knew of a clinic where I could have the baby in secret and afterwards decide whether I wanted to keep it or give it up for adoption.

Fay Ann was horrified. "You lied. You had this planned all the time, ever since we heard about Drew. Does Billie even know what you're doing?"

"She told me it was what she wanted. I've been talking to her since she started coming around."

"Coming around? She's only half-conscious most of the time, like she's drugged or something. How could she make a decision like that?"

"Exactly. That's why I'm taking her to this clinic. So she'll have time to make up her mind. If she gives up the baby her public will never find out about it; safer under the circumstances, don't you think?" As if an afterthought, "Your mother won't know either. That's safer too."

"Alton, you'd better be telling the truth."

"Honey, we all just want what's best for Billie Jo and the baby. Why would I do anything to jeopardize them?"

"Does Nat know about this?"

"Yes. He thought it was a good idea. Other movie stars have had babies there. Don't worry so much. I've got everything under control. You go on to Midland for a week or two; I'll get Billie settled and find us a place to stay; then you can come back to be with her, help her decide."

"Where is this place? What's its name?"

"It's right here, outside of El Paso, a real quiet place; it's called," Alton laughed oddly, "Betty's Hideaway Clinic."

"That's a strange name."

"Well, it's for unwed moms; I guess that's why."

"Why can't I go there to help get Billie settled?"

"Because then I'll have to drive you all the way back into town to get the bus, turn around and go back to the Clinic," Alton told her.

"Are you sure about her care? Are the doctors good?"

"Stop it, Fay Ann."

So Fay Ann took a bus on to Midland, only half convinced that Alton knew what he was doing and totally convinced that she didn't. Frantic at the prospect of lying—what seemed such a transparent lie—she nevertheless managed to follow his instructions to tell her mother that I was too busy with a new film to call, that Alton was looking for work in Los Angeles and that she was back in Midland for a few days because she missed her mother.

It was just sufficiently logical that Mama believed it.

Awake enough to hear the conversation between my sister and her husband, I smiled to myself; no way would I give up my baby. If I'd been stronger I never would have let him bring me so far from home. I wanted Dr. Mauser. I went to sleep again.

When I awoke the next time I was in a room in what seemed to be a small, one-story structure. The walls were blinding white, rough stucco, the furnishings some sort of varnished wood. Green curtains covered the one window, leaving a slight gap where I could see another building, also stucco, in a battered tan color.

"How did I get here?" I asked the pink uniformed woman who

had just entered the room, carrying a metal tray with a plate of unappetizing looking food and a glass full of some sort of juice.

"We brought you in from the car—Mr. Fawcett and I. You were sound asleep. He practically carried you in."

Her accent was slightly Hispanic; her features were regular, pleasant in a swarthy face; the body beneath the nylon of her uniform looked voluptuous.

"Are you the nurse?"

"Yes, Miss Paige, I'm your nurse. My name is Betty. I'll take good care of you. Now have something to drink and eat a little lunch." She poured a glass of the juice and handed it to me, waiting expectantly. I was thirsty, drank about half, canned I knew the minute I tasted it, then put it down.

"I'd like some water instead."

"I'll get you a glass of water; just drink a little more of the juice first."

Not willing to argue but disturbed by her intensity, I wished again I'd never let Alton bring me here. Then I realized with growing alarm that I didn't know where *here* was. I thought he'd said outside of El Paso. What did that mean? This place didn't look like a clinic. But then, what did a clinic for unwed mothers look like?

"Where is Alton? I'd like to see him. Where is my sister?"

"I'll get Alton for you," she said, looking frightened. She scurried from the room. Alton? She called him Alton.

Struggling up from more layers of sleep I heard him say, "Did she drink enough of it?"

There was an answer from the nurse but I was much too tired to understand it. Drew was coming; nothing else was important.

I was awakened by a sharp pain gripping my belly and a suddenly wet feeling between my legs. I cried out.

Betty quickly rounded the open door, took one look at me and called out, "Alton, she's in labor. You'd better get the doctor."

~

Billie describes the onset of labor and the following hours without many details and a forced calm that does not deceive me. The doctor was a man with trembling hands and rheumy eyes, but clean and careful. He was gentle in his examination and gave explicit directions to Betty, who seemed much less well trained. As they wheeled Billie from her room she wondered why the short hall was so empty. No other nurses appeared from behind the few closed doors as they passed them, Billie only half conscious between contractions.

Alton's presence in the labor room—or so they called it—confused her, for why wasn't Drew there? She fought the pain, pushed when told to, knew nothing of the passage of time. It might have been days before they said, "One more push;" she fought for it and the child and Drew and all the lonely nights she would spend without him. She heard a baby's cry, then the doctor's soothing hand caressed her forehead. He told her, "You did fine, young woman. I'm so sorry."

She slept, not strong enough to ask what it was he was sorry about.

Both Fay Ann and Alton were beside Billie when she woke again, asking for her baby. Alton took her hand, stroked it. He too expressed sorrow. Then he told her they had taken the baby away; it had been stillborn, strangled on the umbilical cord; there was nothing they could do to save it.

I thought my heart would break when Billie told me about Drew. This latest blow is almost more than I can tolerate. I feel the tears slip from my eyes as Billie touches my hand, waiting silently for me to recover some semblance of control.

She says at first there was only disbelief, the shock, the tortured, Why? *Then it was as if a section were suddenly stripped from her life; she simply can't remember. Alton had called Fay Ann to tell her the tragic news, warn her not to tell her mother. When Nat called again she was to explain about the baby; as soon as Billie Jo was well enough they would bring her back to Los Angeles.*

Fay Ann's only thought was to get to El Paso as soon as she could. She knew all about losing a child; Billie Jo needed her in a way she never had before.

Alton met her at the bus station, genuinely frightened: for three days Billie Jo had run a fever so high they sponged her with alcohol every twenty minutes. She had been delirious ever since he told her about the baby. The doctor sedated her again, shaking his grizzled head. Now she was so lethargic they feared she would never recover.

~

I jolted awake from a dream: bombs and jungles and searching for something irretrievably lost. Fay Ann stood beside the bed, calling softly, "Billie, Billie. I'm here, honey. It's all right, everything will be all right."

Fay Ann didn't understand that nothing would ever be all right again, that life was a burden I no longer wished to carry. Our family was cursed. I turned my face to the wall, closed my eyes.

I heard Fay Ann ask Alton what kind of a clinic this was, where were the doctors, the nurses? Why was there no sound of babies crying? It looked like just another house to her.

He answered, as they walked down the hall, "The doctors are all on call; the babies are in another building; women wouldn't be here if they wanted the world to know about them."

Fay Ann's angry voice rose; her husband quieted her; that was all I heard.

When I awoke the next time, Alton was beside me again; the synapses in my brain were beginning to connect. He was trying to get me to eat. The thought of food nauseated me. Behind Alton stood Betty, again holding a tray of food.

"Come on, Billie Jo. You have to eat something."

"I can't." I ran my hand across my flattened belly and wished to die.

"Billie Jo, you have to try. Come on, honey, please eat just a little."

I looked around the small white room, green curtains now pulled back to reveal the tan wall belonging to a small house across an alley.

"What happened to my baby?" I whispered.

He took my hand, his face a mask of sorrow.

For one fraction of a moment the mask slipped and beneath it I thought I saw—what? Satisfaction? Evil? Then it was back and I saw only sympathy and grief.

"I told you, honey. The umbilical cord strangled the baby. There wasn't anything you could have done, no way the doctor could have known about a prolapsed cord. I'm so sorry."

"Why did you bring me here? If Dr. Mauser. . . ."

"Dr. Mauser couldn't have saved the baby."

"Go away." I didn't want him; I didn't want anyone. When Fay

Ann came in a few minutes later, I asked her, too, to leave me alone. She sat in the green chair by the bed, stubborn and determined. Betty had vanished, with her the food. Again I turned my face to the wall and finally slept without dreaming.

XIX

They made the drive back to Los Angeles more slowly than they had come, stopping in motels, taking Billie directly to her room and bringing her food there so she wouldn't be seen. She ate little, and that more to please Fay Ann than out of hunger. Her only thought now was to escape the car, to return to the house in Bel Air, to see no one, to curl up on her own bed and remain numb, insensible.

They arrived in Los Angeles on a day of bright blue skies, cleared of smog by the traditional winds of March.

Maria ran from the house, Shadow jumping joyfully at her heels. When she saw no baby, she stopped short, thinking Billie finally had decided to give the child up for adoption.

Billie fell into Maria's arms, appalled that no one had informed her, hating that she had to be the one. Maria wept silently, while trying to comfort her mistress. She led her into the house, then to her room, left Fay Ann to get her to bed while she made tea and brought it with honey and small triangles of toast. Billie looked like a wraith, so thin she was almost skeletal.

She ate one toast triangle and drank the tea, wanly smiling her thanks to Maria. Then she turned over and went to sleep.

It was another week before Billie was able to see and talk to Nat, who had come to the house daily. He was furious at Fay Ann and Alton, for what he considered their irresponsible judgment. He tried to control his normally hot temper for Billie's sake; she gently reminded him that they had done their best; it was no one's fault that the cord was wrapped around the baby's neck.

Hesitantly, Nat asked what the sex of the child had been. Billie answered that she didn't want to know.

She seemed to be recovering her reason if not her strength or, of course impossibly soon, her natural optimism; he offered scripts, to pass the time until she got well, he said. He was sly; he knew her work would be the only thing to bring her back. She understood his game, allowed him the subterfuge, put the scripts aside.

"But," she tells me, "I knew I needed money. Nat tried to hide it from me but my finances were in bad shape; they had been even before I learned about Drew."

She adds, "If I weren't going to be allowed to die, I had to work."

~

All through that spring and summer I was bright and upbeat when I spoke to Mama on the phone, making oh, so logical excuses why the movie I was supposedly working on would never be released. I kept nosy reporters at bay with promises of a role soon; then when I was alone in my room, with just Shadow for company, I fought the depression and the nightmares, asleep or awake.

Alton and Fay Ann resumed their carefree lifestyle but I was never tempted to join them on shopping trips or for dinners at Scandia or Chasen's. I had missed the Oscars, realized when I found the white chiffon St. Laurent in my closet. I stored it away. I didn't even know Julie Andrews had won best actress for *Mary Poppins* until Nat mentioned it in passing one day. I asked if *Goin' Home* had gotten any awards, but didn't really care; I couldn't have attended the ceremony even if I had won.

Slowly I began to gain weight—Nat said I was too thin even for the cameras—thanks to Maria and Fay Ann. By September I was strong enough to seriously consider a new film.

One of the scripts Nat brought was very, very good; exactly the kind of character I could play at this lowest ebb of my life. I vowed, no more fluff; never again would I do a film without real content. In *Nowhere To Hide* I wouldn't need enthusiasm, I would need only to act. Could I?

The mirror told me that my face, though leaner, had changed little. The few gray hairs could be easily dyed; my eyes were different, the sorrow in them starting deep inside and reaching the outside world where only the perceptive would see it.

We began shooting in November. I still took no interest in events around me, came straight home from the studio and begged off any social commitments.

Then, for the first time since the letter about Drew, I felt an unexpected tremor of pleasure when Nat came to me with an offer to play Amanda in a new production of *Glass Menagerie*, on Broadway. I accepted without hesitation.

The anniversary of my baby's death passed, Fay Ann watching anxiously for any signs of a relapse. I held myself together with the glue of an upcoming Broadway show.

When we finished *Nowhere To Hide* I left my sister and her husband in Maria's care, made the trip to New York by plane, as myself, all the mischief and joy of disguise abandoned somewhere in my past with Drew and our child.

It was a successful run; I played the part just short of melodrama, received rave reviews which was nice, was relieved to return to an impersonal hotel room at the end of each performance, earning an even more hermit-like reputation. When I had the energy, I spent any available time discovering New York's unlimited museums and galleries. I even went shopping occasionally, buying gifts which I shipped back to Mama and my sister, reserving some of theirs plus Maria's and Nat's and his family's for my return.

A New York winter, sometimes with blizzard conditions and mounds of snow, was a novel experience; Texas had never been so cold. But in the fall I decided that winter at home was preferable to another one in New York. That's why I turned down a new play by Harold Pinter and went back to L.A. when Sue Lyon took over for me in *Glass Menagerie* in October. I had been away for a year.

I spoke to Nat, told him I'd see him in a week, that I was well, just tired. He sounded relieved, told me to take all the time I needed; then please come to his office. He was just happy I was back to normal. I wondered what normal could possibly be.

The week of rest under Maria's critical eye restored me. I felt almost human again. Shadow remembered me, barked a lot and licked my hand in welcome. My sister seemed happy to see me, also, though she spent a lot of time in her room. Alton stayed away, perhaps looking for work. I was glad to have the house mostly to myself.

We met for dinner, but afterwards I begged to be excused, claiming, truthfully, that the year on legitimate stage had been very wearing.

I drove to Nat's ultra modern office on Robertson Boulevard. He greeted me with a hug so tight it almost took my breath away, then leaned back to appraise me. "You look more like yourself, Alana. I'm happy to see you getting healthy again. New York was good for you."

"Yes, it was," I agreed, sinking into the nearest chair. The soft gray upholstery, the subdued art lessened the stark impact of the angular desk, and steel and glass tables. The room was chic but comfortable.

One wall was almost hidden under photographs of Nat taken with movie stars and behind-the-camera personnel in diverse settings, from golf courses to ski slopes, wearing everything from swim trunks to three-piece suits or tuxedos.

I looked around for any new pictures of Teri and Nat's daughter, now a teenager, found the latest on his desk.

"I have a fine script you should look at."

"I think I'd rather wait a while."

His reaction to this was not what I expected. His mouth turned down and he made a slight clucking noise; I realized with surprise that Nat's hair was mostly gray, his warm brown eyes partly hidden by half glasses. My friend was getting older.

"I hate to hit you with this when you've just gotten home, Billie. I would have come to the house but I thought we might need to talk in private."

"What?"

"Money," he said with a sigh.

"I made a fortune in New York," I protested.

"Yes," he said grimly, "and it's shrinking fast."

"You have to be kidding. How?"

"Your family here has been—shall we say—a little careless about their expenditures."

This was a blow. Stunned, I said, "I had no idea. I thought Alton sold the dealership. I thought he was spending," I laughed bitterly, "his own money."

" 'Fraid not, honey. I didn't want to tell you until you got back. You had enough to worry about, playing eight shows a week."

"How bad is it?"

"You never got your cards back from Alton. I asked him for them. He just laughed at me. There are dozens of charges on them, all sorts, from biggies to drug store items."

"Oh my God. With...everything...I forgot." I heard myself groan as I covered my eyes with my hand. "I charged a lot in New York on my other cards, too."

"Not all that much, really. Your hotel and food and a few purchases—gifts, I'd bet.

"I'm not saying all your money is gone, Billie. What I'm saying is you have to put a stop to Alton. I haven't been able to make an investment for you in two years and you certainly don't want to sell what stocks you do have."

"No," I said faintly, "Of course I don't. This means I'll have to confront him, doesn't it?"

"I'm afraid so."

Returning from Nat's office, I looked for my sister, hoping to talk to her first. She was by the pool, sunning. When she heard me open the patio door she grabbed her towel, pulling it across her body.

"I didn't expect you so soon, Billie Jo."

She hadn't been quick enough. For the first time since I'd arrived home I really looked at her. There were circles under her eyes; her arms and right shoulder were bruised, purple.

"Oh, no."

"Well, I know it looks bad but I fell; the tiles in the bathroom are slippery...."

"Bullshit, Fay Ann," I exploded, with no remorse for the shocked look on her face at my unaccustomed profanity.

"How long has it been going on this time?"

The tears started immediately.

"Ever since you went to New York." She seemed embarrassed, like a recalcitrant child caught misbehaving. "It wasn't bad at first; he just hit me once in a while. But lately it's been getting worse. And especially if he's been drinking. What should I do, Billie?"

"What should you do?" I yelled at her. "You should leave the bastard like you should have done years ago."

"I keep thinking if I can just get it right, he'll stop."

"Honey, don't you know it's not you? It's Alton. He's a wife beater. He always will be. Even I thought he'd stopped, but I guess it was just a—time out!"

Alton walked from the house, dapper in a cashmere sport coat over navy slacks, contact lenses back, hair somehow thicker than when I'd left L.A. I hadn't noticed.

He spoke around the cigarette he had just lighted. "What's a time out?"

"You bastard," I said, clenching my fists to stop me from gouging his eyes.

"What's your problem?" he barked, immediately angry.

"This is my problem: you've been beating my sister. You're out of here."

"What's that bitch been telling you?"

Fay Ann gasped. I looked at this man who had, for a short time demonstrated extraordinary kindness and concern for my welfare; I wondered if he were capable of a deception so complete.

"You're to be out of here tonight," I said, quietly. "And give me all my credit cards. Nat told me about the way you've been spending money."

I heard a, "What are you saying, Billie?" from my sister, ventured a glance at her. She looked confused and upset.

"What's it to Nat?" Alton asked with a nasty laugh. "It's your money, isn't it?"

"That's the point."

Alton's face hardened, then became bland again, all in the flash of a second. "All right, Billie, if you want, but Fay Ann's going to be disappointed. I was going to take her to Mexico for a couple of days." He tossed down the cigarette, ground it to bits against the flagstone.

"Mexico? What are you talking about, Alton?" She pushed herself off the chaise, took one step towards her husband.

I inhaled deeply, knowing my sister's pride and how ashamed she would be. Nevertheless, it had to be said. I looked her straight in the eye.

"I gave Alton some of my credit cards when you first got here. I guess everything he's bought ever since has been charged to them."

Fay Ann went white as a geisha.

"All the travel, all my clothes, all the restaurants, everything? Alton?"

"You knew the agency was bankrupt, Fay Ann."

"You said you'd sold it. I had no idea," she said.

"You really are stupid," sneered her husband. "Where did you think the money was coming from?"

"That's enough!" My outrage exploded. "I'll pay the current bills. Just give my cards back and get out. Get a job. Or ask your father for help."

"My father has just about disowned me," he snarled, "the son-of-a-bitch. He could have saved the dealership three years ago but he wouldn't."

"Maybe that's because he knew you'd been embezzling money from it," I risked.

There was another gasp from Fay Ann.

From Alton dead silence. Then, "Who told you that, your supercilious bitch of a mother?"

"Out, just go. Fay Ann can stay with me as long as she wants, but I want you gone. Don't bother giving back my cards; I'll cancel them."

Fay Ann was standing rigid, horrified. "How could you? Billie has been so good to us. She's family; you don't cheat family. And," her eyes blazing, "don't you ever speak of my mother that way again."

I waited for Fay Ann to confirm that she was leaving her husband at last.

"Go pack our things, Fay Ann," Alton said, not moving his eyes from mine.

Baffled, I saw Fay Ann start towards the house; what would it take? I was dimly conscious of her stopping at the door, saying something about being sorry, she didn't know what to do.

But I was watching Alton's face, fascinated. The mask he had been wearing for so long began to crumble; I saw for the first time the dishonest, cruel, evil man he had become. Yet I still had no idea.

"You, Alana Paige," he said with contempt. "You're just Billie Jo Payner after all, as stupid as your sister. Go ahead, cancel the credit cards. All the money in the world won't buy back what you've lost."

Somehow I was afraid to hear any more. Then I heard myself whisper, "What do you mean?"

"Your baby," he sneered again.

A memory tried to break through to the surface of my mind, which was about to spin out of control.

"Don't you remember when the baby was born? Didn't you hear it cry? Strangled babies are dead when they come out. They can't cry." His voice was vicious, tearing apart my life. I thought I would faint; perhaps I did. Yet I was standing there, one hand on the metal brace of the lounge chair, supporting my weight as my knees began to tremble. "What are you saying?"

"You'll never know, you black man's whore; for all your money and fame, you'll never know if I'm telling the truth, if some little bastard is running around with your precious Drew's blood in its veins."

My sister stared in horror. Time stopped. Suddenly Alton's voice sounded muffled, as if weaving its way through layers of cotton. In a vacuum I was aware of my sister standing by the patio door, rigid. Her voice was strangled in her throat. "What are you talking about? You said the baby died."

"Did I? Did I really say that? I wonder if I could have made a mistake," he drawled sarcastically. "Maybe I just thought the baby died and really it didn't. Maybe I just didn't want it cluttering up Alana's life."

"Your life you mean," Fay Ann screamed at him. "You were afraid a baby would ruin her career—and income. *your* income. Oh you're wicked, evil," she screamed again, and flew at him. He slapped her; she stumbled backwards, falling into a bed of impatiens, blood from her cut lip smearing the white petals.

I was still standing, frozen, caught in a morass of uncertainty: was he saying this to torment me, as punishment for forcing him from my home? Or did I dare to hope that my baby was alive?

Now I saw nothing as the memories crystallized: the small room, the strange doctor, the nurse who seemed to be less than familiar with the process of birth; the order to push one more time, the cry of a baby, then silence. Yes, I did hear a baby's cry through the pain and the unbearable knowledge of Drew's death that never left me.

Somehow I managed to get out the words in a voice I didn't recognize as my own. "Is my baby alive? Tell me the truth, Alton. Is my baby alive?"

He blew a hissing breath past clamped teeth. "I don't have to tell you anything."

"You can't be this cruel." Then a more frightening thought struck me. "You didn't…you couldn't have…."

For the first time I saw him blanch. I had frightened him.

"You're talking murder. I never said anything about murder."

I believed him; he hadn't the courage. "Then the baby *is* alive."

He recovered. "Yes, the baby is alive. But you'll never find it."

It seemed the world was disintegrating right in front of my eyes.

~

This day has been so emotional that I've come back to the hotel, ordered room service, showered, and am sitting in sweats and socks, besotted from a double bourbon, in front of a mute TV set. The pictures in front of me are meaningless: forms and figures gesticulating, colors vibrating.

I switch them off; news has no interest for me tonight.

I left Billie looking totally exhausted, no surprise. Though I tried halfheartedly to stop her before she reached this point, she wouldn't allow it. She is driven to get the story out, all the childhood memories preamble to the central event. It is such a devastating tale of loss and betrayal and human greed. Did Alton really kidnap the child? Did Billie find it? Is her son or daughter living in the next town or even next door?

When I left her late this afternoon, Billie asked if we could go for a drive tomorrow. Much as I hate waiting any longer to find out what happened, I also feel guilt for the long hours of torment this is for her. A drive? At this point?

I'm exhausted also. I have to sleep.

I awakened late; no time to stop for breakfast. If Billie has tea I'll be fine. I wouldn't hesitate to ask for it; we've become close enough for me to be that informal.

It's a hot day; I'm wearing a linen dress, sleeveless, and sandals, but

I have a sweater in case the air conditioner is turned high. I wonder if Billie might again be dressed in silk, as she has been most days, or perhaps today in casual slacks, perfectly tailored to fit her slim form. Her clothes continue to delight me; I feel as if I'm a part of her generation when I see the Faths and St. Laurents and Norells. She wears little jewelry, just earrings usually, with an occasional ring or bracelet.

My nerves are so on edge my thoughts are frivolous. What I expect this morning, drive or not, is to find out about Billie's child. The terrible idea occurs to me that we're going back to the cemetery and there will be another grave. Each time I ask questions, I'm told to have patience. How is that possible?

Please, Billie, tell me the baby lived.

XX

Fay Ann was standing, brushing crushed flower petals from her leg and trying to stop the blood dripping from her mouth. "I don't believe this," she mumbled over the hand at her already swelling lip. She looked stunned, disoriented.

I wanted to go to her but was afraid my legs wouldn't hold me.

"You can't mean what you're saying, Alton. It would be illegal; no clinic would allow. . . ."

"What clinic? That wasn't a clinic. That was just a house and a drunken old doctor my. . . Betty found."

"Your what?" Fay Ann yelled, looking at her bloody hand, distracted. "Who is Betty really? She's not a nurse, is she?"

I didn't care if Betty were another wife. I had to know the truth about my child.

"Does this 'Betty' have the baby? You must tell me, Alton."

His mouth clamped shut. He glared at me for a moment. Then without looking at her, he asked his wife, "Are you coming?"

She laughed, a short hysterical burst. "I've had enough. Billie's right. Get out, just get out."

"No," I blurted, shocking them both. "You can't leave until I know."

Alton smirked, walked deliberately to a chair and settled himself, one elbow resting casually on the arm. "Well now, that's better. Treat me nice and maybe you'll learn something."

"When?"

"When I feel like it."

"That's blackmail." From somewhere an icy calm had sheathed me like a cloak; this was no time to feel sorry for myself. I would learn what I needed to know from this pathetic excuse of a human being, then boot him into the next state. Maybe, I fervently hoped, even into prison. He had kidnapped my child.

"Oh I know what you're thinking," he said, blandly, "you're thinking you might be able to put me in jail. No way; I heard you say you were going to give the baby up for adoption so I was just helping. Betty heard it too."

"Whoever Betty is, neither of you heard anything of the sort because I never said it."

"Your word against mine, sweetie," he said, saccharine, "but after all, Alana Paige couldn't afford to have a black baby out of wedlock then hope to have a career; you wanted the baby out of your life."

"Is that it? My baby is black? And you thought I wouldn't want it?" My fingers curled into fists; I longed to use my nails to rake his self-satisfied face to the bone. "Tell me about my baby. Was it healthy? Is it a boy or girl?" I demanded.

Alton stared at me. Then, with astonishing insolence said, "I'm going to Saks this afternoon. Would you like to come with me, Fay Ann?"

"You are despicable. I never want to see you again," she answered.

Alton rose just as casually as he had seated himself, walked to Fay Ann, who was standing by the door, uncertain whether to run or attack.

Alton stopped in front of her, then, in one swift motion, slapped her face again, turned and sauntered into the house, calling over his shoulder as he went, "You'd better not cancel those credit cards, Billie Jo."

In mutual accord, without speaking, we followed Alton through the living room to the front door where he waved jauntily. He climbed into his Galaxie, and waving again, started the car and headed towards the gate. It occurred to me to be surprised that he hadn't bought a Porsche or a Mercedes.

Still unnaturally calm, I went to the kitchen to get ice for Fay Ann's lip. Maria was singing accompaniment to the radio. I hesitated, then said, "Maria, Alton hit my sister. I want you to see her face." I couldn't tell her what I'd learned until I had time to think what I must do next. But having a witness to violence might be important later on. For what I wasn't sure.

She nodded at me. "Not the first time, Miss Alana. I seen it a lot this last year. I even tried to talk to her once but. . . ." she shrugged her shoulders eloquently.

I wrapped the ice in a towel. We went back to Fay Ann, who now had livid finger marks on her cheek as well as a lip swollen to twice its normal size.

Maria took one look and clicked her tongue, shaking her head. She said, "Maybe you should have a picture of that, just in case,"

I cursed myself for a fool, went for my camera and took several shots, not only of her face but also of the purple bruises on her shoulder and arms. Trust Maria to be sensible. Maybe *she* could figure a way to get the information from Alton. I needed to think.

After trying to explain to my uncomprehending housekeeper that Alton would still be staying with us for a while, in spite of the circumstances, I called Shadow and went for a walk.

"Tell me what to do, Shadow." I said, burying my face in her fur. "If I make him leave he'll never tell me; if I let him stay he'll drag it out until I'm crazy—then maybe not tell anyhow. I can't play that game.

"And there's Fay Ann to consider. How violent is he liable to get? I can't let him use her for a punching bag. Answer me, Shadow." She looked at me as if she knew what I was asking, whining as dogs do when they know their human is in trouble. Whom could I go to?

Well, of course; to whom had I always gone? I turned, called, "Com'on, Shadow," and raced back into the house.

"That weasely little bastard. I knew something was wrong the first time I saw him."

"He was just a kid when I first met him. I never thought he would be capable of something like this. My child is eighteen months old, Nat, and I've never seen it. I don't even know what sex it is, what it looks like—Oh, God, calling my baby 'it!' This is a nightmare. What can I do?"

"What about buying him off? Yeah, yeah, I know. Just the same, how much would he want?"

"More than I have, I guess. No. He won't take a lump sum and leave. He's in for the long term."

Nat rested his elbows on the desktop. He took a deep breath, said, "Billie, don't get mad. This is just a question."

My stomach seized; I knew exactly what he was going to ask.

"Have you given any consideration to the consequences if you find the child and bring it home?"

"You sound just like my brother-in-law. What consequences? Rejection by my public? Losing my career? Do you think that would matter to me? You know me better than anyone, maybe even better than my mother. You know what's important to me. I want my baby back. If I have to wait tables—well I've done it before."

Nat rose from his chair and came around to me, settling one buttock on the corner of the desk.

"You're a brave lady, honey. I'm proud of you."

"I don't need your pride, Nat. I need your help."

"You got it, babe. What do you want me to do?"

The glimmer of an idea had begun to assert itself in the part of my brain that was still capable of thought.

"Take me to El Paso."

~

After arguing unsuccessfully for almost an hour, Nat finally agreed to go with Billie. This wasn't yet the era of paparazzi, but in the highly competitive world of the screen, if Alana Paige planned to make a movie in a comparatively small Texas city, it was news. Billie needed Nat as a buffer between herself and any interference in what she planned to do. The idea of disguise occurred to her but she hadn't the strength or inclination for it. So Nat let it be known that they were scouting a location.

They flew into El Paso the following day, Billie leaving Fay Ann in Maria's care, avoiding Alton, aware that he would find out soon enough where she had gone.

They rented a car at the airport, checked in at the Hilton Hotel, garnering looks and whispers from stray passersby who weren't too involved in their own affairs to notice.

Adjoining rooms were available; Billie opened the connecting door and rapped loudly on its opposite. She wanted to start immediately. Nat sighed and agreed.

It was a futile gesture. There was no way to trace the small white house next to an equally small tan one. Driving on the outskirts of town for two days only left Billie frustrated and Nat disgusted.

In this Texas city of almost half a million, there also was no hope of finding a doctor whose name they didn't know, especially if, as Alton claimed, he was an alcoholic who might not be a practicing physician at all.

Four days after they arrived, Billie told Nat he had been right; it had been a waste of time and energy. The futility was compounded by the overeager news people who camped out beside the entrance to the hotel in the hope of getting an interview.

They flew home

"But Alton," I ask Billie, "was he still such a...." I start to say asshole, think better of it, not because I'm afraid she'll find my slang offensive, but because it isn't a strong enough epithet to describe him.

She interrupts, saving me the search for something appropriate, telling me that he refused to say a word.

Nat hired a private detective who retraced their steps in El Paso, found a house on the outskirts of town that fit Billie's description, took photographs. When they were developed, they showed a white stucco building next to a tan one. It could have been the right house. Except that it looked exactly like every other set of white and tan houses on the street.

The neighbors said it had been rented several times in the past two years, each tenant staying for only a short while. The owners either knew the tenants or the rental had been found in the newspaper; there was no FOR RENT *sign in front and the house was currently unoccupied.*

When the detective asked if Billie wanted him to pursue this line of investigation, she told him no; it could as easily be the wrong house. It seemed a dead end.

Billie says she retreated back into a depression, again not eating, refusing even to consider reading a screenplay.

If I find this daunting to listen to, how painful it must have been for this valiant lady to live through. Again I'm struck by the insignificance of my own problem. I'll tell her about it one day; I think she, more than anyone, will understand.

My whole being yearns to comfort Billie but all I can think of to do is ask if she'd like to take a break and have lunch in town.

She smiles at me, says she would love to. Off we go, though how I'll be able to eat when I'm full to the brim with anxiety, I have yet to figure out. How can she be so calm?

At the restaurant we're seated at a corner table by a small window overlooking a garden. I love seeing Billie's face when she responds to those in town who know her. She lights up with an inner brilliance, always remembering their names, telling me tidbits of gossip about them when we're alone. I notice that the gossip is never malicious, just little stories about their lives and work or children. She exudes genuine warmth; she cares about people. Absurdly, I find myself hoping it will take a lot more time to bring us up to the events of 1995. My editor has begun calling, leaving messages, putting on pressure. Which reminds me that I've not yet looked in the envelope she sent. I resolve to open it tonight.

~

Fay Ann's scream brought me to the surface. I noted with surprise that it was bright in the room, almost noon I would guess. As I dragged myself from the bed, I struggled to separate the sounds from the dreams, again jungles and bombs and blood, babies' blood. Then she screamed again.

It electrified me. While I was trying to sit out life Fay Ann was exposed daily to her husband's sadism. How long had I been lying there, concerned only with my own misery?

These thoughts raced through my head as I dashed towards the sound, unaware that I wore only a tee shirt.

Outside my sister's room I ran headlong into Maria, carrying a rolling pin. I almost laughed.

We nodded to each other and threw open the door. Alton was standing over Fay Ann, fist raised to strike. She was bleeding from her nose; one eye was puffed and blackened.

"No," I yelled and Maria raised the rolling pin over Alton's head. He saw it coming, ducked and it slid harmlessly past his shoulder. Fay Ann was sobbing, trying to scrabble away from Alton's feet.

"Out," I shouted. His eyes ran up and down my body.

He came close to me, ran his hand under my tee shirt, lifting it until it exposed my breasts, and said, "Looking good, Alana. You could pose for Playboy." He laughed. "Don't do anything you'll be sorry for later. I was thinking about giving you a little information soon, since your trip to El Paso was such a bust." He laughed again, turned away, leaving Maria and me standing, mouths agape, while my sister continued to sob on the floor. The odor of alcohol trailed behind him as he left the room.

Maria helped Fay Ann up; she was bent double, holding her side.

"He kicked me," she cried.

"We're going to the emergency room. You might have internal injuries. Get her to the car, Maria. I'll get dressed."

Fay Ann had a badly bruised hip as well as a black eye and bloody nose. This time she *had* fallen in the bathroom—but it was Alton who caused it. She begged not to stay in the hospital, saying there was nothing they could do we couldn't do as well. Against my better judgment I brought her home and urged her into bed; with Maria's care she would recover quickly.

Shadow whined to be let inside; I left her guarding my sister though she probably would have cowered away from Alton; she had never grown to like him.

Fay Ann was despondent. The gritty youngster who had shot a rattlesnake, the young mother who had cared with unparalleled devotion for an impaired child, the woman who had tolerated a sick and brutal husband, was finally reduced to a weeping, helpless female, unable to make a decision or take a stand.

I dragged her to West Los Angeles to report the incident to the police who seemed more interested in my next production than in a case of what has come to be called "domestic violence." But to put Alton in jail Fay Ann would have to prosecute. I had accomplished only one thing: the incident was on record. That was important to me. Even then, I believe, I knew what was going to happen.

It took three weeks for Fay Ann to heal. By then she was able to walk around with only slight discomfort. Her bruises had faded. She had stopped crying finally, but was too afraid even to consider filing charges against her husband. She kept asking if I thought he would ever tell me about my baby, adding that he certainly wouldn't if he went to jail.

Alton stayed away. Where he spent his time was a mystery; I checked with my distraught mother who said he had not shown up in Midland. Mama begged me to send Fay Ann home to her. I said as soon as she was well enough we both would come.

I pulled my luggage from the closet where it was stored and took Fay Ann's .22 from the pocket where it had remained since I found it on the shelf in her closet in Midland.

In Texas everyone handled guns; though I hated them, I knew how they worked. I cleaned it, reloaded the bullets, carried it to my office and put it into a desk drawer.

Alton slammed on the brakes of the Galaxie just in time to keep from plowing into the gardenia bushes along the driveway. Fay Ann and I were in front of the television set, sharing a bottle of wine as we watched a Linda Darnell rerun. Some wine slopped over as she shakily put the glass on the table.

"Come with me, Fay Ann," I said, then called Shadow who had been sleeping in the corner of the room.

"Why?"

"Just do it," I ordered, and she rose to follow into my office, as the dog bounded next to us.

"What are we doing? He'll just come looking."

"Sit down," I said, taking one of the two chairs grouped around a table in the corner of the room. "We've been sitting here for about fifteen minutes, haven't we, honey, talking, while you decide if you want a divorce." Shadow curled up at my feet, chin on front paws.

"What…? What are you saying?" Fay Ann asked, sinking into the chair I had indicated. "Alton won't let me get a divorce."

"He won't have a choice. Do you understand me?" I asked, as sternly as I was able.

"No, I don't…."

Alton's voice was unsteady as he came down the hall towards us. "Where are you two? The TV is on; you must be around somewhere."

"What do you want, Alton? Where have you been for the last month?"

"Ah, the dulcet toned Alana Paige. I thought you might be back in El Paso, hunting down Betty and that decrepit doctor. No? Well, I just came from there. Betty is fine; she sends you…nah…she doesn't send love, just wonders if you still are looking for that baby she…."

He stumbled, realized he was talking too much and snapped his mouth shut.

"You're drunk, Alton. When did you start drinking so much?"

"Once in a while, my lovely wife, once in a while. Tonight I needed to fortify myself before I came home to you."

"You aren't going to get anywhere near her, especially in your present condition. And I warn you, Alton, I've decided to press charges about the baby if you don't tell me where it is. *Now*."

He made a deprecating noise. "What baby, Alana Paige?" he asked, smugly. "Oh, you mean the baby you asked me to find a home for? Hey, wifey, com'on over here and tell your sister how you helped me find a home for that baby."

Aghast, Fay Ann cried, "How could you even think up a lie like that? What's happened to you? I don't know you anymore."

He walked across the room towards her. "You'll tell anyone who asks you that we both helped place Billie's baby to help her; she asked us to."

"Never. I couldn't do that."

"You will," he repeated, menacingly, lifting her from the chair, "because I said you will. Or…."

"Or what?" she cried, finally the defiant sister I knew. "I don't even know where the baby is! You said it was dead." She struggled to free herself from Alton's grasp.

The fur on the back of Shadow's neck rose stiffly. She lifted herself onto her front legs, growling.

"Shut that fucking dog up," Alton said, aiming a kick which made contact more by accident than intent; Shadow yelped and retreated under the desk, her yips of pain adding to the tension in the room. I moved to the desk, knelt down, stroked her fur, afraid to lift her for fear of hurting her more. She continued to whine.

Fay Ann took a stand at last. "Let me go, Alton." She stopped struggling, tossed her head. "I want a divorce."

"I'll kill you first," he said in a low, deadly voice. He threw a punch directly at Fay Ann's face, a knockout blow. She tumbled backwards and landed in a heap across the room, unconscious.

I jerked the desk drawer open; the gun was in my hand, as Alton stared stupidly at what he'd done. "You have one more chance to tell me about the baby before you leave here."

His head came up; his lip curled. "Don't threaten me, Billie."

"I've given up, Alton. Now I just want you to go and never come back."

"Put down the gun, you crazy bitch or I'll give you the same as your sister." He advanced across the floor towards me; again Shadow growled, crawling from her position under the desk.

I pulled the trigger once, the echo reverberating in the enclosed space, then pulled it again, aiming at the ceiling.

Alton fell, and with him my last chance to learn the whereabouts of Drew's child. The gun dropped from my fingers; I tried to go to Fay Ann, but halfway there sank onto the floor, stony cold and disbelieving. That's the way Maria found us all as she ran into the room seconds later.

XXI

It's morning. Too agitated to rest, in spite of another double bourbon I spent a sleepless night. Somewhere after midnight, giving up on the TV, unable to concentrate on notes or novels, I tore open the envelope from my editor, prepared for more reviews on my Gable/Lombard book plus a written lecture on the procedure of interviews, and how to get them done in a timely manner.

I was already formulating offensive phrases about my irritation in words I would never send, but along with the reviews and a page or two on her letterhead, there were several photocopied clippings. On a Post-it was scrawled a note,

"Look what I found! Quite a shock, huh? There are lots more, but these will tell the story. Has she talked about it yet? I'm holding my breath!!!!"

Would I have felt less shock at Billie if I had read these articles before hearing her story? I can't say. Certainly I would have been better able to ask questions. I was too dumbfounded to ask any yesterday.

The articles began on a Tuesday and are dated, from the first to the last, over a period of several weeks.

I re-sort them now and quote from a few of them in order:

December 5, 1966
Los Angeles Times
STAR INVOLVED IN SHOOTING
by Ann Murdock
Associated Press Writer

(Beverly Hills, California) In a shocking incident involving the famous star, Alana Paige, a man, thought to be her brother-in-law has been shot and killed.

Miss Paige, a notoriously reclusive actress, much like Garbo, lives in a home in exclusive Bel Air, barricaded behind a wall covered in foliage, the only entrance a gate controlled from the house.

A call came in to the West Los Angeles Police Department, allegedly from Miss Paige herself. She reported that she had shot a man in defense of her sister, who was found unconscious from a beating by her husband, on the floor in Miss Paige's office, where the crime took place.

There is so little known about the hermitic star that the existence of a sister was a surprise to everyone.

As of now there is no confirmation that Miss Paige did the shooting, though she has been detained by the West L.A. Police....

December 6, 1966
Variety
STAR HELD IN SHOOTING

(Bel Air, California) Alana Paige has admitted to shooting a man who, according to sources, is her brother-in-law, Alton Fawcett. Her sister had received a beating at the hands of her husband, the man found dead on the floor of Miss Paige's office.

Miss Paige was defending her sister from further attack when she used a .22 hand gun to shoot him twice....

December 8, 1966
Hollywood Reporter
STAR KILLS BROTHER-IN-LAW

(Beverly Hills, California) The reclusive star of screen and

stage, Alana Paige, has shot her brother-in-law to protect her sister from further beatings by her husband..

Miss Paige has been in films since the early fifties, shining in such productions as Pharaoh, Some Kind of Magic, Goin' Home, *in which she was an Oscar contender, and most recently, the critically acclaimed* Nowhere To Hide. *She also completed a successful run on Broadway this year, playing Amanda in Tennessee Williams's* Glass Menagerie.

An inquest has been ordered to determine whether the district attorney has cause to prosecute. Miss Paige was not detained....

December 30, 1966
Los Angeles Times
INVESTIGATING JURY EXONERATES STAR
by Ann Murdock
Associated Press Writer

(Beverly Hills, California) An inquest held in the death of Alton Fawcett, husband of Fay Ann Fawcett and brother-in-law of the brilliant and beautiful actress, Alana Paige, has exonerated Miss Paige of second degree murder and ruled the death justifiable homicide.

Maria Nogales, Miss Paige's housekeeper of several years, and Fay Ann Fawcett testified that Mrs. Fawcett had been beaten many times in the past year and there were both hospital and police records to confirm that report.

Nathan Reinhold, the well known artist's manager, also testified as to the beatings. Mrs. Fawcett identified the gun as one belonging to her, brought legally from Texas, where the couple lived.

Miss Paige, dry eyed but obviously shaken, confirmed that she had fired the gun at Mr. Fawcett after firing a warning shot into the ceiling.

"He wouldn't stop," she said....

The other articles were duplications of the sometimes erroneous reports in the first few, all of them making much of Alana's reclusive life style, none of them mentioning a baby. Though some of the articles abound in rumor, from origins in Mississippi to Alana being married at fifteen to a bus driver, they tell astonishingly little about Billie Jo Payner. She had appeared abruptly on the Hollywood scene in a trivial film, Texas Belle, *and remained there still, now an exquisite, untouchable luminary.*

I sit back, totally confused. Billie told me, only yesterday, that she shot into the ceiling after *she shot Alton. That might make the crime manslaughter or second-degree murder. Somehow she had contrived to ignore her actions and claim the equivalent of self-defense. The case never went to trial—no Dr. Mauser to testify, no baby, no revelations about Drew—for if it had, Billie's life would have been exposed to an insatiable press, ferreting out the slightest detail that would improve their ratings. How Billie and Nat managed to keep the story quiet is a minor miracle.*

I now know what Billie meant when she told me she could be ruthless. Will I ever be able to accept her explanation for the lie about the shooting? She moved Fay Ann into the office where the gun was hidden. Does that make it premeditated or did she simply want the protection if she needed it?

Am I the only one she's told? Would the courts have ruled differently if they had known?

Billie has indicated no guilt whatever. I wonder if I would feel any, under similar circumstances. I think not, though I've yet to decide. Part of me says it was plain and simple murder, the other part says Alton had to be stopped. I don't wish to judge Billie. A coroner's jury did that many years ago. My only obligation is to tell the truth in the book I'll write. But how much of the truth?

I'm very late this morning, very troubled. It's time to hear more. I must dress and go.

~

Maria stood in the doorway, as if frozen, her usually ruddy complexion gone gray.

"Maria, we must call the police. Can you?"

She shook her head, mute.

"Then give me the phone; you see to Fay Ann."

"Is she…?

"She's not dead, Maria, she's unconscious. He hit her again."

She took a deep breath, crossed herself and brought me the telephone with trembling hands.

My voice was steady as I told the officer who answered that I had shot a man and needed an ambulance. He stuttered at my name, called me Miss Paige, asked for my address and said he would send a car and ambulance immediately.

Maria was at Fay Ann's side, brushing the dark hair from her battered face. "We call the doctor?"

"An ambulance is coming. We mustn't move her. The police will be here in a few minutes."

Maria glanced sideways at Alton's body, blood leaking from the wound in his chest, shuddered and looked away. "I cover him?"

"Just let the police in, please. And call the vet for Shadow. He kicked her." I already could hear a siren in the distance.

I waited patiently for the police to arrive, my mind once more blank, heard Maria answer the gate phone; a moment later a car screeched to a halt in the driveway.

My sister was moaning as the first police officer entered the room. He knelt beside her, felt the pulse in her neck, found it strong, said, "The ambulance will be here in a minute, Miss Paige. Are you injured?"

"No, I just can't seem to stand up."

The second officer went to Alton's body, checked both wrist and neck pulse, then shook his head, confirming what I already knew. "He's dead. What happened here? Do you know this man?"

"Of course; he's...he was my sister's husband."

I heard someone say he would call the coroner.

They helped me into a chair, as the ambulance pulled noisily into the driveway. One of the patrol officers wrote industriously in a small notebook. We all waited wordlessly until the attendants wheeled in a gurney, fussed over Fay Ann for a little while, then lifted her, conscious now, onto the wheeled stretcher and said, "We'll take her to UCLA, Miss Paige."

I nodded my approval, forced myself to look at Alton's body and bent over, gagging.

Maria sidled back into the room, came to me, anxiously viewing the police officers. "Can I take care of Miss Alana?"

"I'm all right, Maria. Did you call the vet?" Shadow was back under the desk, whining.

"Dr. Trent sends someone for her."

"Oh, good, that's good," I said, tonelessly, wondering how much longer we would have to wait for whomever would arrive. Maria vanished again, gone to the kitchen to make coffee, no doubt.

It seemed hours before one of the officers said, "Here they are."

I looked up; I'd not heard the gate phone ring but still another vehicle had followed a car into the driveway. My thoughts wouldn't coalesce; time moved thickly, like poured honey.

Someone had taken Shadow. I dimly remembered them saying she probably had a cracked rib; they'd take care of her.

As I expected, Maria brought a tray of mugs, with a brimming coffeepot, cream and sugar, into the room, poured me a cup which I held in hands shaking as if palsied. She let the police get their own and now was standing at the door to the office watching the proceedings warily.

Two men in business suits walked into the room, nodded to the standing uniformed officers, stood apart from me talking to them, taking notes.

One of the men began photographing; I could have told him a lot about angles and lighting. He wrote some kind of information down as he moved around Alton's body with his camera, then took pictures of the room and close-ups of the gun, still lying on the floor where I had dropped it.

While he did all this, the other, taller of the two investigators came over, introduced himself as detective Grossman. He asked, "Can you tell us what happened here, Miss Paige?"

"He was hitting my sister. I couldn't make him stop."

"It was your sister they took to the hospital?"

"Yes."

"So she shot him?"

I stared at him. "No, It was I. I shot him. Fay Ann was unconscious."

"I see. Excuse me, please." He conferred again with the policemen and the other detective, returned to me. "They confirm that your sister was unconscious when they arrived. Can you tell me exactly where you were standing when you fired the gun?"

"I was there, by the desk."

"How many shots did you fire?"

"Two. I warned Alton but he just kept coming towards me, so I took the gun from the drawer. I fired into the ceiling first. I thought it would scare him off."

"Was he threatening you?"

"Yes. He said he'd kill Fay Ann if she tried to divorce him. Then he hit her. When I told him to leave, he said he'd…I think he said, 'Be careful or you'll get the same.'

"That's when I shot him."

Now another group of men had crowded into the room. One was the medical examiner Detective Grossman greeted as "Doc." The others were a crime squad who bent over Alton's body taking measurements. They talked a lot about angle of trajectory, marked the floor with chalk, just like in a movie, and finally carried him out on a gurney in some kind of bag. This time I couldn't look.

The detectives came over to me, suggested they should contact a doctor. I said no I was fine. Breathlessly, I asked if I were under arrest.

"No, Miss Paige," said Grossman. "But we'll need to ask you some questions and you'll have to come down to the station to give a statement. I'm sure there'll be a coroner's inquest." He shook his head as if to himself, saying, "This looks pretty cut and dried to me. I don't think they'll take it to the Grand Jury."

I took a deep breath, focused on the two men for the first time; Grossman was extremely tall and thin, with gray hair over a beetled brow, shaggy eyebrows framing expressionless eyes in a lined, weary face. The other man was shorter, with a compact muscular frame, blond curly hair and blue eyes that examined me with intense curiosity.

I thought I could trust them both.

~

Now is the moment for me to ask why Billie told the police she had fired into the ceiling first. She glances from the fabric of her dress, creased into wrinkles by her nervous hands. My emotions are in almost as bad a state as hers. I've not told her about the clippings yet. They're folded into a pocket of my purse.

We sit silently until Billie smiles weakly at me, asks why I'm so quiet today. I reach into my purse and take out the clippings, hand them to her without speaking.

She nods her head, takes a short breath and says, "Ah. No wonder," then asks if I had had them when I first came to Midland. When I answer, she tells me that from my attitude she had assumed not. She adds how surprised she was that the reporters got so many details wrong, that she certainly didn't mind. In spite of the situation and the discomfort between us now, I'm amused at the glimpse of mischief in her comment.

"I think you must tell me the rest, Billie," I say. She nods again and resumes her story.

~

It was, as could be expected, another nightmare. I knew what I had done, knew that if I had waited Shadow might have attacked Alton, driving him away...that, perhaps, I would not have needed to shoot at all. But his words were ringing in my ears; there was no doubt that Alton would carry out his threat to kill his wife if she tried to divorce him. Where had this man come from? He was the son of well-known, well-liked parents, raised in our small town like dozens of other young men. What had turned him into this dangerous, frightening person who could beat his wife and, simply to further his own comfort, steal his sister-in-law's child?

That was the one thing I must never reveal: that I had a reason to hate Alton; if they learned about that, not only would my life be torn apart for the hungry press, but I would probably be charged with murder.

The short ride to the station in West Los Angeles passed in a blur; the news was out; the reporters already were waiting. The detectives shielded me as best they could, walked me into the building to a room where they took my fingerprints to compare with those on the gun. They were trying to make sure I had not lied trying to protect my sister, though she certainly had an even more rational reason for killing Alton than I did.

My statement was a repetition of what I'd said earlier; Detective Grossman asked questions while the other, younger man watched me with animal-like intensity, searching my eyes as I answered. It was disconcerting, which I suppose he intended it to be.

But I am an actress: the truth was simple, the one distortion not much more difficult. It was pure instinct that made me shoot into the ceiling; it was pure instinct that I lied about the sequence of the shots. I perjured myself. I felt no guilt.

By the time I got home Mama had called. She had been listening to the news on a local broadcast and was hysterical; I could hear Howard in the background trying to calm her.

At last convinced that Fay Ann and I were in no danger, she was able to understand what I was saying. She offered to come. After the many times I had invited her, this was not the time to accept.

I was able to reassure her that Fay Ann was not severely injured, that I believed I would not be charged in Alton's death.

There was one of Mama's long silences until she finally said, "God forgive me, I'm glad he's gone."

My sister remained in the hospital for a week, a guard at her door; strange: when she returned to me, bruised and emotionally traumatized, she looked healthier than she had since Johnny's birth. She would recover, and with any luck at all, make a happy life for herself. She certainly deserved it.

The inquest was held in a courtroom in downtown Los Angeles. It was, of course, mobbed, the news people crowding in for quick statements from all of us, taking pictures as fast as their strobe lights could recycle. Obsessed voices screamed for autographs, as if this were a premiere instead of an investigation into a death. It was terrifying and bewildering.

Nat, bless him, said not one word about my pregnancy, nor did Fay Ann or Maria. Dr. Mauser never contacted the police. I could hardly call to ask why but Nat might have had something to do with it. There was no one else who knew except the woman named Betty and the doctor. They must have heard what happened; the national press carried the stories. But they would have been implicated in a kidnapping; they kept their distance. If they had risked coming forward I might have located my baby. I also might have ended up in prison.

It was a grand and glorious time for journalists who cared about films and everything connected with them. Well into 1967 they kept hounding me, calling from the gate, approaching Nat or anyone else who came into or out of the property.

Mama called every day begging for us to come but there was no way to get to Texas.

I told her, "Mama, if I try to go out the gate, even in disguise, they'll be on me like locusts on a field of grain. I'll send Fay Ann home as soon as I can. Nat will smuggle her out and get her on a plane as soon as possible. I can make her up and give her a wig. It'll do. We'll let you know what time to be at the airport.

"Take care of her, Mama. What she needs now is rest and some peace."

Ironic! Suddenly I had become a hot property in a way talent alone had never made me. Nat brought stacks of screenplays submitted for my approval; I examined them desultorily, knowing I must go back to work soon. Would I ever again get the joy from acting that had brought me here and maintained me for so long?

As luck would have it, the right script and the young detective arrived on the same day.

XXII

When Maria announced the homicide detective I panicked. I put the papers I was holding down on the new desk in my bedroom—the office door was locked and would remain that way—leaned back gaping at her, fear racing around with my blood.

"He's not with the other one."

"Alone?"

"Yes, just asked if you were home. I let him in the gate; now he's at the door; is that all right?" she asked, anxiously.

"Of course, Maria. Tell him I'll be out in a minute."

My clothes were presentable; I was wearing an old pair of navy blue Dior slacks with a matching sweater, and loafers. But the mirror showed an apprehensive face; that would never do. I touched my lips with gloss, ran a comb through my hair and checked again. Better.

In the living room, the detective stood in front of the window, gazing out at the gardenia bushes; he was casually dressed in blue jeans and a sport jacket over a pink shirt.

He turned at the sound of my footsteps on the parquet. I was struck with his composure and presence. He was a handsome man, with a graceful, compact body, not particularly tall, yet somehow imposing. His blue eyes sparkled; a smile softened the angular planes of his face, the chin hidden behind a neatly trimmed beard. He was not the least bit intimidating, but I was still nervous.

"Miss Paige."

"Yes, Detective. Sit down, please. What can I do for you?"

"Oh, just a few follow-up questions."

"The inquest was supposed to be the end of it."

"This is more for my own benefit than anything official."

"I see." I did not see at all.

"Is your sister fully recovered?"

"Yes, thank you. She went home last week."

Maria appeared with tea and some *petit fours* from Paradise Pastry on Westwood Boulevard; her concern was obvious.

"Thank you, Maria." If I'd been less tense I would have giggled.

The lieutenant smiled at me as Maria left the room.

"She loves you."

I relaxed a little. "Yes. And it's mutual. She's a wonderful woman. She takes very good care of me."

He studied me for several moments while I poured tea, struggling to keep my expression serene.

"Thank you," he said, taking the cup from my icy hand. "Why are you so nervous?"

"Why are you here?" I countered.

"Stalemate." And he laughed. "Nothing very threatening." Now he grew serious. "I've thought a great deal about this case. I've always been disturbed by the two bullets." His intense gaze fastened on my eyes. "Why did you fire into the ceiling?"

My heart began to race. The cup rattled as I replaced it in its saucer. There was no double jeopardy after an inquest; the case could well be reopened if there were new evidence. "I told you, I told the coroner: I tried to warn Alton off."

"It's been my experience," he said, "that a warning shot is fired next to the person you're trying to warn, not above him."

"I'm not that good a shot. I might have hit him, when all I was trying to do was make him leave."

"Not a good shot. Right." His eyes were narrowed, piercing. "Then how were you able to shoot him through the heart?"

"He had no heart," I snapped, without thinking.

There was a long pause.

Finally the lieutenant nodded his head. "Yes, I think that was true. I've done a little research on Mr. Fawcett."

I stayed mute.

"It seems your idle brother-in-law found a great deal to keep him busy. Did you know he was having an affair with a dancer from the Seven Veils? That's a strip joint in Venice."

The air blew from my mouth as both eyebrows flew up in a totally unrehearsed expression of surprise. "I had no idea."

"He did a lot of out of town travel the last couple of years, too. He rented a car a few times, drove out of state, usually as far as Albuquerque. That's where I lost track of him. He stopped using credit cards, paid with cash instead. Hard to trace."

"Why do you think…?"

"That's what I hoped you could tell me."

"I haven't the faintest idea," I claimed, though suddenly my suspicions jelled: Betty. It had to be Betty Mama was talking about when she first mentioned a girlfriend, how long ago?

But a dancer—dancer?—from a bar in Venice?

He was watching me carefully, could see I was disturbed. Could also see I hadn't known.

The tension in the room somehow magically dissipated. When I lifted my head to see his face it was calm and pleasant, no hint of doubt.

He shocked me. "I have a confession."

He had a confession?

"I checked on him so I'd have reason to come back. I wanted to see you again."

To my amazement, he was blushing.

"Do you think…could I take you to dinner sometime?"

I stared at him. He was serious.

Shadow galloped through the door, skidded to a stop in front of the detective and sat, her tail thumping the floor.

"Come here, girl. What's her name?"

"Shadow," I answered as she went to him, put her head on his knee and wagged her tail blissfully as he scratched behind her ears. A pain clutched my stomach; she had done the same with Drew.

"She's all recovered, isn't she? You're a beauty, aren't you, girl?" He raised an eyebrow. "Well?"

"Well what?"

"Will you have dinner with me? Soon?"

I was completely disconcerted. "I don't go out much, detective."

"You could make an exception. We'd go somewhere quiet where you wouldn't be hassled."

I had no idea where that could be. "I don't know," I faltered, wondering why I didn't simply say no.

He declined to pursue but in his eyes was an undisguised plea that charmed me.

"You could come here," I said, not really believing the words had come from my mouth. "Maria would fix us something."

His face lit up like a little boy's. "Do you mean it?"

Irritated more at myself than at him, I answered, crossly, "I wouldn't have said it if I didn't."

"Tell me when. I'll be here. Then maybe you could stop calling me 'detective'. I'm usually called JD."

That was the beginning.

~

Talking about JD has put a little color back into Billie's waxen face; or perhaps it's the cerise blouse she wears with her gray linen slacks. She doesn't dress this casually often but looks, as always, beautiful.

The change in her demeanor is remarkable. She has lost the pained, tortured expression she's worn since she first talked about Drew's death. I can't begin to imagine how difficult this all has been for her. But now it seems easier. I can only hope it means she has found some peace in the years since. The proper and overused term is, "Life goes on." It's true. And again puts my own life in perspective. It no longer seems so terrible. I'll tell her about it when we finish the interviews.

I love this woman, whatever she did.

~

JD was delightful company, funny and gentlemanly in an old fashioned, unexpected way. He was a movie buff and we enjoyed picking apart the directing and acting. He liked old films the best; I laughed at him when he told me he actually had seen *Texas Belle.*

"That dog? That was my first role."

"I know. It was on TV a few weeks ago. You were great."

"Great! I barely knew what I was doing."

"Didn't show. Hey, this is delicious; what does Maria call it?"

"It's stroganoff. You're uncouth if you've never had it."

"I'm just a cop; whaddaya expect?"

"Right. And I'm just a hick from Texas."

He sobered instantly. "Are you, Alana? Why have you always tried so hard to keep that hidden?"

Sorry I had let it slip, though he must have known from the investigation, I tried to shrug it off.

"Have to be from somewhere."

"Is your family still there?"

"My mother and stepfather live there. Fay Ann has moved to Arizona. I think—I hope—she's found a nice guy who will treat her well."

"Fawcett was a bastard," he said, darkly. "I'd be willing to bet a lot went on with him we don't know about.

Suddenly faint, I agreed, "I'm sure you're right."

The policeman was instantly alert, all detective for a moment, studying me intently, looking for what? Then he relaxed. "Wonderful dinner. Thank you. And thank Maria."

I smiled, realized I'd enjoyed it as much as he did. Impulsively, I suggested, "Come back again."

"I'd like that."

When I returned to work it was impossible to keep any kind of schedule, as is always the case. Occasionally JD would show up at the studio; we would have drinks or dinner afterwards if it weren't too late.

I found myself thinking of him often, remembering the boyish look he would get when pleased or his job was less trying than usual. He understood when I couldn't make plans, since he was so often in the same position, forced to cancel our casual dates at the last minute.

We saw each other or spoke when time and degree of fatigue permitted. I was wrapped up in the film, totally involved in a script in which I had faith. It was *Blind Fury*, my first effort since the inquest. I'd been afraid of the reception I might get on the set but if anything it was warmer than before, as if in sympathy for the awful events I had lived through. Men who beat their wives were not uncommon but they certainly weren't approved, either. My defense of Fay Ann was applauded secretly, especially by most of the women.

After *Blind Fury* I went on location in Canada to film *Contagious*.

They were both successful pictures and my coffers were again full; Nat was happy; I was relieved.

JD and I had spoken almost nightly, sharing the events of the day, exciting or boring. He met my plane when I returned from Montreal on a wet and foggy afternoon. I was remarkably happy to see him. We chattered all the way to my house, where Maria and Shadow both greeted us, Shadow with leaps of joy, Maria more sedately.

JD carried my bags inside, turned to me, gathered me into his arms and whirled me around until I was dizzy.

"I'm so glad you're back. I missed you."

"Put me down, JD," I said severely, then relented and told him I'd missed him, too.

In one of his mercurial mood changes he asked, "Did you, Alana, did you really?"

"I really did." I reached to muss his curly hair but he caught my hand in mid stroke. He grasped my wrist, levered me to him and put his arms around me.

"Don't you know how much I love you, Alana? I have from the first, when you told me that ridiculous story about firing into the ceiling before firing at Alton."

I gasped. "How…?"

"Shush; quiet. I want to kiss you."

His mouth covered mine gently; I responded. Drew and our baby were gone; but perhaps my life was not over after all.

XXIII

Maria was smiling when I went into the kitchen after JD left. She had the radio on, as usual, humming along with Jeannie C. Riley's "HarperValley PTA."

"What are you grinning about?"

"I think," she said, "you like Mr. JD."

"You're incorrigible. Yes, I'm amazed; I do like him."

"You need."

A typical Maria comment. She was right. I did need.

"This is good. When he come back? I fix a special dinner."

"All your dinners are special," I told her. "Com'on, Shadow. Let's go for a walk."

My next film was in preproduction so I had free time. But JD was working a case, which meant long hours and circles under his eyes. The next time he visited, after dinner we were watching a rerun of *Odd Man Out* with James Mason, when he fell asleep. I covered him with an afghan Mama had made for me and went to my room. I was still awake when he tapped softly on my open door and called, "Alana?"

"Come in."

"Thank you for covering me. Sorry I fell asleep."

"You needed to; no sense waking you."

He sat on the bed, looking around the room in the silvered light from the half moon shining through the windows.

"It must be a beautiful room in the daytime."

"It is," I agreed, waiting.

"It suits you." He was motionless, like a male Galatea awaiting his Pygmalion.

"JD."

He reached for me.

My first thought on awakening the next morning was: you are a traitor; how could you give yourself so completely to this man when Drew was everything to you? I felt the heat behind my eyes, as JD rolled over, one hand slapping lightly against my side.

He was instantly awake, half sitting before he remembered where he was.

"Alana. I'm sorry. Did I hurt you?"

"No, you barely touched me."

"Then why...what's wrong?"

"What makes you think something is wrong?" I asked, turning my head away.

"Oh, com'on. I can read you pretty well; that's my job, you know." He settled back down, drew me close to him. "I want to know what you're thinking, what you're feeling; probably be too nosy for my own good."

The urge to tell him was so strong. I remembered my thought when I first saw him: that I could trust him, felt he would understand—at least part of it. It couldn't hurt to tell him about Drew; certainly would be better for him to know.

I raised myself, slightly upright but still leaning against him.

"I should tell you...." It was more difficult than I had expected. His eyes took on the intensity I had learned was his facile mind concentrating.

"I had a lover...." Again I stopped.

"You are probably nearing thirty years old, Alana."

I snorted and interrupted, "Thirty-one, as a matter of fact."

"Whatever. I would have expected you to have a lot more than one lover. In fact, I'm astonished you haven't been married a bunch of times like the rest of Hollywood. I'm a lightweight, only married once. Now tell me."

"He was...he was killed in Vietnam."

"Oh, shit! That's so hard. I'm sorry." He thought, then added, "That's dishonest. If he were alive, I might not be here with you this morning. Still...."

"I wanted you to understand...something. I'm not sure exactly what."

"That there'd been someone important in your life? I'm glad there was. You shouldn't spend your whole life alone, like some kind of hermit or ascetic." He kissed my shoulder, then my cheek, then turned my face to him and kissed my lips. "I'm in love with you now, today; everything before this is history." There was no guile, no pressure to make some major decision; there was only this moment, these emotions, this wanting. If I had pulled away he simply would have kissed me again and not been angry or hurt. It was good I had told him; there must be honesty between us.

Honesty? What was I thinking? That was inconceivable.

"I know there's more. You'll tell me when you're ready." JD turned my face towards him again. "I'm in no hurry. I just love being with you—out of bed—or in."

Though the pleasure in it was gone, it seemed wiser than ever to go in disguise when Mama called to say Howard had suffered a stroke and might not live. My grief at the news was for her; I was indifferent to this man who had been willing to betray my mother all those years ago. I wondered if he had found any other young, innocent girls to "teach" about men.

I called JD and Nat to tell them I'd be gone, and why. They were appropriately sympathetic and asked me to convey their wishes to Mama. Maria, as always, would keep my home undefiled while I was away.

When I arrived in Midland I rented a car as usual and drove to the house. Fay Ann, looking healthier than I had seen her in years, in an above-the-knee, light cotton dress, dark hair falling softly to her shoulders, had already arrived. It took her only a moment to recognize me behind the makeup and wig. She greeted me with a hug, then shook her head as I entered the house.

"I don't think he's going to make it."

"How's Mama?"

"She's as good as can be expected. You know our mother."

At that moment Mama walked into the room, saw me and began to cry. She took me by surprise for she had gone completely gray. I realized that while I had hibernated in Hollywood my mother had aged; I quickly calculated her to be fifty-seven. How had that happened?

Well, it happened the same as everything else that had escaped me for the past few years. All the turbulence of the last half of 1966 and 1967 had slipped by without my noticing. I had been insulated in my own pain, one small human in a cataclysmic cycle of losses. A twinge of guilt assailed me.

"This is the first time I've seen you since Alton's...since Alton died and you don't even look like yourself."

"You know how I hate to be recognized, Mama. Please don't scold. I wanted to get here without anyone stopping me."

"I'm sorry, honey. I hardly know what I'm saying. Thank you for coming. I've just talked to the hospital. They told me to come back."

"That means...."

"That means he's dying." She sobbed, stifled it, and said, "We have to go now."

Fay Ann was pale; I knew the funeral must be painfully reminiscent of the last ones she had attended in this same cemetery. Alton's body had been returned to his family here, where he was buried next to his son, an irony of which I was well aware as, of course, were Mama and my sister. Fay Ann pointedly ignored his grave site as she stopped briefly at Johnny's grave.

Later, when the well-meaning neighbors had left, their casseroles and cakes safely stored, Mama said, "Howard was a good man. We loved each other. I never gave him reason to regret being married to me and I feel the same way." She was crying, tears streaking her cheeks. I never would tell her about Howard's attempt at infidelity; there was no reason for her to know.

Fay Ann was searching my face, seeing something there that I preferred to keep hidden, even from her. Later she asked me what I'd been thinking. I merely smiled at her and told her it was nothing. It would serve no purpose to ruin Howard's reputation. She looked at me dubiously but let it pass. The thought crossed my mind that JD would have seen right through me. He was that perceptive and already knew me that well.

I turned to Fay Ann, asked, "Are you happy? Do you like living in Tucson?"

"I'm happy; I like Tucson." She blushed. "I have a boyfriend. He's gentle; he would never hurt me."

I hugged her. "I knew there was someone. It's time you had some luck. Tell me about him."

"He's a widower. I met him the first day I went to work for the county. He's a contractor." She smiled. "He has two children, a girl eight and a little boy, five."

"Do you like the children?"

Her eyes glazed over. "Yes," she said, brushing away a tear. "I like them. Even if I were young enough I'd be afraid to have any more of my own, after Johnny. The doctor tells me that's silly and I'm not too old, but I'm afraid just the same. If everything works out with Dennis I'd have two great kids."

My own eyes avoided hers. Where was my child now? He? She?—would be three and a half years old.

My sister's hand was on my arm; she was saying, "…so sorry. I forgot. It was thoughtless of me."

"I asked," my shoulders shrugging off the hurt. "We can't change what happened. I'm thrilled for you."

"Is it awful, Billie? Being alone, I mean. You live in that beautiful house with no one but Maria. I wish you could find a…a companion but you never go anywhere except to work. Are all the men you meet there…? I don't know what you'd call them."

"'Egotistical' would be reasonable," I laughed, happy to turn from melancholy. "That's not fair, of course. Look at Nat; he's been my mentor and guide and friend for years."

"But not your lover."

"No, never that." I hesitated, then thought, what the hell. "I do have a lover."

Fay Ann was so delighted she bounced in her chair, spilling iced tea all over her skirt. She dabbed at it, ineffectually. "Wonderful. Who?"

"You won't believe me. One of the detectives from…."

She blanched. "From Alton's…investigation?"

"Yes. The younger one."

"I remember a good looking man asking me a million questions when I was in the hospital. He was at the inquest, too. Is that who you mean? That good-looking blond?"

I laughed again. "Yes; that good-looking blond. He is a really nice man. Intelligent, caring, funny."

"Hmmm. Somehow it never occurred to me you could be interested in a detective."

"You'd understand if you met him." Suddenly I realized just how interested I really was in that detective.

Mama said she would come for a visit as soon as she got everything settled. When I asked what had to be settled she hedged; I was forced to ask if Howard had provided for her.

"Yes, he made some good investments and left an insurance policy. He got it when he was working for Exxon and he kept up the premiums. The mortgage has been paid for ages; the house is free and clear. But there are a few matters I'd like to take care of. You go home, honey. I'll come later."

"I'll send you a ticket to be sure. You've never seen my house; in fact you've never been to California. There's so much to show you. Of course I might be in production on *Having It All.* But we'll manage."

It had taken fifteen years and the death of her husband to get my mother to Hollywood.

The timing was perfect. Shooting was scheduled to start in January so we had the whole Christmas season to enjoy. Mama was in good spirits though there were times I found her with eyes red and swollen. It was hard for me to refrain from telling her that I understood too well her heartbreak.

Several times I tried to share Drew with her. Through the years, when she had followed up her effort to find out about the mysterious man I had mentioned, I always had brushed off her question with a flick of my hand and some facetious comment about my bad judgment. I had kept my secret too long, too assiduously. It was too late to reveal it now. I found it beyond my ability to talk about him. Heaven knows what she thought.

She and Maria were instant buddies, sharing recipes and gossip of some sort. When I entered the kitchen in the mornings Mama was already there, seated at the table, one hand holding a coffee cup, the other stroking Shadow's fur, while Maria bustled around making breakfast.

I took her out to dinner to every four-star restaurant I knew of, plus a tourist's view of Hollywood, Los Angeles, Santa Monica, even along Mulholland from Laurel Canyon to Havenhurst for the spectacular view of the San Fernando Valley and the snow on the Santa Susanna Mountains.

Then we drove up the Pacific Coast Highway from Venice to Santa Barbara, my mother as enchanted with her first glimpse of the Pacific as I had been when Mary Lee took me to the beach so long ago. I saw more of my city in three weeks than I had seen in all the years I'd lived there.

We shopped at I. Magnin's and Bullock's Wilshire, had lunch at the Brown Derby, examined the hand and footprints at the Grauman's Chinese Theater, spent a morning at the Los Angeles Art Museum, ate at the Egg and The Eye. Truth to tell, I think I enjoyed it as much as she did, in spite of whispers from other shoppers or diners and the occasional autograph seekers. I caught Mama preening when I signed my name for someone. She was proud; I loved her for it.

Mama liked JD from the moment she met him. He would tease her unmercifully, then get serious, talk about cases from the past, ones he could discuss without compromising himself or anyone else.

He was tactful, avoided asking to stay over while she was with me, nevertheless kissing me hello and goodbye without restraint, in her presence. It was, as much as anything else, I suppose, his way of telling her how he felt about me.

Since I never objected, it also telegraphed that I felt the same for him.

Mama asked, before she returned to Midland, whether we had any plans.

"We've never discussed it. I think we're both happy with things the way they are."

She made a face, shook her head, "I don't understand young people these days."

"I'm not so young, Mama, and JD is nearing forty."

"Handsome young man," she said, ignoring my information. "I could go for him myself; I like broad shoulders and slim hips."

"Mama!" I couldn't help grinning; she delighted me and made me laugh. I'd miss her. "It's been so much fun having you here. I wish you'd stay longer."

"No, honey, it's time to go home. Besides, you have to start work next week. You don't need to be worrying about showing me places. I could tell by how surprised people were, seeing you, that you don't go out much. I sure did like watching them make that movie and meeting the other stars. Thank you for taking me to the studio."

"Look for Butch and Sundance in about September."

"I will; two more handsome blonds."

"Will you come back, Mama," I cried, ignoring the heads turning to stare at me, as she walked towards the jet way.

"I'll be back," she waved jauntily and entered the plane.

XXIV

Billie tries to describe the loneliness she felt when her Mother left, entirely different she says, from the wrenching desolation she suffered each time Drew was called away. Her mother was available—everyday by phone if desired—and less than a full day's travel away. She missed her, but as with every project she'd done, Having It All *consumed her, leaving her little time to brood.*

She was as popular a star as ever, still radiantly beautiful, with a greater maturity that she brought to roles she and Nat chose carefully to optimize her talents.

Our meetings are less strained now; she hasn't mentioned the child lately, so I hesitate to do so. We've recovered the camaraderie we had built earlier: back to tea or brandy, a luncheon out yesterday. Billie has been consistently dressing less formally, though always in perfect taste, today in green linen pants and a white cotton shirt. It's almost as if the dresses from the past were a sort of armor she no longer needs.

We've just returned from a drive into the flatlands surrounding Midland, wind rolling the tumbleweed in front of the car, and always in the distance the insect-like pumps, sucking oil from the ground for an insatiable public.

"JD was a wonderful lover," she begins, surprising me. I'll gladly let her continue.

~

He had asked me many times to come to his home in Santa Monica Canyon. I had begun to feel self-conscious, refusing so often. So one rainy weekend, when we both miraculously had some free time, I agreed to meet him there. I don't know what I expected. What I discovered was all redwood and glass, tucked away in a snug canyon, neat, with Navajo hangings and a cabinet of Kochina dolls taking up space along the wall opposite a fireplace.

The kitchen had a round picnic table in the middle under hanging copper pots; the appliances were shining white. In the window over the sink were plants; when I got closer I realized they were herbs. Something on the stove smelled marvelous.

The bedroom was small but had a fireplace of its own; the king size bed, covered in a colorful quilt, filled most of the room, with only enough space left over for a bureau.

The bathroom, conversely, was large, with a huge orange and red tiled tub recessed in a window looking out on a canyon, wild with manzanita, oak, azalea and eucalyptus. When I asked him about the tub, he said, sheepishly, "I got carried away."

"You mean you designed it yourself?"

"Actually, I built it myself."

I felt my eyes widen. "How much of it?"

"This was an old shack from the twenties. I got it cheap and spent about ten years rebuilding."

"I'm truly impressed."

A balcony circled three sides of the house, just wide enough for some lounge chairs and a small table or two. The branches of an oak tree came through the flooring at one corner. It was beautiful: a miniature gem.

Leading me back into the kitchen, JD said, "I don't find much time to cook, but I like it. I made us stew; it's been simmering all day."

Too wet to eat outside, we sat at the picnic table, already set with Mexican pottery. The stew was savory with herbs, the beef tender. Icy beer in heavy mugs, crusty French bread completed the meal.

"You can cook for me any time. Maria has real competition."

We were on the sofa in front of a crackling fire that warmed the room and painted leaping flares of color on the off-white walls. The rain was driven across the balcony by the wind, dribbling down the windows in streaks. I watched, fascinated by the patterns it created. His silence caught my attention. I turned towards him.

"Do you mean that?" He was solemn, blue eyes hypnotic in their intensity. His hair fell in a tangle across his forehead, blond curls glinting. I could see the tension in his biceps under the short-sleeved sport shirt he was wearing.

I didn't know what to say. He waited.

"Since Drew…I haven't…."

"Drew is gone," he said gently; "I'm here. I'm asking you to marry me, Alana."

"Oh," I breathed in, like a startled child. "Somehow I never thought…."

"I'm in love with you. Maybe that isn't enough. Certainly it isn't if you don't love me. Do you?"

"There's a lot you don't know about me," I began, watching the rain again.

"I know there's more. I've hoped you'd tell me; maybe you will eventually. You haven't answered my question."

It was my turn to search his eyes. He was patient, but the longing was so apparent it hurt.

"If you can…I can't hide anything from you if we're going to…." What was the matter with me? He had asked a question. I knew the answer. "Yes, I love you. Yes, I want to marry you. Yes, yes, yes."

The boyish grin lit his face as he grasped my hands. "You make lots more money than I do. I'll probably have a problem with that. My job is a terror and I'm a bastard when I'm in the middle of a tough case. I get drunk about once a year and have a hangover for three days." He was laughing.

I laughed with him. "I've lived alone so long I'll probably try to boss you around all the time. I need to be by myself sometimes and I'm cranky when we're filming; we go on location, so I'd have to be away." I knew my face was as aflame as his.

There was a bubble of joy trying to escape; I felt it in my chest and in my throat; I feared it. I had been joyous with Drew.

"Now what? You keep retreating."

"Drew. When I think of him it frightens me. You're in a dangerous job too."

"Is that it? Don't believe your movies; being a detective isn't as dangerous as being a uniformed cop."

He put his arms around me. I molded my body to his, almost reassured.

"I can never replace Drew; I know that," he told me softly. "But I love you very much and believe I could make you happy."

No arms could ever hold me or warm me the way Drew's had. Yes, this was different but when JD kissed me I let go of that thought and with it all the fear and anguish. I saw the words from Drew's letter; this was what he had wanted for me.

JD's lips were delicious, full and tender. My body grew languorous. He lifted me, "The couch is too short," deposited me on the bed. We made love as if our whole lives depended on giving each other the maximum pleasure.

It was perfect, fulfilling, healing. It was a promise and a commitment and we both knew it.

When we were satiated, still entwined, we talked as lovers frequently do.

"You've never told me about your first marriage, JD. I haven't wanted to ask. If you'd rather not," I added hastily, "I'll understand." I expected to hear of a wife who grew tired of a detective's hectic schedule, and divorced him.

His lips tightened as did his arms around me. "Maureen had picked up our son from Little League and was driving home. We lived on one of the side streets in Venice, along the canal. A drunk driver doing about sixty-five came down the wrong side of the street, plowed into our car and drove it all the way into the water. The canal isn't deep, but they were unconscious. By the time they were pulled out it was too late."

"My God, how terrible." I watched his face twist in pain in the dancing firelight; his grief merged with mine. "I didn't know." My arms drew him closer.

His smile was crooked, pinched. "It was twelve years ago. It gets easier but you never lose it completely."

"No, you don't. I wish I could comfort you. I know about that kind of pain. My baby.…." I stopped.

"What baby? What about your baby?"

"If I tell you, it could tear us apart. You might find duty stronger than love." I was aware of sounding Victorian, but it didn't stop me.

He sat up, opened a drawer by the bed, took out a package of cigarettes. "Yeah, sometimes I need one," he said sheepishly to my inquiring glance. He lit the cigarette and blew the smoke away with a twist of his mouth. "I'm listening."

"You aren't making it any easier."

"Let's get this behind us. We need to go forward."

I took a deep breath, gathering courage. If this were to destroy us there was nothing I could do.

"I was pregnant when Drew left that last time. He didn't know—well, I didn't know either. Alton.…you remember."

JD nodded, stubbed out the cigarette, muttering something about, "….awful tasting things." He took my hand.

"I was bereft, only semi-conscious. Alton took me to El Paso; I didn't really understand what was happening. I kept thinking I was going to meet Drew.

"He took me to some kind of clinic that wasn't really a clinic. He made up some excuse for Fay Ann. She didn't really understand what was going on any better than I did.

"Did I ever tell you that Drew was black?"

"No, you never did."

"Alton thought having a biracial baby out of wedlock would ruin my career. Maybe it would have. If so it also would have ruined his means of support," I added bitterly. "I had no idea at the time that he was spending my money faster than I could earn it."

"Did you lose the baby?"

"Not in the way you mean. Alton said it died. It was almost a year later before I found out he was lying. He had given it away like a puppy from a too-large litter. He never told me where. He never told me if it was a girl or boy."

"Are you saying he took the baby from you without your consent, gave it away and refused to tell you where it was?"

"That's what I said."

"Jesus Christ!"

"I still don't remember much about that whole time. We drove there in Alton's car and when it was all over we drove back."

"Fay Ann?"

"He lied to her as much as to me, sent her home to Midland long enough for me to give birth, sent the baby somewhere, then got her back to help take care of me. I guess I almost died. I wanted to. Mama still doesn't know.

"The child is four now." My eyes grew hot. "I wish I could cry. I never have. Never."

"You cry inside, love. I know; I do, too."

I kept waiting for JD to say this put Alton's death in a different light; that I had motive other than the defense of my sister. He was quiet.

"You can reopen the case, can't you?"

He looked at me in surprise. "I suppose I could. If all this came out there's a chance they might find the death a criminal act. You could be indicted."

"I was afraid you'd arrest me if I told you."

"Don't be paranoid." He snorted. "Do you for one minute think I'd turn you in? I didn't when I knew the bullet in the ceiling was your second shot, not your first."

I bit my lip. "How did you know?"

"I just knew."

"But you didn't say anything."

"There was no way forensics could have proved anything. It was cop instinct, that's all." He kissed me again. "Did you really think I'd arrest you?"

"Yes."

"Well," he scoffed, "how absurd. It would serve absolutely no purpose. Everything else was true, wasn't it?"

I nodded. "Yes, everything."

"Well then, you were justified; the inquest finding was correct. If it went to trial they'd never convict anyway." He paused. "I don't know if this is something I have to report. Will I be derelict in my duty if I don't? I'm not sure how the boss would take it."

JD leaned back thoughtfully. Then he gave me one of his "detective" looks and asked, "This will be a tough one: are you absolutely certain the baby was alive?"

"You want to know if Alton could have murdered my child," I said, and noticed my voice wavering. "I feel certain that he would never have had the nerve to murder anyone. He was only capable," I finished, sarcastic, "of kidnapping."

"And you're sure it was El Paso you went to?"

"Of course I'm sure; Fay Ann confirmed it, so it's not just my shaky memory."

"Tell me again," JD ordered, "every detail you can think of."

I told the story again, elaborating extensively from details I thought long forgotten: the white house next to the tan one; the picture the detective had brought back; the quiet of the building, as if I were the only occupant; the doctor who had seemed kind, if less than competent; the woman named Betty in her pink uniform.

I described as best I could the nightmare trip from Los Angeles, the even more nightmarish one back, the frustration Nat and I felt at the impossibility of finding the right house or tracing one questionable doctor; the additional frustration when the detective came back with nothing useful to add to our sketchy information.

"Alton was totally inflexible. He wouldn't tell me anything."

"Describe this woman, Betty."

"All I can see," I said, closing my eyes, "is a dark, Hispanic looking, youngish woman, very pretty, with a lush body. Even that might not be accurate. I was almost completely out of it. I do remember that she seemed scared. Yes, when the baby started coming, she was scared."

"So she probably wasn't really a nurse."

"That must be right. But what difference does all this make? Why are you asking me all these questions?"

He slid down in the bed beside me. "Just more cop stuff."

His hands roved over my body and I forgot to ask what kind of "cop stuff" he meant.

~

Billie is calm as she relates all this. Hearing JD's experienced assessment of the facts surrounding Alton's death, I find myself relieved, as if I no longer have to fight against making judgment.

What it causes is a return to my earlier impatience. Not that I object to hearing everything Billie can tell me; just that I wonder where all this is going.

Finally I can't wait and ask her if they ever got married. She smiles, says it's late, she's tired and we can continue tomorrow; I should come for breakfast.

I find myself grinding my teeth.

XXV

It seemed wiser to keep our marriage plans secret from everybody. As always, there was the chance that someone with perfectly good intentions would slip, the news—for I was still news—would spread, we'd have reporters camped outside the gate and also at the house in the canyon. We wanted our privacy more than we wanted our legitimacy. It didn't seem to matter. Given our schedules we spent as much time together as if we were married. Maria seemed more concerned than either of us, though I think she only grumbled because she liked it when JD teased her.

The one interruption to our haphazard lifestyle was Fay Ann's wedding—a most welcome interruption.

I went to Tucson, met her Dennis and the children, and knew that she was truly happy at last. She glowed, slim and lovely, as she had been when she was a youngster, before the disaster of Alton, her pregnancy and Johnny.

She wore a simple pale pink full-length dress; a tiara of roses anchored a short veil to her dark hair. The groom watched her every move as if he believed he was the luckiest man in the world. I thought perhaps he was.

After the ceremony I went back to Midland with Mama, spent a week with her. We talked far into the nights, hot chocolate returning me to childhood and the days before my father left, when I was an innocent and Fay Ann not much older. I told Mama about JD, his proposal and my acceptance. She was so pleased that she didn't scold about our casual attitude as to when the wedding would take place.

Nat called for me to return to Hollywood to sign the contract for *Falling Apart*, a film that would have been better suited to me a few years before, though of course I couldn't have done it then.

Nat wasn't at all certain I could handle the role of a woman slowly going mad, but I wanted it. The chance to work beside Jack Nicholson, directed by Robert Altman was too challenging to miss.

Trust Nat. He had always seen through me.

He said, "If I didn't see all the signs of you in love for the first time since.... well, I'd worry more about the part."

"We haven't wanted to tell anyone. All the same old privacy reasons." He nodded, watching me out of the corner of his eyes, expecting Lord knows what. I took a deep breath and blurted, "It's one of the detectives from Alton's investigation."

"You're kidding." It wasn't often I saw Nat taken by surprise.

"I'm not. He's a wonderful man." I laughed. "A dual personality: the detective, tough, intelligent, as tenacious as a bulldog; and the lover: gentle, honest, compassionate. Each side of his personality complements the other. And the bonus is he loves the movies and he's funny."

Nat rose from his desk, hugged me as hard as he ever had. There was a suspicious moisture in his eyes; he didn't say a word.

Yes, I was right: *Falling Apart* was a challenge. I had never been so tired in my life. JD and Maria fussed at me constantly. I didn't mind a bit.

Now, with JD so much a part of my life, I tucked away the hollowness my lost child left in my heart; I took no precautions when we made love, convinced that if I were to get pregnant, it was meant to be.

But I didn't conceive and as I progressed further into my thirties, I became discouraged, though not resigned.

Falling Apart was in the can. JD was between cases. We were in his bed, champagne glasses discarded, the sheets tangled, the fire only glowing embers, when he said, "I have to talk to you, Lani."

He sounded so serious I was frightened.

I wanted to make light with some flippant remark but it seemed stuck in my throat.

He rolled over and wrapped me in his arms. I thought, He doesn't want me anymore; I struggled to pull away but he kept me tight against him.

"Hold still. I've found your baby."

The blood drained from my head, leaving me dizzy and disoriented. I couldn't speak; there were no words to express the rush of emotions that overwhelmed me.

JD brought me a glass of water, rubbed my wrists, wiped my face with a cold cloth. "I didn't know how to tell you without it being a shock. I wasn't too gentle, was I?" he asked, ruefully. "I'm sorry."

"Are you sure? How did you.... How do you know it's mine? Healthy? Boy or girl? Where...."

"Whoa, whoa. Let's take it one step at a time. Are you all right?"

"I'm not sure. But I have to know."

"Try to settle down," he ordered, and slid back into bed beside me. "I'll tell you everything."

~

When Billie told me, I gasped, as astonished as she must have been. I look at her expectantly. "Yes," she says, "I'll tell you exactly as JD told me. I still remember lines from my first films; it's easy to have almost total recall of everything he said that day."

I roll my eyes in wonder. She probably can quote pages of dialog, whole scripts. This is what JD related to her, as she quoted it directly into the tape recorder:

"After you told me about Alton's deception, I put it together with the information I'd gathered when I was investigating the shooting. I went to the dive in Venice to see if I could track down the dancer he was seeing. The bartender recognized the description you gave me of a woman he called Serena Gay—wow, they sure pick some exotic names—said she'd left without giving notice, didn't even pick up her costumes or collect her paycheck. The date was just after Alton died. I figured he brought her to LA so they could keep up the affair, then when he was killed, she panicked and hightailed it home.

"I told you Alton had done some traveling out of state for a while, always losing me in Albuquerque, which is less than a day's drive from

El Paso. He stopped those trips about the same time Betty—or Serena or whatever she liked to call herself—started working at the Seven Veils. The timing was right.

"When you went to Arizona for the wedding, I flew into El Paso, called in a favor from a friend on the PD there.

"We tried to track down the house, but you were right: there wasn't much chance, like the detective you hired said. A lot of housing all looks alike.

"Then I remembered the uniform. Even if Betty wasn't a nurse, she had to look like one. How many nurses do you know wear pink instead of white? I started canvassing uniform shops; there aren't that many in town; I figured it was worth a shot. I sure as shit had nothing else to go on.

"In the fourth shop, the owner remembered selling two pink uniforms to a woman who fit Betty's description. He said he had ordered half a dozen a few years before and still had four of them left. That's why he remembered.

"He took out a box of receipts that must have been around for twenty years and started leafing through it. It looked hopeless to me, but the guy had everything filed by year, said he kept it all to make sure the IRS never had any reason to up his taxes. He was a funny old guy.

"But sharp. It didn't take him long to find it; he had underlined the 'pink'; pretty disgusted with the lack of sales. He asked me if I wanted to buy his remaining stock. I told him to give it to the Salvation Army and handed him a hundred dollar bill.

"Seems Betty—that is her name, by the way, bought the uniforms on her credit card. Hooray for credit cards! I had a last name and an address.

"Nothing is quite that easy, though. She'd moved, of course. Actually she'd moved more than once. My time was running out. I knew you'd be back in a couple of days. If I had to stay over I'd have to tell you why; I didn't want to lie and say it was a case. Actually it was a case though, wasn't it? Anyhow, I didn't want to get your hopes up if this all fizzled.

"Well, my friend ran her name for me. There were two Betty Espinozas in town.

"The first one was a secretary at an insurance firm. She weighed about two hundred pounds and had hennaed hair; definitely not our girl.

"I found her dancing at a club downtown. She looked good and still had that quality that's right for a stripper, whatever it is. After the show she left by the back door, bumped right into me. I flashed the shield fast, so she couldn't tell it was from out of state, scared her to death.

"We went to a coffee bar that was still open; I proceeded to scare her more. By the time I was finished with her, she was happy to tell me about El Paso and what happened to you and your baby."

Billie stops. It's as sudden as if I had pulled an invisible plug. I look at her usually expressive face. It is shut down, revealing nothing. She has withdrawn into herself as if she hesitates to reveal more, almost as if she is frightened.

Yet at this critical point she stares at me with a fervor she's never shown before. It is beyond me to try to read her. I'd give a great deal to be able to see what goes on behind that sometimes inscrutable mask she wears.

She asks for my forgiveness. I don't understand and tell her so. To this she simply acknowledges my confusion, adding that I will, very soon.

Then abruptly, in a mercurial mood swing, she laughs. I know the expression on my face is one of bewilderment. One minute an image in marble, cold, emotionless; now animated, almost loving. Is she schizophrenic? Or has life so squandered her emotions that she hardly knows which one she feels.

But then I must remember she is an actress: which Billie do I believe?

XXVI

It's evening, unusual for our meetings but somehow an appropriate time of day to learn about the child. I feel certain Billie will continue, though she is nervous again, her hands holding tight to each other as if to prevent them from flying up in pointless gestures.

We're settled in our usual chairs, coffee cups nearby, though Billie would be unable to hold hers.

A strange excitement grips me but as I search her eyes I see sadness not triumph and I grow anxious at what I'm about to hear.

She tells me it was a devastating time. She clung to JD emotionally as she did physically. Without him she would have sunk into total despair.

The tears Billie never sheds fill my eyes. I turn away, many questions yet to be answered. Strangely, now I'm no longer in a hurry. She continues:

JD said,

"I had some help along the way, things I couldn't have found out without friends here and in other places. It all came together for me; no way I ever would have mentioned any of it to you otherwise. So:

"Betty and Alton had been lovers for a long time. She was an exotic dancer, very young, really quite good looking with a dynamite figure. He met her on a genuine business trip to El Paso. Shortly after that he began making trips there that had nothing to do with business—unless you want to count monkey business.

"He gave her gifts, sometime extravagant ones. She didn't know where the money was from, never cared. Now we know it was from the agency, filched. He was in trouble. His father had stopped bailing him out; the dealership was going down the tubes; he was trying to sell it before it went bankrupt.

"When Johnny died he saw you as an easy mark. Your concern for Fay Ann was obvious and you were making a fortune in Hollywood. He reasoned that he could play on your sympathy and you'd take them in.

"He was a slick con man; he played you just right, so he ended up living in a beautiful house in a glittering city and to top off his good fortune, you loaned him your credit cards. He was in pig heaven, blinded by the glamour of restaurants he'd never expected to see, much less frequent, and shops whose names are nationally known.

"Then the shit hit the fan.

"Not only were you pregnant, you were pregnant by a Negro. Never mind that Drew was in Vietnam serving his country, that he was a good officer and, from all I've been able to discover, a fine man. Alton's only concern was that your career might be damaged or totally ruined, stopping his free ride cold.

"It was close to your due date. He called Betty in El Paso. He knew she'd had an abortion, actually the doctor had aborted her more than once. His license had been revoked and he'd spent some time in jail. They couldn't get a legitimate physician to do what Alton wanted, but this guy had been a genuine doctor, was controllable, down on his luck. Perfect—Alton had no intention of losing you to a quack.

"They worked out a plan. Betty tracked down the doctor and promised him a bundle, rented a house, set it up as best she could, bought herself a couple of uniforms—pink, fortunately. She said wearing a uniform was bad enough but white clothes are boring; she found a lawyer who dealt in 'black market babies.' She sure knew the underground.

"The lawyer was delighted; usually he had to search for expectant mothers, then pay up to ten thousand dollars for a baby, the girl in trouble some scared teenager whose parents hadn't known about the pregnancy 'til too late for an abortion, even if they would have allowed it.

"Here was someone offering him a child, then agreeing to take less money. He didn't even have to tell some couple anxious to adopt that there was less cash involved; he could keep the extra for himself. Everybody would be happy.

"Did it occur to him the mother of this child might not know what was going on? Not according to him. Betty says she passed herself off as a maid in the household, told him the usual tale of unwanted pregnancy and distraught parents: it was a society family; their daughter was too young; they couldn't handle the disgrace if it got out. Better no questions asked.

"She made no mention of parentage, figuring, perhaps rightly, that the attorney would refuse to place the baby if it were biracial; he was, after all, a southern gentleman. Betty said she didn't know what they'd do if the baby had been born dark-skinned but as it turned out it wasn't a problem; it was lighter than Betty.

"Alton called her from your house to make sure everything was ready. He usually—though not always—went out to place his calls but she said he'd freaked at the last minute. She calmed him down, made sure he'd covered his tracks with Fay Ann and the others, told him to get you in the car and bring you to El Paso right away.

"He fed you, of all things, Benadryl, to keep you asleep, brought you to the 'clinic' that Betty had created, to see the doctor who was practicing illegally and well could have killed the baby and you, too, because he'd become a drunk. But I guess he remembered some part of the Hippocratic Oath, sterilized everything properly and did what he could for you. I traced him. He died last year. Never did get his act together; was found on the street."

~

By now, as you can imagine, I was frantic for JD to tell me about the child. He still hadn't said whether it was male or female, healthy or ill, if it had all it's fingers and toes, if there was any indication of Down Syndrome.

I wanted to scream at him. He took another cigarette, lit it, puffed it once and again stubbed it out.

"Why aren't you finishing? Is something wrong? Did the baby die after all? Tell me, JD. You're torturing me."

"The baby was a healthy little girl, about six pounds, Betty thought. She cried on cue, the doctor cut the umbilical, told Betty how to clean her up, delivered the placenta and left instructions for your care. Alton paid him, warned him to keep his mouth shut, making dire threats he'd never have had the nerve to carry out, and dismissed him.

"The only other time he saw you was when your fever got so high they thought you'd die. He came back, medicated you, gave them more instructions and disappeared into whatever hole he'd climbed out of.

"They needed Fay Ann to help take care of you but had to get the infant away before she got there. Betty took her to the lawyer who had a setup for newborns, to care for them until the adopting 'parents' arrived.

"He called them, told them the baby was premature—she was a little, wasn't she?—but ready for them to take immediately. He never wanted to keep the babies any longer than necessary. All he cared about was a healthy infant and the money.

"I talked to him at Huntsville; they nailed the bastard on a different case and gave him the maximum. Sometimes there is justice."

JD stopped talking then. He hadn't told me whether he knew where my child was now. He had said nothing about the family who took her. I had to know.

"Please, JD, tell me the rest."

He nodded assent, took my hand and kissed it.

"It's very good and very bad."

My heart thumped so hard I could hear it. "What?"

"They're an older couple who evidently had tried to have a baby for a long time, then tried legal adoption with no success. To them this baby was a miracle.

"They came to El Paso the next day, anxious to see their daughter and take her home as soon as they could."

"Why did you say it's bad? She isn't sick, is she? Where do they live? I want to see her. How soon can I take her?"

"That's the bad part, Lani. I saw this coming but it seemed more important to find out about her than to leave you forever in limbo, wondering for the rest of your life. I'm not sure I did the right thing."

He held my hand tightly against him. "The lawyer always had forged birth certificates for the new parents. Your daughter is, to all intents and purposes, their child."

My breath whooshed from me as if I had been hit with a baseball bat.

Why hadn't I foreseen this? From the moment JD said he'd found her, without once considering the consequences I had envisioned some sort of fairy tale ending: they had taken her illegally; she was mine!

"Betty? The lawyer?" I cried. Can't we make them tell the truth?"

"Maybe."

"Well, then. . . ."

"Think, Lani. She's five years old; it's the only family she's ever known." He paused, glanced outside to another rainy day. "I wouldn't say this if she were in any sort of dysfunctional family, if there were the slightest chance that they were doing her harm. I'd go after them like a bat out of hell. But my source says she's a happy, well adjusted little girl, goes to kindergarten, plays with other children and her…" he hesitated, "…parents love her."

As he spoke a numbness crept over me, smothering my hopes like a blanket over a fire. "I can't have her?" I whispered.

"I can't lie. It's a legal long shot, even if we subpoenaed Betty and the attorney to testify. But the point is, I know you, Lani. Even if you could take her from them, I don't think you'd want to do that to her."

I stared at the rain, the last shred of hope sliding away like the drops down the windowpane. It was inevitable; I should have known.

"I can't have her," I whispered again.

JD took me in his arms, cradling my head against his chest. "Oh, Lani, I'm so sorry."

After a long time, I asked in a voice I didn't recognize, "Do you think I could see her?"

He kissed my hair, my cheek, the cleft in my chin, then my hair again. "I think we can arrange it, love. I knew you'd ask. I've already talked to my source."

"Who is this 'source?'"

"Harold Levi, a friend of mine who used to be a cop; he's a private detective now. He knows where she is and can take us there." He tipped my head up, looked into my eyes. "Are you sure you want to do this? Are you sure it won't make it more difficult for you?"

"Even if it does, I want to, JD. I want to see my baby."

The next Monday we went to Harold Levi's office. In just these few days I had lost weight; my clothes hung loosely; JD watched me with worried eyes and Maria tried stuffing me full of goodies, but I couldn't eat.

"Harold knows everything. He's been helping me for the last three months," JD said, by way of introduction.

"Then you know how my...how the little girl is. Please tell me about her."

"She's a beautiful little girl, dark hair, dark eyes, graceful and smart as a whip. She gets along well with her playmates, is reading, doing okay in school; I've talked to her teacher. And I've interviewed her parents."

"How could you do that?"

"Easy, Miss Paige. I have cards from every imaginable type of business. I use the most appropriate one for the situation.

"The parents were cooperative as soon as I convinced them I wasn't a cop getting information about their daughter. I said I was researching family interaction for my dissertation." He laughed. "I'm pretty old to be getting a Ph.D. but it's not unheard of.

"They didn't really want to talk much about the past. I could tell it was painful. Couldn't push too hard without arousing their suspicions; no reason to make them uncomfortable. So I was only able to get a little background.

"They were both from Europe. I had the feeling that she might be Jewish but there weren't any tattooed numbers on her arm, so if I'm right, she managed to hide out for a long time. She's a little older than he is; they were just kids during the war, ended up orphans.

"Anyhow they came over in the late forties. I checked out everything I could without actually going overseas.

"Their story about the little girl is that she was born to them late in life—that's how they put it. I watched when they said it; just a quick glance between them, nothing else. It wouldn't be surprising if she couldn't conceive after her war experiences.

"The child has had the usual kid's diseases, like chicken pox, plus colds and flus; she broke her arm once, falling off a tricycle. But basically she's a healthy child, well loved and cared for. She has no siblings.

"May I call you Lani?" Harold asked.

"Of course."

He looked at me for a long moment. "I just wanted to tell you how impressed I am at the way you're handling this situation." He leaned back in his chair. "I've thought a lot about the custody issue. I don't know whether you'd be able to get it. I doubt that you could. I do know how devastating a court case could be to the child and the family. To you, also. You're doing the right thing, Lani."

I took JD's hand; he leaned over to kiss me. He knew all about the loss of a child. I felt as if I had lost mine twice.

Harold asked, "I understand you'd like to see her?"

"Yes. Yes, I want to very much."

"She goes to school in the mornings. If you're sure it won't upset you, I'll do it. Let me know when you can come back on a weekday."

We were parked in front of a one-story brick building separated from the rest of the school by a chain-link fence that wrapped around the playground, protecting it from strangers. It was equipped with the usual climbing structures and toys. A group of small children romped and played under the supervision of a vigilant teacher and her helper.

Harold pointed to a small girl in tights and a blue dress, hiked almost to her waist as she crawled through a red plastic tube. As she reached the end, her face came into view; I inhaled sharply. Her little face was chiseled and fine, straight nose, creamy, perfect skin, dark hair half tumbled from the pony tail, wisps curling in disarray.

"She looks exactly like Drew."

"No," said JD, shaking his head at me, "she looks just like you."

XXVII

With JD's help and Maria's pampering, the hole in my heart began to heal. It would never fill completely but as time passed, life became not only bearable, but exciting.

I no longer looked like a concentration camp victim. I began to take an interest in the world again, after six years in which I had ignored the murders, the politics, wars, and natural disasters that went on with depressing regularity.

Nat sent scripts for my approval and finally one appealed to me. When JD liked it also, I decided to accept the role of Patricia in *The Rebellion.* We started work immediately.

JD was embroiled in a complicated murder case, as worn out as I when he appeared at my door at any hour, greeted noisily by an enthusiastic Shadow, definitely his dog now. Our schedules clashed too often, yet the separations only made our meetings that much more intense.

Maria cooked all his favorites; she liked him, continued to make sly references about marriage. I promised her that we would—when we had time. She usually muttered something about living in sin, which made me laugh; I knew she didn't care. She would mutter some more and go back to the kitchen and her cooking, singing "Let It Be" or whatever was playing on the radio, as she seasoned meat or chopped vegetables for one of her specialties.

~

The Rebellion *played on television a few weeks before I came here; I watched it, little knowing I soon would be in the presence of the star of that movie. Billie tells me it was a little too melodramatic for her taste but I found it well plotted, with stellar performances by Billie and her co-star, the young and upcoming Harrison Ford.*

Billie is gazing into the distance again but this time there's a smile on her lovely face. Too many times she has been so sad. It warms me to see her reliving good memories at last.

When she finished the picture, Billie talked JD into a vacation in Europe as soon as he was free. She giggles like a school girl when she describes his resistance until she suggested they pool their money, then go however far it would take them.

They flew to Paris. Billie used her real name for the passport, beguiled JD with her disguises. They were able to escape notice—just two more tourists—wander freely down the Champs-Elysée, or into the Moulin Rouge. She led him to her favorite places, as well as into the small, unknown cafés and down the winding narrow streets.

They spent only one week in Paris, rented a car to drive next to Mont St. Michele. She delighted in trapping him on the shore as the tide came in, separating them from the island hotel, until he picked her up and waded across, ankle deep, then made her pay for her prank when they were behind the closed door of their ancient room.

They went to Lascaux to see and wonder at the Stone Age wall paintings; in the countryside they were safe from recognition. They traveled to Switzerland and stayed a week in a chalet outside of Geneva, blessedly alone.

They hated to return.

~

We spent as much time at JD's house in the canyon as we did in mine, and somehow we were able to maintain the secrecy of our relationship for longer than we had any right to expect.

When we were discovered at last, it was at the Sandcastle in Malibu, where we had thought I could go without interference since Malibu was the home of so many film people.

After dinner we stood inhaling the fresh salt air, watching the playful, noisy seals, JD behind me, arms crossed over my shoulders, pressing me tight to his body against the chill. We were laughing at the comical barks and grunts, when suddenly we were startled by a flash of light in our faces; a figure scurried towards the parking lot.

JD started after the man, but I grasped his sleeve. "I don't mind if you don't. We can't always stay at home. It might be easier if we don't try to dodge them every time we leave the house."

He kissed the scar on my lip, then kissed me harder. "As long as it doesn't bother you or interfere with my job." We turned back to the seals.

Later, in JD's bed, we laughed at the foolishness of it all, then turned to each other to make love. He aroused me with ease and I never stopped teasing him at how quickly I could coax him erect.

Along with the pleasure of my time with JD was the gratitude. I felt I never could thank him enough for his persistence in tracking down my child. We received regular reports from Harold and pictures, many pictures, which I treasured, entering them into albums, occasionally caressing the face that turned, unaware, towards the long lens of the camera.

Then the photograph from the Sandcastle showed up in a tabloid at the market checkstand. I was recognizable, barely, but JD was partially turned away from the camera; you would have to know him to identify him; as a photograph, the sea lions were in better focus. But it started a rumor, so I was besieged with calls about my "secret lover," whom the papers called, "Mr. Paige."

Nat was disgusted—he admired JD and the four of us dined together periodically—saying the old days were nicer. Even Mama and Fay Ann called to ask why, suddenly, there were unpleasant articles appearing in the magazines.

JD's superior called him in to warn him that any notoriety would lessen his efficiency and endanger his position. JD had never told him my confession about Alton or his private investigation of my baby's whereabouts. If even once I was followed to my daughter's town where I went when unable to resist, someone might ferret out the whole story. Then JD would be in serious trouble.

~

Billie reminds me that she had always defended her privacy and admits it was extreme. She also reminds me of how drastically times had changed. In the early days of Hollywood's "golden years" there was more respect for glamour, at least publicly, since the studios stringently controlled news releases. But with the decline of the studio system anybody was fair game and everyone who owned a camera thought he was a photojournalist.

People became intrusive and aggressive, gathering in rowdy crowds outside the doors of restaurants or clubs at the merest hint that someone of interest was inside.

So Billie says her avoidance of the media became almost pathological, and JD, trying to balance his career and his time with Billie, began to express his frustration by simply staying away.

She feared that she was losing him.

~

One day, when I had expected JD and he called to say he was too busy, I sat down to count. I discovered that in the nineteen years I had been acting, I had made thirty-one movies with one Broadway show tossed in for variety. It was nowhere near a record, but it was enough. I thought about Peter Bogdanovich's comment that Hollywood had died and nobody noticed.

Scratching Shadow's aging head absently, I leaned back in the chair to think. An idea was stirring in my subconscious; it needed only time to blossom.

Maria found me in the darkening room when she came to ask about dinner."Maria, do you think JD really loves me?"

She looked at me with her head cocked to the side. "Yes, he loves you," she answered. "Why you doubt?"

"Movies are great; I love acting."

"Are you sick, Miss Alana?"

"No, I'm fine. I don't want any dinner, Maria."

"Uh huh. You're worried. I can tell. Well," she added, "you need to marry Mr. JD."

"I think you're right."

I sat at my desk and wrote several letters.

¶

Nat had been negotiating a contract for the lead role in *The Velvet Glove*: Mrs. Bottinger, another part I coveted.

I went to his office the day he called to tell me he had gotten the salary he asked for, the highest I'd ever been paid.

We discussed finances and futures. It was after the contract was signed that Nat delivered the blow.

"I'm going to retire, Billie. Teri wants to move to the desert, now that our girl is in college."

"You can't leave me, Nat. What will I do without you?"

"You're perfectly able to take care of yourself, honey. You're a remarkable woman."

Somehow I'd never even considered the possibility of Nat retiring. Then I looked at him more carefully, aware of how oblivious I could be when I was distracted by my own affairs. He didn't look well.

"Tell me the truth, Nat. Are you ill?"

He took his time answering, his head wagging back and forth as he considered his reply; a cold chill made me shiver.

"Actually, I am. We don't think it's going to amount to much, but my heart has been acting funny."

"Funny how?"

"I've had some angina, you know, chest pains. Doesn't have to be dangerous. But this job is pretty intense. Teri wants me out of Hollywood." He sighed. "I have mixed emotions. I love it. But it's not like the old days and it wears me out. Maybe she's right." He smiled at me. "The doctor agrees, anyway."

"When do you think you'll leave?" I was as close to tears as I ever got.

"We've been looking at a house down in Indian Wells; pretty empty town now, but it's growing. I think we'll make an offer."

"Nat, I don't know what to say. I can't imagine being here without you."

"You have JD. And I'll only be a phone call away if you need advice."

JD had been less than enthusiastic when I told him about *The Velvet Glove*. I'd not yet told him about Nat.

We were in front of the fire in his canyon house, an empty wine bottle on the table, the last wine in our glasses glowing red in the firelight. I approached the subject obliquely. "I'm not too happy at Nat's news."

"What news?" he asked, frowning.

"He's retiring."

"No way. I didn't think he'd ever retire."

"He's having some chest pain; the doctor advised him to get out of Hollywood. Teri agrees. So they're going to move to Indian Wells, you know, outside of Palm Springs."

"I know where it is," he said, annoyed. "It's tiny."

"They don't seem to care."

"Maybe they're right. L.A. has gotten too big and crowded."

My heart thumped like Shadow's tail. "Do you think," I began, casually, "you could ever live in a small town?"

"It might be a nice change."

"What would you say if I told you I'm thinking of following in Nat's footsteps?"

"What do you mean," JD asked, his detective look taking over.

"I want to retire." Saying it for the first time made it real, scary and almost overwhelming.

"Oh, sure," he laughed, but there was a telltale glint in his eyes.

"You don't believe me." I drank the remains in my glass, deposited it on the table and maneuvered myself onto his lap. I felt a satisfying response beneath me. I kissed him, letting my tongue linger on his, then drew back.

"Garbo left the screen in 1941 and never made another film; Dorothy Lamour has only done occasional roles since 1953 and Bardot just retired. Why wouldn't you believe I'd do the same?"

"Bardot retired?" he teased, nuzzling my neck. "Too bad."

"Stop it, you lecher. I'm serious."

"I can tell," he said, reaching under my shirt.

Afterwards, we talked seriously. It took some doing for him to believe I meant it. "*The Velvet Glove* is my last film. If I sell the house Nat says the income from my investments will be enough so I don't have to worry about money."

"Do you plan to camp out in the park in Beverly Hills?"

"I thought you might invite me into your house."

"I might consider doing that. What about Maria?"

"She said she'd move in with her sister and come in days. There's no way I'd be able to exist without her."

"Or she without you," he added. "So you've already talked about it."

"Yes. What do you think?"

"I think," he said, "that I love you very much, Billie Jo Alana Paige Payner."

~

Billie is masterful at leaving me hanging. When I ask if they married, she smiles and says she wants me to take her for a drive; there is something she must do today. My acquiescence is begrudging, almost rude.

I'm quiet as we walk to the car; I wait for instructions, then head out of town on the road we've taken only once before. Beside me, Billie is exasperatingly serene.

My pulse quickens as I remember this road and where it leads. She isn't evading my questions, she's taking me to a part of her life.

When we arrive at the cemetery she leads me to Johnny's grave, though she ignores Alton's marker, which I observe beside it. Next we walk to a marker I'd not seen the first time we came. Her mother's name is there:

JEANNE PAYNER RODINSKI
JULY 20, 1911–OCTOBER 7, 1989
ALWAYS OUR MAMA

We stand for a moment, Billie's lips moving silently; I say nothing; what is there to say? Then she leads me to the grave I remember and suddenly what I should have put together earlier is crystal clear. The name on this tombstone reads: JASON DAVID ELLIOT. JD.

I look at Billie with the question obvious on my face. She smiles wistfully and nods.

So they did marry; the friends in town, the waitresses in the restaurants, all called her Mrs. Elliot if they didn't use her first name. How could I have missed it?

She is still smiling, looking fondly at the memorial and says only that they were very happy together, that she was very lucky.

Again my eyes fill. I turn away, not willing to let her know how touched I am that she at last found some happiness. But she's much too bright not to see my emotion and takes my arm, saying, "Come my dear; it's late; time to go back now."

We return to the car, then drive into town. I don't ask, I go immediately to the restaurant I know she enjoys, telling her I want no argument.

She smiles again, enjoying me as dictator. I love this woman.

XXVIII

In truth, neither of us cared about the legalities. But when JD joined me here we knew we had to marry, because this was still a small southern city and it wouldn't do for the chief of police to have a mistress instead of a wife.

Strangely, of all the letters I wrote, Midland was where the police chief was closest to retirement. It had taken over a year to set up the job for JD. During that time I finished *The Velvet Glove*, perhaps the best performance of my career. When I was nominated for an Oscar, I remembered the white St. Laurent dress I had bought so long ago and ransacked the storage closet for it. It hung neglected at the back, limp and yellowed, far beyond redemption.

This time I would enjoy shopping for something even more spectacular to wear. I went to Neiman Marcus and found a Versace, one-shoulder silk crepe gown, black, that flowed down my body like oil, the hem embroidered in silver scrolls.

JD, after threats and coercion, joined Nat and Teri, in town for the evening from their new home in Indian Wells, and several of my co-stars at the awards ceremony. He looked magnificent in a tuxedo. I wanted to cling to his arm but the stipulation to his presence was pretense that he was Nat's friend, not mine. We sat apart from one another.

Glenda Jackson stole the Oscar from me. I found myself not caring as much as I would have expected; a nomination was honor enough, like a silver medal instead of a gold at the Olympics.

It was a giddy evening. Only four of us knew I would be leaving Hollywood within the year.

When my house sold to a pretentious couple from Chicago I picked up the phone to dial Fay Ann in Tucson. No longer timid or downtrodden, she was a happy wife and mother, absorbed in the growth of her family and her husband's business where she now worked two days a week.

I listened to the children's news with a pang of sorrow, then swept it aside. If I couldn't be a mother, at least I could be an aunt, even if at a distance. I talked to them both, then they ran off to play and Fay Ann asked, "What is it, Billie? You sound excited—or something."

"I am. I have a surprise for you." I took a deep breath. "I'm retiring."

"Oh, come on, Billie Jo."

"I mean it. *The Velvet Glove* was my last film and I've just signed the escrow on my house."

There was a long pause. Then, "You mean it!"

"I mean it."

"Why?"

"I've been thinking about it a lot. I finally realized that I miss the glamour. It's just faded away, like film exposed to sunlight. It's not fun anymore.

"But mainly, I really think if I keep making movies I'm going to lose JD; it's too hard on us both. He's more important to me than acting. And," she would understand, "I can't take another loss."

"No. You shouldn't have to. What are you going to do?"

"I wrote letters to all the reasonable small towns I could think of. Midland, can you imagine? has offered JD the Police Captaincy. He's perfect for it and he's ready to leave here."

"Are you sure?"

"We've talked it over. The only thing we're waiting for is the job. Everything else is set."

"Isn't he mad at you interfering?"

"He was at first; then I convinced him that it was the best way to keep us together."

"But why would you go back to Midland?"

"Why not? We'd have to go somewhere."

"Have you told Mama yet?"

"I'm going to call her now."

Mama couldn't accept that I would give up Hollywood and all I'd worked for to return to a small, unsophisticated city in the south, with a terrible climate and few of the luxuries to which I'd grown accustomed.

I tried to explain it. "Lots of Hollywood people have given up everything, including lovers and families for their careers. Some of them have grown old, been passed over, killed themselves or gotten into strange kinds of trouble, like Hedy Lamarr shoplifting, or poor Betty Hutton. Did you know they found her in a Catholic Rectory? She's the housekeeper there.

"I don't want to 'decline': I want to leave at the top, while my public still knows my name, before it's too late."

"But, honey, you're still so beautiful," protested my mother.

Insulted, I snapped, "Being beautiful won't keep me warm at night. I'd not leave if I had nothing to go to, but if JD leaves with me, I'll be happy."

That Mama understood.

~

There she was, one of the most visible women in the world who had always managed to keep her life as private as an out-of-focus background in a photograph. She left Hollywood as obscurely as she had arrived, Maria accompanying her, JD to follow.

They settled in a quiet old neighborhood across from the park, in a brick house with a wrought iron railing around a spacious front porch. The neighbors, after the initial thrill of having a genuine movie star next door, became friends, which meant they allowed the Elliots to live in peace.

Shadow sniffed out every corner and chose one in the breakfast room for herself, curling up in a spot where the sun hit the planked wood floor in the mornings. She was old now, walking sedately, never jumping, though her greeting to JD when he arrived from California was as boisterous as usual.

Billie describes her own greeting as only slightly less enthusiastic; Drew's ghost had been riding on her shoulder, filling her with apprehension, making the four months they were separated seem like four years.

JD reached Midland in April, 1975; they had more than twenty years together, most as a married couple, more than many were allotted. Billie says that never once has she regretted her decision; she adds that now no one even remembers her name. She says it without rancor; I know better but don't argue.

After her mother's death she discovered what had needed "taking care of" when Howard died. The house in which Billie now lives had been deeded to her and Fay Ann, to be available for either of her daughters in case of need. Their Mama had arranged a trust fund to pay the taxes and some upkeep. In spite of both of the girl's financial independence she never changed it.

Billie made some necessary improvements and, with Fay Ann's approval, told Maria to bring her sister from her deteriorating neighborhood in East Los Angeles, and occupy it as long as she wished. Billie moved here from the brick house when JD died less than a year ago.

Fay Ann is the grandmother of three little girls, another child on the way. Her Dennis has retired and they still live in Tucson, the children nearby. Billie enjoys being great-aunt to her sister's grandchildren; she visits regularly.

It seems that I have come to the end of Alana Paige's story. Here in the hotel room I feel empty, hollow, as Billie must have felt all these years without her child. Tomorrow will end the interviews.

I do not wish to believe that I won't see her again.

She says there is only a little more to talk about. I'm trying to think of a way to gracefully extend our time together. I wonder if she would ever consider visiting me in California. Tomorrow I'll ask.

XXIX

Now that she believes I've finished my story, I wonder what she is thinking, this lovely young woman from California. Does she see me as merely an old woman recalling her past, or does she realize there is much, much more to our meetings?

Is she satisfied with what I've told her? She has been alternately patient and fretful these several weeks, tolerating my pauses and whims with good humor the better part of the time. She has my life on tape—most of it, at least—and now can easily write a biography if she wishes.

I hope I've shown her the love I shared with two fine men without sounding unfaithful to the first, too meek with the second. Lord knows JD and I had some battles after we moved here. I must say that those sessions were always followed by delightful, passionate moments, making up. Quite remarkable really, that we never seemed to get enough of each other. I smile when I think about some of the things we did.

Well, I've left all of that to her imagination. These days one needn't describe lovemaking, just turn on the television set. It was better in the old days; a lot of beauty was lost when everything became so graphic.

Maria said I was crazy to do this. She wasn't very happy to leave me alone, either, even if I did send her on the extended vacation she's always talked about. She's getting much too old to take care of me; I'd better think of having some help for her, though she'll fight it.

I'm rambling. It's nerves, waiting for my biographer to arrive. I hope she thinks well of me and likes me. I hope she understands why I made the choices I did.

I hope, today, I can get her to reveal herself. I don't know how to open the dam she so obviously needs to release. I've hinted, and asked her, too. It's done no good. How will I be able to admit all I know about her?

I'll ask again, as if I know nothing, as if I'm in complete ignorance. Somehow I'll get her to talk to me.

~

Are you sure you want to hear about me? After the drama of your history, I'm afraid you'll find my life story pretty boring, at least until lately. Actually I did want to share some...recent events...with you, get your opinion about something that's bothering me.

I had a very normal childhood, aside from the lack of any relatives; no siblings either. I was born in Petaluma. My parents were considered rather old to be having their first child. But I was healthy and they loved me.

They never talked much about their pasts. I knew they were from Germany and obviously lived through the war since they didn't get to the United States until it was over. It didn't matter much when I was growing up; too involved with myself, I guess. Then, when I got old enough to learn about the Holocaust, I felt uncomfortable asking; they didn't like answering questions. I thought I understood.

I was always fascinated with the idea of writing, started when I was really little with stories about fairies and elves. I took lit. and comp. classes in college; I went to Berkeley. My folk weren't rich but they had enough money to put me through school if I worked part time.

When I graduated I got a job as a copywriter in San Francisco. But what really interested me was Hollywood. That's how I got started doing casual research and sort of fell into writing the book about Lombard and Gable. I have to tell you, I was shocked that it got published.

In the meanwhile I met a man. I thought he was the greatest guy in the world. He was, for a while. We got married, moved to Santa Rosa. I wanted to get pregnant; lucky I didn't.

Glenn had a very good job at Rossi and Jones but his real ambition was to write a novel. When the publisher accepted my Lombard/Gable manuscript he began to act out, getting angry at nothing, yelling and screaming, threatening me. He was just plain jealous, started staying out all night and once in a while got drunk. The only times he was okay was when we visited my parents. Then he couldn't have been nicer.

He and my dad had always liked each other, would go for walks together, letting mom and me get the meals ready, like for Thanksgiving, or other holidays.

I thought that was great. Then things changed for Glenn and me but my parents didn't know, so we just kept on as if nothing were the matter.

I feel myself tensing up. Are you sure you want to hear the rest? I don't want to burden you with my problems, Billie.

Well, last year my parents were in an automobile accident. My mom was killed outright; my dad lived three weeks, then he died, too.

They were in their seventies, a reasonably long life, but that doesn't help when the loss is so sudden and unexpected. If they'd died of natural causes it would have been easier. But they were still vital and would have had a lot more years, I think.

A few months ago, my husband got really pissed off. He hit me. I told him to get out. I won't tolerate violence. Besides, the marriage had been long over anyhow.

He started screaming at me, something about my parents. Then he got real quiet and mean and said, "They weren't what you think they were. You don't really know anything about them, or what they did. And that's my parting gift to you. Go ahead, try to figure it out."

He slammed the door and left me with my mouth hanging open. I didn't understand what he was talking about. There weren't any words that made sense, from the little he had told me.

After I pulled myself together I started wondering about all sort of things: the German background, the lack of relatives, the story that they'd met in a camp—what kind of camp?—the absence of birth certificates, though I had found their naturalization papers. None of that had to mean anything negative. But then why did my husband say those strange things about them, especially that I didn't know what they'd done.

The only conclusion I could come to was that they'd been Nazis, had managed to get here to escape being caught and punished, and that for some reason I couldn't imagine, my Dad had told this to Glenn.

The idea freaked me out.

I began to plan research into their past as much as I could, determined to go to Germany if necessary. I had to know, I had to prove to myself that they weren't.... But you called and I'm here instead. The other is on the back burner for now. I'm almost afraid to pursue it, for fear of what I'll find out.

I never thought I'd feel better telling you, but I do. I've learned to love you, Billie. I can't imagine not seeing you again.

~

Every nerve in my body is singing with tension; there are timpani reverberating in my head.

"There's no need to pursue it," I tell her, gazing at the winged brows, the creamy skin, the chiseled lips.

She stares at me, disappointed, misunderstanding my nonchalant response to her fear.

"I mean," I begin, awkwardly, "that's not what it was. Your parents were refugees; they were never Nazis."

When, bewildered, she asks how I could possibly know that, I tell her, "They were investigated thoroughly. They came here in the late forties, 1948. They had met in a displaced person's camp when the war was over. Your...mother...was a year or two older than your father. They tried to have a baby for a long time. Probably the reason she could never conceive was due to her experiences during the war. It was a terrible time for everyone. People were starving, they were terrorized."

She has a look of incredulity on her lovely face and asks how I could possibly know so much; what do I mean that her mother couldn't conceive; she's here, isn't she? When she adds, "I don't understand," I make her wait one last time and go for the stack of albums that are almost too heavy for me to carry.

Then I tell her to look. I watch her expression as she examines the pages in awe.

It is all there, from the first baby picture Harold Levi borrowed and reprinted, to the last, taken from the screen of a television set the day she appeared on "Oprah" to hype her book.

She recognizes herself from kindergarten, grade school, prom night and graduation, when Harold turned the job of tracking her over to a younger man; then graduation from Berkeley, and a very fuzzy picture of her in a wedding gown, shot from a great distance.

While she turns the pages, I tell her how we followed her all these years, from the moment JD found her, that I knew about the accident and death of the people she knew as her family. About Glenn leaving and her filing for divorce, one of the reasons I chose this moment in time to make contact, knowing that now she needed me as I always had needed her. That also I had to wait for J.D's sake, so as not to jeopardize him in any way.

When she looks at me, the confusion in her eyes breaks my heart. But the look gives way to one of comprehension and wonderment. Slowly she smiles. I believe she means what she said: that she has learned to love me.

"Yes," I say, "you're my lost baby, my beautiful little girl, my strong and fine young woman. My daughter. I have always loved you."

And suddenly I'm crying.